"I'm trying to find your sister."

Bo studied the face of Claudie's brother and began to detect a hint of her in the man's eyes. He put out his hand. "Bo Lester. I'm a private investigator, but this isn't work. It's personal."

"I thought you were in California," Zach said softly.

He knows who I am. "I came looking for Claudie. She left without telling anyone where she was going."

"Musta had her reasons."

Bo sighed. "The reasons are she's stubborn, secretive and ornery as a moose."

Zach's mouth twitched as if in agreement. "She's been on her own a long time," he said loyally.

"I know that. She's also strong, brave and resourceful. But I'm worried about her and I want to be there when—" He stopped. What if Claudie hadn't told Zach?

"She takes on our daddy?" Zach finished. He looked at Bo. "But why do you care what happens to her?"

A lump the size of Manhattan formed in Bo's throat. He had to swallow twice before he could say, "Because I love her."

Dear Reader,

Writing is a process that sometimes amazes me. *Back in Kansas* originated with Bo, who started out as my hero's best friend in *His Daddy's Eyes*. But he wasn't content to be a secondary character. His voice came through loud and clear. Throughout the writing of *His Daddy's Eyes*, I was sure Bo was destined to fall in love with Eve, his archnemesis. I was completely blown away when my editor pointed out the obvious—Bo seemed to be falling for Claudie. "But she's a reformed prostitute!" I exclaimed in shock. I was told that Superromance readers were broad-minded enough to accept that people do change. Not everyone brings an unblemished past to a new relationship.

People often ask how I research my characters and plots. In addition to the Internet, I'm blessed with a wealth of resources right in my own family. My nephew Michael Robson—whom I neglected to acknowledge in my previous book—helped give me a feel for Sacramento; my nephew Mark Knutson and his wife, Mona, did the same for Kansas. My sisters, Jan and Jean, and dear friend Lorry are invaluable proofreaders.

As both a reader and a writer I'd like to lend my support to the Get Caught Reading campaign. I feel a huge part of my life would be missing without books. Believe me, whenever I'm not writing, I can be caught reading everything from Superromance novels to cookbooks. My motto is: A Book— Don't Leave Home Without One.

I want to thank all the readers who have written to me with their thoughtful, often insightful letters. I love hearing from you. My address is: P.O. Box 322, Catheys Valley, CA 95306. Or you may contact me via e-mail through my Web page at www.superauthors.com.

Debra Salonen

Back in Kansas
Debra Salonen

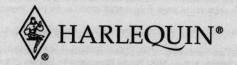

HARLEQUIN®

TORONTO • NEW YORK • LONDON
AMSTERDAM • PARIS • SYDNEY • HAMBURG
STOCKHOLM • ATHENS • TOKYO • MILAN • MADRID
PRAGUE • WARSAW • BUDAPEST • AUCKLAND

ISBN 0-373-70986-2

BACK IN KANSAS

This edition published by arrangement with Harlequin Books S.A.

® and TM are trademarks of the publisher. Trademarks indicated with
® are registered in the United States Patent and Trademark Office, the
Canadian Trade Marks Office and in other countries.

Visit us at www.eHarlequin.com

Printed in U.S.A.

CHAPTER ONE

CLAUDINE ST. JAMES knew the value of a dollar, or rather a twenty-dollar bill. That was how much she'd made the first time she'd sold her body.

"I'll give you eight-fifty for it and not a penny more," she said, keeping her voice as stern as possible. Inside, a rare feeling of frivolity made it hard to keep a straight face.

The old man behind the counter of the Wyoming thrift-store-cum-gas-station gave her a squinty look from his single watery eye—the other was concealed behind a hard plastic cup taped to his face with old-fashioned white tape, the kind that left black tracks behind when you pulled it off.

"Are you trying to snooker me, little girl?" he asked, his voice warbling as if he'd been silent too long.

At five-five, Claudie was used to being called "little," but she was nobody's "girl."

"No," she said, drawing her shoulders back. "The tag says twenty. It might be worth ten. Don't know. Don't care, because, frankly, I don't happen to need it that bad. If you want to get rid of it, then I'll give you eight. If not, keep it." She'd had twenty-seven years to perfect her poker face, and no old man with only one good eye would ever see past it.

He hefted the object in question into the dim light of his storefront window. Claudie assumed a pose of careless nonchalance and looked over the old man's shoulder through the coating of grime that almost obscured the four old-fashioned gas pumps out front.

Sara would kill me if I let the bookstore window get that dirty, she thought.

Claudie winced as an image of Sara Bishop—her friend and the owner of the Sacramento bookstore that Claudie managed—popped into her head. Claudie hadn't talked to Sara in almost a week. She and Ren, her husband of three months, had left early last Friday for their cabin at Lake Almanor; Claudie's impulsive decision to embark on this self-imposed mission hadn't come until later that day when her Internet search turned up a ghost from her past.

Knowing Sara would be worried about her, Claudie had phoned the Bishop home Sunday evening from her motel in Wendover, Utah, but could only leave a message since no one answered.

I hope everything's okay, Claudie thought, poking at various pieces of dust-covered junk while the man debated. *I hope they didn't get caught in that storm that was following me.* A burning sensation in the pit of her stomach made her frown. For a person who'd been on her own since seventeen, Claudie wasn't used to worrying about other people, or vice versa.

"Oh, all right," the man grumbled. He pitched the book to the counter as if to get it out of his limited sight as quickly as possible. "But you said eight-fifty the first time. Not eight. No way I'd be letting it go for eight."

Claudie bit down on the smile that tried to worm

its way to her lips. She jammed her hand into the front pocket of her jeans and withdrew the exact amount, a five, three ones and two quarters. She'd been saving the quarters to call Sara but figured it was worth the sacrifice for an original copy of Mark Twain's *Pudd'nhead Wilson*. Ren, a collector of rare and old books, would keel over when he opened it at Christmas.

Claudie swept the prize into her voluminous purse and hurried to her car. Humming under her breath, she slipped behind the wheel of her 1986 Toyota wagon and pulled on her sunglasses. The car, which had belonged to Sara for most of its hundred thousand miles, was the first possession of any worth Claudie had ever owned. Except for some transmission trouble in Wendover, which had wasted two long days and cost her three hundred bucks, the car was running like a dream.

"Okay, baby, let's hit the road," she said aloud, easing the car into gear. As she waited for the streetlight to change, she glanced appraisingly at the sky. Horizon-to-horizon blue. Yesterday's brief, tumultuous storm, which had stranded her in western Wyoming overnight, might have seemed a figment of her imagination if not for a few residual snowdrifts.

The miniblizzard had reminded Claudie of Maya's ominous forecast prior to Claudie's departure. Maya, the newest resident of One Wish House—the halfway house for ex-prostitutes that Claudie had helped establish—had pulled Claudie aside to whisper, "You can't trust November. One minute it's nice, the next you're buried alive in snow. The weather can be more brutal than a man."

Claudie had shrugged off the dire prediction. It

wasn't like she had a choice. Her baby sister would turn seventeen next month. Seventeen. A grim number that had marked a turning point in Claudie's life. The point when life had gone from bad to worse. She wasn't about to let the same thing happen to Sherry. Claudie only hoped she hadn't left it too late.

No, her trip couldn't wait—which is exactly what she planned to tell Bo. That is, if he was still speaking to her.

ROBERT BOWEN LESTER, JR., or Bo, as he preferred, slammed down the receiver with gusto. "Who the hell came up with automated answering systems?" he muttered under his breath.

His secretary, Karen Kriegen, a sixtyish German with the build of a sumo wrestler and the voice of a porn star, appeared in the doorway of his office. "You break the phone—I'm going home."

Bo knew she was only half kidding and he gave her a look of contrition. "Sorry, Mrs. K. By the time I got to the fifteenth option, I'd forgot what I was calling about."

She made a tsking sound and shook her head. "Where's that happy-go-lucky P.I. I used to work for? I think I liked him better before he fell in love."

"L-lo-ve?" he sputtered. "Believe me, Mrs. K., that's the last emotion on my list where Claudie St. James is concerned."

A ladylike snort filtered past the partially closed door. Karen and the other four members of his staff apparently had put their own interpretation on his impassioned search for Claudie. *They're wrong,* he adamantly insisted, swiveling his chair to face the floor-to-ceiling window at the far end of his office. The tinted glass afforded a pleasant view of the building's Andalusian square, but Bo's mind was not on his surroundings. He'd been plagued by harrowing thoughts of what-if… ever since learning Claudie disappeared.

"She's not here," the Asian girl had told him Friday night when he'd knocked on the door of One Wish House. Bo had cut his Vegas trip short—ostensibly because he'd been bored. In reality, he'd missed Claudie. And he'd been worried about her, too. She'd seemed preoccupied and distant for over a week. "She's gone off on a mission, and you are best to leave this alone," the woman had added, her voice steeped with portent.

She'd have shut the door of the old Victorian house in his face if not for Bo's cop-trained reflexes. "Claudie's gone? Where? She didn't mention anything about a trip when I talked to her last night." But she had seemed tense and distracted—maybe a little down, which was another reason he'd cut his trip short.

"It is not for me to say," Maya—Bo was certain that was the woman's name—had replied. She spoke with a spooky singsong intonation that made him uneasy. "Her wounds are deep and painful. There is much healing to do." For some reason her speech sent a bolt of fear through Bo.

Before he could ask anything else, a tall black woman had appeared in the doorway to add her two cents. "Get lost, asshole. If Claudie wanted you to know where she was, she'da called you. But she didn't, so guess what? You're f—"

Bo hadn't waited around to hear the rest of Rochell's colorful diatribe. He'd dashed to his car and started calling people. First, Sara, Claudie's best friend. *"Hello, you've reached the Bishops. Please leave us a message…"* Bo ended the call with a curse and tried Ren's cell phone but wasn't surprised when a voice told him the number was not in service. Ren seldom turned the damn thing on.

Next, Bo had tried the bookstore. "She came by about four and asked if she could have the week off," Daniel Pagannini, the comanager told him. "I kinda assumed she was joining you in Vegas. Next Monday is a holiday, and she was due for a vacation. Why? Is there a problem?"

Bo's gut said, yes. With anyone else, he might have shrugged it off, but not with Claudie. People like her weren't generally impetuous. They'd learned the hard way that unplanned risks often left you exposed and vulnerable. It had taken Bo months to win her trust— at least he'd thought she trusted him, but apparently he'd been deluding himself. She hadn't even bothered to tell him goodbye.

A staged cough brought Bo back to the present. He spun his chair to find Ren Bishop standing in the doorway.

"Don't shoot," an amused voice said. "My wife's pregnant with twins."

Bo's body gave a little shudder as the wasted adrenaline dissipated in his veins. "Dammit, Bishop, haven't I told you not to sneak up on me?"

"I knocked," Ren Bishop said, moving into the room. He looked around, his expression appreciative. "Nice digs. Beats the hell out of the spare bedroom of your houseboat."

"I moved here in September, you jerk. Is this the first time you've been to my office?"

Ren shrugged carelessly. "Have you been to mine on campus, yet?"

Bo rocked back in his chair and kicked his feet up on his desk. Ren had recently switched from dispensing the law to teaching it. "Point taken. Have a seat. Any word from Claudie?"

"No, she didn't tell Sara where she was going, either. To me that says she didn't want to worry the two people she cares most about."

Bo snorted. "Some way of showing it."

Ren walked to the window, checking out the view. "At the moment, Sara's more worried about you than Claudie. Mrs. Kriegen told her you haven't left this place since Saturday."

"Mrs. K. exaggerates. Besides, I got a shower and a closet full of clothes here. The couch makes into a bed and there's a pizzeria next door. Maybe I'll sell the boat and move here permanently."

Ren returned to the tufted leather sofa and sat down. Bo could see the depth of his concern. "I know you're worried about her. We're all—"

"Screw worried," Bo snapped. "I'm just plain pissed now. I thought we were past that I-don't-need-anyone-and-nobody-needs-me stage. She has a life here, Ren. Responsibilities. A job." He swallowed to keep from saying, "A relationship."

"I'm sure she took all that into account before she left," Ren said equitably. "Claudie's not what I'd call impetuous. This must have been darned important."

Bo shook his head. "Too important to share with the people who care about her?"

Ren sighed and lifted his shoulders in resignation.

Bo regretted his outburst. Mrs. K. was right—this really wasn't like him. "By the way," he said in a more equitable tone, "I know Daniel's managing the bookstore while Claudie's away, but I forgot to ask when I talked to you last night. Who's running One Wish House while she's gone?"

Ren looked up, a bemused expression on his face. "Believe it or not, my mother volunteered. Apparently, Claudie called her late Friday afternoon and said she had a family emergency and asked if Babe would keep an eye on the place until she returned."

"She called Babe but not me," Bo said, not caring how bitter he sounded.

Ren sighed. "Like I told you on the phone, this must be something she thinks she has to do on her own. You're the same way, Lester. Jeez, getting personal information out of you is like pulling teeth. How long did we know each other before I ever met your family? I probably never would have met Matt if he hadn't come to visit you." He waited a second then asked, "Are you still going to New York?"

Bo studied his fingernails—being a judge had given Ren an unfair advantage when it came to reading people's faces. Bo didn't want to reveal how hopeless this case looked. "I don't know. I left a message on Matt's machine, but it's not like we have a lot to go on. I don't even know her real name."

Ren rose. "Here," he said, taking a piece of paper from the inside pocket of his lightweight blazer. "Maybe this will help. Sara found this drawing in Brady's backpack."

"What information could your four-year-old son possibly have?"

"Apparently Claudie was doodling when she baby-sat Brady last week," Ren told him.

Bo took the rumpled paper. He switched on his desk lamp and held it under the light. Claudie had apparently been teaching Brady the alphabet. Beside letters were names. "Do you recognize any of these names?" Bo asked, working to keep his voice even. Just the sight of Claudie's carefully crafted penmanship made a funny ache blossom behind his breastbone.

"Nope. But Brady told Sara they were the names of Claudie's brothers and sisters. He said the two with the sad faces beneath them died."

Bo sat up straighter. "You're kidding. She never mentioned any family." He scanned the names again. "My God, she has two brothers and two sisters still alive, and I've never heard of them. That woman makes a clam look chatty."

Ren shrugged. "That's our Claudie." He turned away but stopped. "By the way, Sara thinks she once heard Claudie say something about growing up near one of the Great Lakes."

Bo groaned. "Terrific! That narrows down the search to the upper third of the country."

"Why don't you come home with me, Bo? Sara's fixing lunch. Maybe we could do some brainstorming."

Bo shook his head. "Thanks, but I'm gonna run over to the bookstore. Claudie told Daniel she'd e-mail him if she got a chance." He couldn't stop himself from adding, bitterly, "I have an e-mail address, too, you know."

Ren squeezed Bo's shoulder. "She's a big girl, Bo. She can take care of herself." He stopped at the threshold and looked back. "Let me know if you decide to go to New York, okay? We still haven't been able to reach Eve. Weird, huh?"

Bo didn't have the energy to care about whatever troubles might be facing Eve Masterson, Ren's former fiancée. She'd chosen her course—a shot at network news, complete with all the fame, glamour and salary that went with it. If anyone could take care of herself it was Eve. Claudie, on the other hand, was as defenseless as a baby chick.

True, Claudie had survived for years in the emotionally desolate world of prostitution. But that was the old Claudie. The hooker. The new Claudie had her GED and was signed up for her first semester of college next spring. The new Claudie was fragile, vulnerable. Bo knew this on a gut level. And his gut was telling him to find her before something or someone could hurt her again.

He studied Claudie's sketch a minute longer. Wedged between *Wesley* and *Valery* was a word he'd overlooked. A name. A surname. "Anders."

This might be the break he needed. Bo buzzed his secretary. "Mrs. K., try my cousin again, please. And see if you can get me on a flight to New York. Tonight."

AS HER CAR joined the easterly flow of traffic on Interstate 80, Claudie heaved a sigh and let her thoughts drift to Bo—where they seemed content to stay way too much of the time.

"Bo's head over heels crazy about you, Claudie," Sara had said last Tuesday as they'd relaxed on the bench of the BART train during their ride back from San Francisco. An array of fancy bags—trophies from their shopping expedition—encircled their aching feet.

"If he is, then he's just plain crazy, Sara. I'm not the girl next door, you know."

"He knows who you are, Claudie," Sara had protested. "He's seen you turn your life around these past seven months and he knows how hard you've worked to help other women get off the street."

Sara's praise had a way of making Claudie squirm—it felt good but somehow undeserved. "I'm no saint, Sara. I'm not the kind of person who deserves a happy ending. Life just doesn't work that way for people like me."

Sara's eyes had filled with tears. "You are so wrong about that, Claudie. And if you think Bo believes that then you don't know Bo."

Their conversation had been interrupted by the train's arrival at the Pleasanton station where Sara's Explorer was parked, but Sara's words had stayed with Claudie during the drive home. Claudie did know Bo. He was a kind, decent man who'd always treated her with respect.

He'd never judged her or questioned her about her years on the streets. The more she came to know him—they were often thrown together thanks to Ren and Sara's situation—the better she liked him. But that was as far as their relationship should go. They needed to keep things superficial.

Friendly. Bo was a friend. Period.

So maybe you're hoping your friend will come look-ing for you, a little voice said.

"No," she said aloud, startling herself by the vol-ume of her denial. "I can do this myself. If I'd have wanted his help, all I had to do was ask."

But that would have meant telling him about her past. That was nobody's business but hers—and Gar-ret Anders's.

A sign announcing a truck stop caught her eye and Claudie impulsively took the exit. The clock on the dash read: three-thirty. She was less than twenty miles from Cheyenne. Her brother probably had a job, which meant Claudie would have to time her arrival. She knew she could call first, but she wanted to sur-prise him. Perhaps just to see if he still recognized her. She was curious herself—was there any of the old Claudie left to see?

She parked near a bank of phones and got out of the car. The wind sliced through her sweatshirt, but the clean, brisk air felt exhilarating. She sat down at a picnic table partially sheltered from the wind and mentally catalogued all that she'd left behind to un-dertake this quest.

First and foremost: One Wish House.

Back in July when Ren first suggested using his partially renovated Victorian home in Folsom, Cali-fornia, as a halfway house for prostitutes, Claudie had laughed in disbelief. But somehow the project had be-come a reality.

The name had come from her friend, Keneesha, a former prostitute who'd turned her life around and was now living in Georgia, raising the son she'd abandoned years earlier. "When I was hookin', I can't tell you the number of times I'd find myself thinking, 'If I could have one wish, I'd ask to start over,'" Kee had said when she'd returned for Sara's wedding.

The home's current residents ranged in age from nineteen to thirty-three. While linked to various bureaucratic agencies, the halfway house was a volunteer residence program.

Claudie feared her absence might undermine all she'd worked so hard to create.

"You know what people are going to think, right?" Davina had fretted as she watched Claudie pack. "They're going to think you abandoned us or something."

"It's dangerous out there, Claudie," the world-weary Maya had added. "I've been across this country more than once—bad things can happen. And this is a terrible time of year to travel. Storms. Snow this high," she'd said raising to her tiptoes to hold her hand above her head.

"*Sí,*" Davina had concurred, "you shouldn't do this alone. Meester Bo would go. I know he would. He likes you."

A foul epithet had introduced Rochell's opinion. "She don't need a man to do this. She got off the street on her own, didn't she? Why do you always act like men are the answer?"

"Bo's at a gadget fair in Vegas until Monday," Claudie had interjected. "This can't wait. I'll call him from the road and let him know I'm okay. Besides, we're just friends, you know."

Sally Rae, a willowy blonde and youngest member

of the group, made a snorting sound. "Yeah, right, like we believe that."

Claudie had grabbed her jacket from her closet and faced the group. "Hey, this isn't a best-case scenario, but I've got to go, and you all know why. Babe Bishop's going to check in on things from time to time."

Their simultaneous groans summed up their feelings about that topic. Claudie flinched. "Sorry, but she's on the board of directors. If you need any help, call Sara."

Davina, the most spontaneous of the group, surged forward, clasping Claudie in a hug. "Don't worry. We will be okay, Claudie. And I will pray for you and your little sister."

The women walked Claudie to the door. A sober stillness hung in the foyer as she opened the door. Beyond the porch, a steady drizzle fell, cold and uninviting. Claudie feared she might not make it over Donner Pass without chains. She'd debated about waiting until morning to head out, but the weather report showed a big storm approaching from the northwest.

Maya spoke softly. "You are a warrior on a quest, Claudie." Her obsidian eyes had seemed capable of viewing the core of Claudie's heart. "Find the truth and it will release the pain you keep locked away."

A warrior on a quest, Claudie silently repeated, gazing across the windswept vista. *Bo would love that one, wouldn't he?*

Guilt made her grimace, but she closed her mind to Bo's image. She couldn't think about him right now. She had to stay focused.

She rose and started toward her car, but detoured at the bank of phones. She counted her remaining coins—only enough for one call. *If I call Sara, she could give Bo a message.*

Coward, a voice whispered. A cowardly warrior on a foolish quest. *Yep, that about sums things up,* she thought, shaking her head to keep the wind-induced tears at bay.

BREATHLESS FROM her run to catch the phone, Sara croaked, "Hello."

The voice on the other end triggered a flood of emotion. "Claudie! Thank God you're okay. Tell me you're okay."

"I'm fine, Sara J. Don't get all worked up. That can't be good for the babies."

An immediate sense of relief made Sara's knees weak. She sat down on a stool and caught sight of the notepad and pen Bo had left beside every phone in the house. *Notes. Bo said I'm supposed to concentrate and take notes. Impressions. Background noises.* "Where are you? Why'd you leave without telling me? You are coming back, right?" Sara asked, picking up the pen. It was hard to be a sleuth and talk at the same time.

Claudie's small laugh sounded sort of lonely and sad. "I'm a bad penny, remember? I keep turning up."

Sara's eyes misted over. "You'd better come back soon. Brady's missing you, and Bo's going nuts."

"Bo's one of the reasons I left without telling anyone. You know Super Snoop—he'd have his nose in this up to his eyebrows. I have to do this on my own, Sara."

"But we're your friends, Claudie. Can't we help? That's what friends do."

"Between keeping up with Brady and getting ready for the new babies, you've got your hands full at the moment, remember?" Her friend was obviously not going to reveal much, so Sara tried to focus on the noises coming through the line.

She hastily jotted down "Trucks? Freeway? Interstate?" Sara decided to gamble. "Does this have anything to do with your family?"

In the moment of stunned silence that followed, Sara heard a tinny voice give the call letters of a radio station. She wrote them down. "How do you know that?" Claudie asked, her voice tense.

"You left a piece of paper in Brady's backpack. There were names. Brady said they were your brothers and sisters."

Claudie blew out a breath. "I keep forgetting how smart that little guy is." Sara added the notation: *She misses Brady...and us.* "Well, all I'm gonna say about it right now is that I'm trying to find my half brother. Hopefully Yancy can put me in touch with the rest of the bunch. A regular old-home week," she said her voice sounding less than pleased by the prospect.

Sara added a few quick notes to her list. "That sounds wonderful. I'm happy you're reuniting with your family."

Claudie's chuckle didn't sound encouraging. "I haven't seen any of these people since I left home ten years ago. I doubt they're going to be thrilled to see me, but that's just tough. This is something I gotta do. Period.''

Sara recognized the determination in her friend's voice. ''I know you, Claudie. You'll do whatever you set out to do. I just wish we could help. We're family, too, aren't we?''

''You're my California family, Sara, and I know you want to help, but this is the past. My past. Believe me, it isn't pretty. And I don't want my future god-children exposed to any of it.''

Sara swallowed loudly. ''Then Bo. Couldn't he help?''

''No,'' Claudie responded. ''This is something I ran away from a long time ago, and if I learned anything from you and Ren it's that the past has a way of catching up with you. I have to deal with it. I can't sit by in my safe little world and let Garret ruin another girl's life.''

''Who…?'' Sara tried to ask, but her question was interrupted by a mechanical voice asking for more money.

''My stepfather, that's who,'' Claudie snapped. A second later, she sighed, as if regretting her disclosure. ''I'm outa change, Sara J. Gotta go. I'll call again soon. Tell Brady I haven't forgotten his birthday. I'm going to send him something. And tell Bo he can yell at me all he wants when I get back. Bye.''

The line went dead and Sara replaced the receiver. She walked into Ren's office and turned on the computer. Within minutes she was online; seconds later she'd found a page dedicated to the call signs of radio stations. She pushed the button to access the other phone line and hit the speed-dial number of Bo's office. As soon as he picked up, she said, "Hi, it's me. I think she's in Wyoming."

CHAPTER TWO

KNOCKING ON the door of her brother's house turned out to be harder than Claudie expected. Her heart pounded in her chest as she forced herself to take a deep breath. The raw Wyoming wind penetrated through her Sacramento Kings sweatshirt making her shiver. The November sun was already sinking below a stratum of thin, horizontal clouds—eye-catching ribbons of tangerine and magenta.

The hollow tinny sound her knocking produced didn't seem substantial enough to magnify past the wooden inner door. She looked for a doorbell but found a piece of frayed duct tape over an empty hole.

Her hand was poised to rap again when she heard a loud, hollow thump. A moment later the inner door opened with a swoosh. A tall, trim man in a worn plaid shirt greeted her with a curious, ''Yeah? What can I do for you?''

The lanky auburn hair was familiar even if the long handsome face wasn't.

Claudie swallowed. ''Yancy?'' she asked in a small voice.

He bent down slightly and put his face closer to the screen. ''Do I know you?''

''It's Claudie,'' she said, suddenly realizing her wind-combed, Meg Ryan hairdo probably bore little resemblance to the girl with long dark hair that he'd last known.

He stepped back as if someone had yanked him by the collar. His mouth dropped open and he shook his head. "My *sister* Claudie? Really?"

Claudie's heart galloped against her ribs. She'd visualized this moment a dozen times. She just hadn't expected to feel so…tearful. "Yeah, it's me."

Yancy stepped forward again, this time fumbling with the latch on the metal screen door. "Well, I'll be… It's been ten years, ain't it? Good Lord, I'd never have recognized you. Come on in."

Gratified to find her legs still worked, she stepped over the threshold and moved in enough for him to close the door. Once inside, she was struck by conflicting odors: overly pungent male cologne and the too-sweet stench of chlorine. He must have noticed her nose crinkling. "We're bleaching the toilets," he said apologetically. "We all had the flu since Sunday, but everybody's better today."

Claudie smiled—not sure what to say. Yancy seemed just as tentative. His big, coarse-looking hands made start and stop motions as if he wanted to hug her but wasn't sure how to do it. Finally, he indicated the room to her right. "Let's go sit down. This is just too weird. I can't believe it. Zach and me were sure you'd died or something."

Claudie picked her way past an assortment of shoes, toys and old newspapers, which Yancy apologized for with another reference to their recent illness. The couch was a plush navy sectional adorned with a dozen throw pillows in a rainbow of hues. She nudged aside a plump square of sunshine yellow and sat down.

"I've been living in California. Sacramento, mostly," she said.

"Really? I been through there. I used to drive long hauls but I've been with a cement company the last six years. Closer to home. Wife likes it that way." He lowered himself to a dusty piano bench across from her. Behind him sat an electric keyboard enveloped in an opaque plastic cover.

"You're married," Claudie said, looking around. A brass frame on the end table held an eight-by-ten photo of a woman with long blond hair and two young boys, one dark, one light. "Is that your family?"

"One of 'em," Yancy said, making a wry face. "My first wife, Becca, lives in Denver with our daughter Darcy—she'll be seven in January."

"Wow," Claudie exclaimed, mentally doing the math. Yancy was two and a half years her junior. "You started young."

"Yeah, you think you know everything when you're seventeen. Hell, I didn't even know enough to use a rubber. Becca was six months along when we got married. It was a mistake from the start."

Claudie nodded as if she understood.

"You married?" he asked.

"No."

He opened his mouth as if to speak but just then a small child burst through the front door then slammed it resoundingly. Yancy poked out one long arm and grabbed the boy before he could escape.

"Slow down, Pika. Your Aunt Claudie's here to visit. Say hi."

The child, who looked a year or two older than Brady, squirmed like a fish on a line. "Hi," he said, not making eye contact. From what Claudie could see, he was the spitting image of his father at that age—wavy auburn hair, all legs and arms.

Yancy let him go and the boy dashed down the hallway.

"What did you say his name is?"

"Pika. As in Pike's Peak. Renee says that's where he was conceived when we were on a camping trip. Hell if I know. I was probably stoned or drunk."

Claudie kept her expression blank. She'd known plenty of men who wanted sex when they were stoned or drunk. If she'd been the dishonest type, she could have ripped them off when they passed out. But she wasn't a thief.

"Who?" a woman's voice asked in the distance. "Yancy, is someone here?" she called out a moment later.

"Yeah, Renee, my sister's here." Yancy shook his head once more as if the idea still boggled his mind.

A shuffling sound preceded Renee's arrival. Curious, Claudie sat forward. The woman who appeared in the doorway looked far different from her photograph. Her bleached locks hung limp beside her long sallow face. Her pale skin was blotchy and a large cold sore festered at the corner of her lip.

Dressed in baggy red sweatpants, heelless mules and a paint-splattered Mickey Mouse T-shirt, she attempted to fix up her hair and clothes but gave up with a sigh, "Oh, hell," she grumbled, extending her hand. "I'm Renee."

Claudie rose and shook her hand. "Claudie."

Renee's chin turned abruptly toward her husband. "*That* one?"

Claudie's hackles rose until Yancy said, "Yep, my long-lost sister who ran away from home when she was sixteen."

"Seventeen," Claudie corrected. "I was sixteen when Mom died, but my birthday's May 7, and I didn't leave home 'til the fifth of June."

He nodded. "That's right. We were still in school, which was how come Val's teacher offered to take her in."

Renee motioned for Yancy to move over so she could sit down beside him. Claudie sat back down, uneasily. She hadn't talked about that time in her life for ten years, and she wasn't sure she wanted to do so with a stranger present.

"How long have you been married?" she asked, stalling.

Renee shrugged. "Four years next week. Pika was six months old when we tied the knot. We'da done it sooner, but his divorce from the Barbie doll wasn't final."

Yancy's grimace told Claudie his ex-wife was a sore spot in his current marriage.

"And you have a second son," Claudie said, nodding toward the photo.

"Laramie. He's three. He's over at his grandma's— my mom's house. She lives across the alley. He still ain't feelin' too good."

"Oh." Claudie looked at her brother. "They're pretty close together, aren't they? Like you and Zach."

Yancy frowned. "Yeah, but that's all we're having.

Two, not ten. I already went in and had the operation just to make sure there weren't any *accidents*."

Startled by his vehement response, Claudie glanced at Renee. Her scowl said this was another sore subject.

"Renee wanted to try again for a girl, but like my pal Andy says the first rule about holes is, if you're in one, stop digging."

Renee snorted then looked at Claudie. "Like Andy knows shit from shinola—he's single. You got kids?"

Claudie pictured Sara's adopted son, Brady. At times he felt like her child. At times she wished he were her child. She shook her head. "No."

Yancy made an understanding sound. "Not surprised. With Mom sick so much toward the end, you were practically raising the rest of us." To Renee, he said, "Claudie had to drop out of school after Mom passed away to stay home and take care of our little sister, Sherry."

Claudie looked down at the floor. Sweet darling Sherry hadn't been the problem. If Garret hadn't started drinking…

She put the thought aside when Yancy asked, "So, Sis, what brings you to Cheyenne?"

Claudie swallowed. "I ran across your name on the Internet. I couldn't find anything on Zach or Val, so I thought I'd get a hold of you and see what you know."

He nodded. "Searching for your roots, huh? A guy I work with's big on that genealogy crap." He shrugged. "Not me. Past's behind us—right where I like it."

A year ago Claudie would have agreed with him wholeheartedly.

"So you're online, huh?" Renee asked. "We're talking about getting a computer. I have one at work, but our boss is like Mr. Scrooge—if he thought you were using his toys for anything but work he'd fire you."

"We have several computers at the bookstore where I work," Claudie said, picturing the new office space Sara and Ren had created at the rear of the bookstore—one cubicle for Daniel, one for her.

"You work in a bookstore?" Yancy asked, obviously surprised.

"Part-time. I manage a halfway house, too." She'd told a watered-down version of her story so many times, it almost sounded like someone else's life. Here, she thought, uneasily, is someone who knew the truth.

"You mean like for ex-cons?" Yancy exclaimed. "How weird! You know Zach's gonna be getting out of jail in another year or so. Maybe he could go to your place."

It was Claudie's turn to sputter. "Zach's in jail?"

"South Dakota State Penitentiary. Vehicular manslaughter. Drove his rig into a car one night when he was drunk. Killed two people."

Claudie grimaced. A part of her wasn't surprised to learn that her brother's life had turned into a nightmare. As the eldest son he'd borne the brunt of his father's demands. He'd also been the most devastated by their younger brother Wesley's death.

"I didn't know that. How long ago?" she asked.

Yancy looked at Renee. "Four, maybe five years ago. We write each other once 'n a while."

Renee snorted. "Like once a year if you're lucky."

He gave her a black look, and she stood up. "Listen," she said to Claudie, "I'd like to stay and chat, but I gotta finish up before Mom brings Laramie home. And, don't forget, Yance, you promised to take Pika to the video store if he cleaned up the dog shit," she told her husband.

"Did he do it?" Yancy asked.

"He said he did. Go look for yourself." With that she turned away, but stopped and said, "It was nice meeting you, Claudie. I'm sorry we can't offer you a place to stay tonight, but, believe me, you don't want to catch what we just got over, and Laramie might still be contagious."

Claudie hadn't thought about her plans for the night, but she definitely didn't want to catch the flu. "Thanks, but I need to push on anyway. I've got a lot of stops to make."

After his wife was gone, Yancy heaved a sigh. "Families are such fun."

He'd meant it as a joke, but Claudie shook her head. "Not ours."

He flinched. "Are you gonna bring all that stuff back up? 'Cause I don't want to hear it, Claudie. What's done is done, you can't take it back."

She cocked her head. "What do you mean I can't take it back? Do you think I lied about what happened?"

He shrugged. "The old man said you did. He claimed you just wanted to get out of staying home with Sherry. He tol' the police you were mad 'cause he made you miss the prom or something."

A fury so deep and massive it nearly choked her made Claudie leap to her feet. "That bastard. That lying scumbag. He raped me, Yancy. He was supposed to go to jail. Miss Murray promised he'd go to jail if I told the police what happened.''

Yancy drew back. ''Well, I don't know about any of that. Once the police came and took us all away, me 'n' Zach never got to go home. We saw Dad a couple'a more times at the courthouse, but the judge said it was apparent Dad couldn't handle us. The judge said me'n Zach needed more discipline and structure than we were getting at home, so he sent us to a group home in Emporia.''

Claudie saw a hooded look descend over his face. ''It sucked big time. The food was bad, the beds stunk. Only good part was we were together most of the time. Zach learned to work on engines and they helped him find a job with a trucking company when he turned eighteen. I was supposed to stick around another year, but I split when Zach did. We went to Omaha.''

''What'd you do there?''

''Zach drove truck. I was a dishwasher mostly, but then I met Becca. Her dad owned the company Zach was working for.''

''How'd you wind up here?''

He shrugged. ''Long story. Could we save it for later? You kinda caught us at a bad time—what with the family being sick and all.''

She got the hint. ''Look, Yancy, I came here for a reason. I think Garret—'' she couldn't bring herself to use the word Dad ''—might do to Sherry what he did to me. I want to go back there and make sure it doesn't happen.''

Yancy looked stunned. "You came all this way 'cause…" he slowly inhaled. "He really did it, huh?"

A fist clenched in her stomach. "Did you think I'd lie about something like that?"

He shrugged. "Zach said maybe you got knocked up by Darren Blains and just stirred things up so you could get away without anybody noticing."

Claudie frowned. "Darren and I did it a few times, but I wasn't pregnant—no way was I going to wind up like Mom. But I didn't lie about Garret. It happened the day he lost his job. He came home drunk and…" She squeezed her eyes closed, blocking images that skittered about on the edge of her consciousness.

When she looked at Yancy he was doubled over, hands folded between his knees. "Shit." He was quiet a minute then asked, "Was it just the once?"

Claudie fought to keep her expression even. "Yes. Does that make it all right?"

He flinched visibly. After a long pause, he let out a sigh. "What do you want from me?"

"I'm going back and I want you to come along."

He snorted. "Yeah, right. Just drop everything and head back to Kansas because you're afraid the old man might be playing hide the salami with Sherry, huh? How do you even know he's still alive? I ain't heard from him since we left. Maybe he's dead."

Claudie open the purse at her feet and withdrew three sheets of paper folded in half. "He's not that old, Yancy. Fifty-one or two. I found his Web page on the Internet. That's what made me come looking for you."

She handed Yancy the papers. Even seeing her step-father's image produced a sick feeling.

Yancy read for a minute. "He's a preacher? I thought he was Catholic. Remember all that church stuff we had to do up 'til Mom got sick?"

Claudie remembered—it was one of the reasons she hadn't stepped inside a church in ten years. "I don't know how he got to be a preacher but it's him."

Yancy flipped to the second page. "He's on radio?"

Claudie nodded. "Makes sense if you think about it. He always was a salesman. Mom used to say he could sell sand to Arabs. Now he's peddling God."

She rose and walked to her brother's side. When he turned to the third page she pointed out a paragraph she'd highlighted in yellow. "See. It mentions his teenage daughter named Sherry."

Yancy grunted.

"So? Will you go with me?"

He paused as if considering her request, but in the end his answer was the one Claudie expected. "I can't, Claudie. I got a wife 'n' two kids, an ex-wife and child support, a mortgage and two car payments. I leave 'n' the whole damn thing goes to hell. Just being home sick the last two days means I gotta pull weekend overtime to break even."

Claudie swallowed her disappointment. When he handed her the papers, she carefully folded them and picked up her purse. "Could you at least put me in touch with Zach and Valery? Maybe they can help me. I don't like the idea of going in there cold." A lesson she'd learned from watching Bo at work.

He scratched his head. "Zach ain't hard to find. The

prison's in Sioux Falls, and he won't be going anywhere for a while.'' He rose. ''You gotta call ahead to make sure your name is on his visitor list. Yours probably ain't, but they might make an exception since you come so far. I got the number of the prison around here somewhere.''

He disappeared into the room across the hall but returned a few seconds later. ''Here,'' he said, passing her a scrap of paper. ''I don't have a clue about Val. She changed her name when she got adopted, but I can't remember what that teacher's name was.'' He sighed. ''Ask Zach. I think he said he got a Christmas card from her last year.''

Claudie left without telling her sister-in-law goodbye or meeting her youngest nephew. She gave her brother a hug—the first in ten years, but somehow it didn't produce that warm, fuzzy feeling greeting cards always talk about. As she walked to her car, she sighed, surprised by the deflated feeling that engulfed her.

What the hell did you expect? she asked herself severely once she was sitting behind the wheel.

Suddenly, out of the blue, she felt the need to talk to Bo. He'd understand, she thought starting the car. Impulsively, she pulled into the first gas station she found. Its lighted telephone booth stood on the side of the building.

After three rings a familiar voice requested the caller to leave a message or try Bo's cellular number. Taking a deep breath, she said, ''Hi. It's me. I'm sure as hell glad you're not there to get this call—you'd just yell at me and I'd end up hanging up on you.'' She smiled, knowing it was the truth. ''I'm just calling to let you know I'm doing fine. You know me—the Energizer Bunny—I keep going and going.''

She shook her head at the inanity of her dialogue. ''Listen, I'll make this quick. I don't expect you to understand, but I'm doing something I need to do and I didn't tell you because I thought you'd freak. Sara probably told you by now I'm tracking down my long-lost family.'' She tried to keep her tone light. ''I just saw brother number two and now I'm on my way to see number one. Apparently there's no big rush—he won't be going anywhere for the next three to five,'' she said dryly.

She could picture the look on Bo's face when he heard this message. He'd be mad…and hurt. ''Well,'' she said, trying to keep her tone from betraying how much she missed him, ''I'll call you later. Bye.''

BO PLAYED the recording a third time. According to the machine's log, he'd only missed her call by ten minutes. He glanced at his watch. Less than an hour until his flight.

Karen Kriegen walked in—a sheaf of papers in her outstretched hand. ''Here's the latest on those names,'' she said. ''Looks promising.''

Bo took the inch-thick stack and shoved it in his briefcase without looking at it. ''I'll go through it on the plane. Anything from Matt, yet?''

''Not yet. I'll give him your flight information if he calls before I leave for the night. If he doesn't call, I'll make sure the switchboard has the details.''

''Great. Thanks. The less time I have to spend in New York the better,'' Bo said, suppressing a shudder. He wouldn't have made the trip at all if he wasn't banking on his cousin's help. Matt, who was four years younger than Bo, was a cop. But he'd been injured on the job and relegated to a desk job. He was also apparently doing some kind of computer tracking for the FBI. If anyone had access to the information Bo needed, it would be Matt.

Bo flipped open his answering machine and pocketed the recording of Claudie's voice. He told himself Matt might be able to use it to help track her whereabouts, but in all honesty Bo had decided their best bet would be to figure out where she was going, not try to guess where she was at the moment. "Do we have any more tapes for this thing?" he asked, nodding at the empty machine.

Karen nodded tolerantly. "Go. I'll take care of it."

He gave her a grateful smile then turned to leave.

Bo was halfway across the parking lot when he bumped into Ren and Sara. Sara's face, already a little puffy with pregnancy, was flushed from hurrying.

"Hey, Sara, if you don't slow down you're going to have those kids in three months instead of six."

"My doctor said walking is good for me," she told him breathlessly.

"Walking. Not wind sprints." He looped his arm around Sara's shoulders. "What are you guys doing here? I'm on my way to the airport."

Sara squeezed him briefly. "I know. Ren said you were going to New York. That's why we came by. I wanted to give you this." Bo had to trot to keep up with her. He took the folded piece of paper she passed him.

"More drawings?" Bo asked, stopping to look it over.

"No," Sara said. "I just remembered something I thought might be important. When I was helping Claudie study for the GED, we got in an argument over the capital of Kansas. I didn't believe it was Topeka. She was right. She said she'd lived on a farm about twenty miles north of there. I thought she was kidding. I mean, can you picture Claudie as a Kansas farm girl?"

Ren added, "When Sara told me that, it triggered something. Last week, Claudie asked me about the statute of limitations on rape. I told her it would depend on the state, and she said, 'How 'bout Kansas?'"

"You think she was raped?" Bo asked, his voice catching.

Sara nodded. "It's possible. She mentioned her stepfather the last time she called. Something about not letting him ruin another girl."

"What's this?" Bo asked, fingering a yellow Post-it note adorned with a florid scrawl.

"That's Babe's theory. She's home with Brady."

Bo's heartbeat quickened as he scanned the note. "Revenge? She thinks Claudie may be on her way to Kansas to kill the guy who molested her?"

Ren grimaced. "I told Mother I thought that was a bit extreme, but you know Babe."

"Bo, you've got to find her." Sara's voice broke.

"I will, Sara," Bo said, touching her shoulder supportively. "But I don't believe Babe's theory." He added the paper to his briefcase. "Listen, you guys, I gotta run. Don't worry, Sara. I'll make sure nothing bad happens. I promise."

With a wave, he left his friends behind. Impatient now to begin the search, Bo started his car and pulled into traffic. Ren and Sara's news had brought additional worries he didn't need. If his researchers had been more confident in their theory, he'd have skipped New York and gone straight to Kansas, but Bo believed in being prepared. He wanted to learn as much as he could about Claudie's past before thrusting himself into the middle of something he didn't understand.

Accelerating, the Mazda joined the cars headed north on I-5. If all went as planned, he'd be in New York shortly after midnight. And, if his cousin was as proficient at the computer as his mother claimed, Bo might beat Claudie to Kansas.

If that's where she's going, he reminded himself.

MATTHEW ROSS kicked the door closed behind him. The dim glow from the night-light he'd left burning in the guest bath was just enough for him to negotiate the narrow hallway with his arms wrapped around two full bags of groceries. Ashley was coming for the weekend, and he'd stocked up on all her favorites— Goldfish crackers, apples, toaster waffles with honey—not syrup—and praline fudge ripple ice cream. Ashley was easy to please; her mother, on the other hand, made the Middle East peace talks look like a negotiator's dream job.

He carefully lowered the bags to the counter in his kitchenette then dug past the four-pack of toilet paper to reach the freezer bag. The nightmare of New York City traffic never ceased to amaze him. Even though he'd grown up in New Jersey, and, as a cop with the NYPD he'd learned to deal with the decaying infrastructure and moronic drivers, the state of the roads seemed to be getting worse by the day.

Or you're just getting too damn old to take it, he told himself.

Once the ice cream was safely stored in the freezer section of his small refrigerator he took his time putting things away. As he leaned down to stow the box of crackers he noticed the number two in red on his answering machine. He checked his pager first, but saw no new messages so figured the calls were personal, not work-related.

He cracked open a Heineken before lowering himself to the stool where he kept a pen and paper handy.

"Yo, Cuz, this is Bo," the first message began.

Matt almost choked on his swallow of beer. He hadn't spoken with his cousin, Bo Lester, in ages. As he listened to the message his surprise intensified. A woman. Missing. A friend. Something told Matt the mystery woman was more than a friend.

He scribbled down the time and flight number of his cousin's plane. Sure, he'd meet the plane and provide a bed—or rather, a couch for a couple of nights. Matt's guest room with its four-poster bed and down comforter was still at his ex-wife's house—along with his daughter and the better part of his life.

"Matthew," the second message started, causing Matt's beer to curdle in his stomach, "Ashley won't be able to make it this weekend after all. I know this is your regular weekend but something wonderful came up that she couldn't resist. She feels terrible about this and will call you later to explain." There was a pause and Matt could picture the troubled look on his ex-wife's face—she never could lie without frowning in a way that made a crease between her eyebrows. That giveaway point had been what alerted him to her affair. "Please try not to blow this out of proportion, Matt. You can have her next weekend, which technically is our weekend, but I'm prepared to be flexible if you are. This is about Ashley's happiness, not her parents' schedules."

Matt gripped his beer bottle, willing himself not to smash it against the wall. Sonya knew just how to manipulate his emotions. She knew how much he loved his daughter, and she constantly used Ashley's state of mind as a weapon against him.

"Call when you get this message so I can explain about the dressage school. Bye."

Matt polished off his beer with a long gulp then tossed the bottle in the garbage. It wasn't as satisfying, but it beat the hell out of cleaning up broken glass— he'd learned that one the hard way. A glance at his watch told him he might as well head to the airport. There were plenty of bars there, and since Bo was a reformed drinker, he could play designated driver.

CLAUDIE SAT in the middle of the bed, her legs crossed Indian fashion. She'd changed into sweats and heavy socks the minute she got to her room. Beside her lay the road map, and she studied it as she sipped on the frappe she'd picked up at the pizza place down the street. Her motel wasn't much to look at, but the price was right.

She'd opted to stay in Cheyenne rather than drive any farther. For one thing, she didn't know where she was going—South Dakota or Kansas? Her decision would depend on Zach—or rather, whether or not she could get in to see him.

I'll worry about that tomorrow, Claudie told herself. Tonight, she planned a long soak in the tub. The tension of meeting Yancy and the long hours in the car had given her a stiff neck. What she wouldn't have given to have Bo there—Bo with the great hands.

She closed her eyes and pictured him. Not tall and startlingly handsome like Ren, Bo's looks kind of sneaked up on you when you weren't looking. Strong and compact, he emanated power when he chose to or slipped into obscurity when it suited him. His wardrobe was a joke, but Claudie knew he dressed to fit an image he had of himself—nondescript. What he didn't realize was, he was anything but.

Rolling her chin to stretch her tired muscles, she imagined him massaging her neck. It had taken months of patience on his part before she let him so much as hold her hand. The massaging part had come two weeks ago after a game of tag with Brady when she slipped on the wet grass and wound up sprawled flat on her back.

"Do you need a doctor?" Bo had asked, kneeling beside her, concern written all over his face.

Brady had draped himself over Bo's shoulder, his small face pinched with fear. "Claudie hurt?"

"I'm fine, silly boys," she said, but when she tried to sit up, a twinge of pain shot from her hip to her neck.

Bo's sharp eyes caught her flinch, and he moved closer, placing one hand on her shoulder to keep her from moving. "Brady boy, run get your mama. Okay?"

The lad shot off toward the house. Claudie had groaned more from the fuss than the pain. "Now, hush, sweetheart," he said, situating himself squarely at her back so he could place both hands on her neck. "Let me check this out."

Claudie hadn't been able to keep herself from reacting. Not that his touch felt bad—in fact, it was wonderful—but she wasn't used to such intimate contact. His fingers froze in place until she let out the breath she'd been holding.

"Does this hurt?" he'd asked, his voice low, just inches from her ear.

The roar of blood racing through her veins had made it impossible to speak. She'd tried to shake her head, but his hands kept her chin still. "Don't move. Just relax. Close your eyes and feel my fingers. If I hit anything sensitive, yell."

Yell? Good grief. Everything you touch is sensitive. If I open my mouth, the entire neighborhood's going to hear me.

The whole episode couldn't have lasted more than two or three minutes, but it changed Claudie's life. She went from hating touch to craving it. Maybe this urge to protect her sister wasn't the only reason she'd taken off so impulsively. Maybe she was afraid she couldn't trust herself around Bo anymore. When she was with him, she wanted things she couldn't have— like a relationship, a boyfriend-girlfriend relationship. But that meant sex. And for Claudie, sex was commerce and she was out of that business for good.

Jumping off the bed, Claudie walked to the bathroom to draw her tub. She turned on both handles full blast then set out her washcloth and shampoo. She paused before the small, old-fashioned sink and mirror. She eyed her image critically. Nothing fabulous, but not bad. Maybe a little older around the eyes than she'd have liked, but nowhere near as wasted as some of the working girls she'd known.

Over the din of the water, she repeated the vow she'd taken last January when she made up her mind to change her life. Her lips formed the words with reverence: "No sex. No cigarettes. No drugs. No excuses."

She was finally beginning to like Claudie St. James, and she wouldn't give that up for anything or anyone. Even Bo.

CHAPTER THREE

BO TUNED OUT the droning voice of the flight attendant telling the passengers to wait until the plane came to a complete stop to unfasten their seat belts. He closed his eyes and tried to focus on his objective, not his fatigue. Normally, while on a job, he could go for days with a bare minimum of food and sleep, but for some reason, Claudie's leaving seemed to rob him of his ability to concentrate. He kept imagining her in bad places.

"We can go now," his seatmate, a white-haired woman who'd snored softly most of the way, told him.

Apologizing, Bo rose, leaving his laptop computer on the seat. He wrangled his carry-on bag from the overhead compartment then removed the woman's overstuffed paisley tote as well.

She rewarded him with a smile. "I wouldn't worry if I were you," she said, cryptically, "your girl will come around in time."

He leaned forward. "I beg your pardon?"

Her powdered flesh crinkled in a road map of wrinkles. "Your gal," she repeated, as if he had a hearing problem. "She'll come around." Her watery eyes twinkled from the overhead light. "I peeked at your computer board when you were in the toilet," she said, motioning toward his laptop.

"Oh," he said, marveling at his sloppiness. He'd walked off and left his laptop open? Jeez, he was slipping.

He picked up the lightweight machine and stuffed it in his briefcase. As he reached for his carry-on bag, the woman said, "You must love her a lot to follow after her like this. At first, I was thinking you might be one of those stalkers I'm always reading about, but I can tell you've got a good heart."

Bo couldn't decide whether to be angry or amused. She seemed harmless so he asked, "How can you tell?"

Her elfin grin made him smile back. "I'm old. You know these things when you get to be my age."

Bo courteously moved to one side to allow her to pass ahead of him. She patted his arm and told him, "That's very kind, but you'd best run along and find her. She won't wait forever, you know."

Bo chuckled then bowed slightly and hurried up the aisle and out the door. He put the woman's remarks out of his mind as he scanned the terminal for his cousin. No tall, broad-shouldered guy with wavy black hair in sight.

"Where are you, Cuz?" Bo muttered as he walked along the corridor, picking his way through throngs of incoming passengers.

"Bo," a voice called.

Bo stopped and looked around. A familiar face peered at him between some artificial greenery. Bo wound his way through a maze of tall stools. The place differed little from the dozens he'd visited in airports around the country—only the colorful logos of the city's sport team changed.

"Hey, man, how ya' doin'?" Matt asked, not bothering to stand.

Bo sat opposite him and ordered a Pepsi from a waitress who drifted past. "Still not drinking, huh? Good for you," Matt noted, his speech slightly slurred.

"How long have you been here, Matt?"

Matt pushed back the sleeve of his leather bomber jacket to look at his watch. He blinked, finally closing one eye to gain the focus he needed. "A few hours and twenty-two minutes. Give or take."

Bo paid for his soda with a five then hastily gulped half of it. "Hand over your keys, Cuz. I hope you still live in the same place 'cause I'm not sure I trust you to give me directions."

Matt drew himself up offended. "I may be intoxicated but I'm not decapitated."

"Thank God," Bo said, helping his cousin to rise. "I was worried about that."

The long trek to the parking lot seemed to help clear Matt's head to some degree. Bo thought Matt's limp seemed more pronounced than it had the last time they were together, but he didn't say anything. He wanted to ask about his cousin's recovery and physical therapy but decided to hold off until morning. He knew how sensitive Matt was about the injury that had nearly claimed his life.

Matt handed Bo the keys to his Jeep Cherokee without protest. Once they'd exited the parking lot, Bo asked, "So what's this about? You've never been what I'd call a big drinker."

Matt slumped down as far as the seat belt would permit. He kept his face aimed toward the passenger window. "Your basic drowning of sorrows, I guess. Turn off the antennae and go blank—booze helps."

Bo understood. In his youth, alcohol had been his drug of choice. By the time he was sixteen he'd lost count of the number of times he'd puked his guts out. Bo counted himself lucky that more exotic drugs hadn't been readily available or he might have fried his brain before Larry Bishop and his son came along to help him find sobriety.

"It's a little late in life to become an alcoholic, bud. I really wouldn't recommend trying—it just prolongs the agony of whatever it is you're trying to escape from."

Matt didn't respond.

"Is it the divorce?" Bo caught Matt's negative motion but his long sad sigh said otherwise. "What's it been? A year?"

"Almost two," Matt muttered. "Sonya and Alan have been married a year."

Bo nodded. "How's Ashley?"

"Great—considering her parents are immature jerks who fight for every spare second of her time," Matt said bitterly. "That's what set me off tonight. This was my weekend to have her but Sonya called at the last minute to say Ashley had been invited to a dressage sleep-over."

Bo frowned. "I thought dressage had something to do with horses."

"It does. That's Ashley's new passion. It goes with her age, I guess. She and a couple of friends are sleeping at the dressage school."

"Isn't that an expensive hobby?" Bo asked, knowing it was none of his business.

Matt's sigh sounded heartfelt. "Money isn't a big problem when your stepfather is the nose-man of the stars."

"I take it you're referring to plastic surgery, not cocaine."

"Dr. Al," Matt said, snorting with disgust. "Don't get me started." He sat up a little straighter. "Want to tell me what you're doing here? Isn't New York the last place on earth you want to be? You heard about your old man, right? He moved in with his mistress a month or so ago."

Bo's stomach gripped what was left of his airplane food and punched it toward his throat. He swallowed the taste of bile. "Yeah, I got the lowdown when I spoke to my mother."

"How's Aunt Ruth taking it?"

Bo shrugged, grateful the traffic wasn't as constipated as usual. He pictured his mother at Ren and Sara's wedding last August—his father had claimed a prior commitment. Short and a little pudgy, Ruth Lester never seemed to change. She'd worn her salt-and-pepper hair in the same style—a chin-length page-boy—for twenty years. "She sounds more resigned than hurt," Bo said truthfully. "I got the impression she finds his behavior a bit silly but not all that surprising given his age and gender."

Matt seemed to swallow a laugh. "That Ruth is one cool lady. My mother would have my dad's balls embalmed and strung on a necklace."

Bo smiled. He hadn't planned to see either of his parents this trip, but a nagging sense of guilt made him wonder if his mother was truly as blasé about the news as she'd sounded. Maybe he'd find some time tomorrow to look in on her at work.

Following Matt's pointers, Bo pulled the Jeep into a parking garage three blocks from Matt's apartment building. "How much does this set you back a month?" he asked, curious.

Matt groaned. "Enough to send my daughter to Harvard. I'm seriously considering moving. Maybe Sacramento," he said, flippantly. "Got a job for me, Cuz?"

Bo had never heard such a defeated tone in his cousin's voice. Matt was the proverbial golden boy— the person to emulate. Handsome, smart, top student, heroic cop. He was four years younger than Bo— which would make him 36 years old. What happened? Bo wanted to ask, but he knew that would have to wait for the morning, too.

CLAUDIE TOOK her time admiring the chiseled faces of the Mount Rushmore National Monument. When she'd called the prison early that morning, she'd been told her name would have to be added to Zach's visitor list before she'd be allowed to see him. Her disappointment must have traveled through the phone line because the control-room guard told her they would try to expedite the process. She was told to show up Saturday at twelve-thirty and they would let her know.

Since Claudie had never traveled as a tourist, she decided to make the most of this opportunity, starting with the Black Hills of South Dakota. She'd headed north out of Cheyenne and soon found herself in some of the prettiest country she'd ever seen.

She'd stopped for breakfast in a cute little town called Custer, then paid a remarkable fee to see a hole in a hillside, which if you squinted was starting to take on the shape of Crazy Horse. The project truly was a labor of love, and she hadn't regretted the expenditure once she learned the whole story behind the mammoth undertaking. After Rushmore, she planned to hit a few tourist spots around Rapid City, ending her afternoon with a tour of the Badlands. Tonight, she planned to stay at a place called Wall Drug, then on Friday she'd complete her trip across the state to Sioux Falls.

As Claudie leaned forward for a better view, an older woman accidentally jostled her elbow. ''Oh, dear, I'm so sorry,'' she said.

''That's okay,'' Claudie said, slightly embarrassed by the way she'd jumped back. *Old habits,* she thought, moving away to take a seat at a small bench. She watched the woman interact with a man, presumably her husband. The couple were taking turns snapping pictures of each other with the four faces in the background. Without really intending to, Claudie rose and approached them. ''Would you like me to take one of the two of you together?'' she asked.

The woman let out a small of squeal of delight. ''That would be great. This is our fortieth anniversary. We were married in The Little Chapel in the Woods,'' she said, apparently assuming Claudie was familiar with the place.

''Congratulations,'' Claudie said.

The husband put his arm around his wife's shoulder and hugged her close. He was a distinguished-looking man with a kind face. Claudie snapped two photos then handed the camera back to the man. ''Thank you, miss,'' he said with a pleasant smile. "Do you have a camera? We could return the favor.''

Startled by the question, Claudie realized she'd never owned a camera, and aside from the photos of Sara's wedding, she had very few pictures of herself. "No, I don't, but that's a good idea. I saw one of those disposables for sale in the gift shop. I think I'll buy one.''

He nodded and smiled, as if pleased to have contributed to her trip. "Well, we'll be drifting around here for another hour or so. If you want to find us, we'd be happy to do the honors.''

She hurried to the shop and made the purchase before she could change her mind. *Maybe if they turn out, I'll give one to Brady,* she told herself. *And Bo.*

BO AWOKE to the smell of coffee. Grudgingly he opened one eye. Sunlight streamed through the room's single window, highlighting spots of rust on the ornate bars. "Why does a cop have bars on the windows?'' he asked, sensing his cousin's presence in the adjacent kitchen.

"Ex-cop,'' a disembodied voice returned.

"Is that official?'' Bo asked, sitting up.

There hadn't been much chitchat once they'd reached the apartment last night. Matt's eyes had been at half-mast. He'd handed Bo a set of sheets and a blanket and pointed to the couch. "It folds out or you can sleep on it that way. It's not bad,'' he'd said. "I slept on it for a full year before Sonya kicked me out.''

His cousin entered the room carrying two steaming

mugs. "With sugar, right?" Matt asked. "Mom always called you Mr. Sweet Tooth."

Bo took the cup, inhaling the aroma. "Yep, and your sister always called me Mr. Sweet Spot. I bet Aunt Irene didn't know that." Chuckling, he asked, "How is Deborah, anyway? Last I heard she was married to a banker and had a dozen kids."

"Jack's a stockbroker and they have four kids, two are adopted. Deb's great. Is there something about this 'Sweet Spot' name I should know?"

Bo laughed at his cousin's suspicious look. "You ought to be ashamed of those incestuous thoughts. Deborah used to tickle me until I'd cry. At the time she was bigger than me, but I bet I could take her now."

Matt visibly relaxed. "Do you want something to eat? I bought Cheerios...for Ashley."

Bo planted his feet on the floor and rose, stretching. "What time is it?"

"A quarter after eleven," Matt said sheepishly. "I guess neither of us thought about setting an alarm."

Bo experienced a momentary jolt of panic, but took a deep breath and let it out. "No biggie. You're gonna crack this case wide-open in a matter of minutes, right?"

Matt started to roll his eyes, but flinched and put his hand to his head. "Just as soon as my head goes back to its normal size." He rubbed the crease between his brows. "Now I remember why I don't drink."

Bo gave him a conciliatory pat on the shoulder. "Hangovers suck. I haven't missed them at all." He carried his cup to the window and looked outside. The weather actually seemed halfway decent. "Anyway, as soon as you're up to it, I'd like to get cracking on this. Did you get my fax?"

"I just found it," Matt said, stretching his neck as if he were the one who'd slept on the sofa. In a baggy, NYPD T-shirt and faded gray sweatpants and bare feet he looked like a grown-up version of the kid Bo used to tease on those rare occasions when Ruth had taken him to visit her brother's family.

Estranged from her family for most of Bo's childhood, Ruth had reestablished contact with her brother after their father's death when Bo was eleven. Relations between the siblings remained tentative at best, but the two sisters-in-law became friends.

"So tell me what's going on with you and the force," Bo said.

Matt rose and walked to the window. He was silent a minute. "They've tried to be diplomatic and make a place for me the best they can, but what do you do with an eleven-year veteran with a gimpy knee? They loved the FBI gig because then they didn't have to see me every day, but that's just temporary." He looked over his shoulder. "I doubt if they're looking forward to my return any more than I am."

Bo yanked on his canvas slacks and tucked in his undershirt. He'd shower and change as soon as he had an itinerary in place. "Listen, I know our circumstances weren't the same, but I went through my own kind of burnout in the force, and, believe me, I've never regretted going out on my own."

Matt looked interested, but Bo could almost hear the cautionary words of advice barking in the back of his cousin's head. "I know I don't have child support payments and I'm sure the cost of living hasn't gone down since the last time I lived in this burg, but you do have options, Matt. You asked me last night if I was looking for employees, and the answer is no. But I would consider taking on a partner. You could handle everything east of the Mississippi, and I'll keep my side of the continent.''

''No problem,'' Matt guffawed. ''Half a country is more than enough for me.''

Bo withdrew a map from the inside pocket of his ancient winter topcoat. ''Consider this a test case. You help me find Claudie, and we talk business.''

Matt turned away, but not before Bo caught the spark of interest in his eyes. ''I'm a desk jockey now, Bo.'' He pointed to his knee. ''I'm not too hot in the hundred-yard dash any more.''

Bo spread the finely detailed map on the table. ''Trust me, Cuz, neither am I. This job is ten percent physical, ninety percent mental. I'll hustle jobs, you handle the computer and we'll hire some young jock to take care of the rest.''

Matt laughed outright. ''You're just as whacked out as ever.''

''Yeah, and you're just as uptight. You remind me of Ren. Thank God Sara came along and loosened him up.''

Matt shook his head. ''I still can't get over the fact he was engaged to Eve Masterson, and called it off to marry someone else.'' He walked across the room to join Bo at the dinette. ''Who in their right mind gives up a chance to sleep with the hottest woman on network news?''

Stifling a sigh, Bo picked up his briefcase. He focused on the tumbler locks. "Listen. For your information, Eve's a decent enough person, but she was all wrong for Ren. If they'd gotten married, they wouldn't have lasted a year. Sara's like a Broadway musical where Ren's concerned. Eve was intermission. But, now that you mention it, Ren wanted me to check up on Eve while I'm in town. Sara's worried about her."

Matt's face scrunched up in confusion. "Sara, the wife, is worried about Eve, the ex-girlfriend?"

Bo nodded. "You'd understand if you knew Sara."

Matt took a sip of coffee. "Eve hasn't been on the air for a couple of weeks, you know. I heard a rumor she jumped networks. Word has it there's a guy involved."

Bo shrugged. "Personally, I can't picture her putting anyone above her career, but who knows? Remind me to call her later, will ya? But, first, let's get cracking on finding Claudie. Time is of the essence, as my father would say."

"Particularly *now*," Matt said with a snicker. "Keeping a twenty-something girlfriend happy can't be easy for a man in his sixties."

Bo grimaced. He slammed his pen flat and leaned over the map. "Here's where my crew thinks she was born. Maybe you'll have better luck pulling up the hard facts. I'll give you what we know, or think we know, and you tell me where we go from that."

Matt joined him at the table, his shoulder a few inches from Bo's. "Okay. I'll do it—on one condition. I get to call Eve. Who knows, maybe I'll get lucky."

Bo looked him straight in the eye. "No problem, but might I remind you, you have limited bargaining power here? You're working off an old debt, remember?"

Bo bit down on his inner cheek as the color rose in his cousin's face. "Bite me, Lester."

"After you, Ross."

The two men looked at each other a minute then chuckled simultaneously. Matt's quick temper was a trait Bo remembered well as were Matt's grit and determination—characteristics Bo hoped would serve them well on the task ahead.

MATT STUDIED the highlighted notations on the map, his brain vaguely listening to the sound of the water running in the shower. Thanks to his hangover, it had taken him all of Thursday and part of this morning to construct a viable profile of the woman called Claudine St. James, from her birth in 1973 at the St. James School for Unwed Mothers, where her birth certificate read Claudine Yvonne Smith—to the present.

The fundamentals of Matt's computer program were neither new nor revolutionary, but the interactive format was user friendly and fast. Normally, a project this complex might take two or three days to finish, but Matt had worked nonstop to complete the analysis. This way Bo could get going, and Matt wouldn't have to miss Ashley's school play tonight.

Bo, whose antsy energy just about drove Matt up the wall, spent his time on a weak attempt at locating Eve Masterson but came up empty-handed. "You can run this program on Eve after I leave," Bo had told him. "If it's as good as you say, you should be able to tell me where she lives and what she had for dinner last night, right?"

Matt had laughed. "You make me sound like Big Brother." Sadly, the program did have invasive connotations if used improperly, which is why he couldn't market it for "big bucks," as his ex-wife had suggested.

As he highlighted certain events in Claudie's life—a shot record admitting her to kindergarten, the 1981 record of death for Timothy John Anders, age one day—Matt's mind flashed back to his cousin's earlier comment. *Payback*, Matt thought. This little job would eradicate a twenty-year debt of gratitude.

He tried to picture himself at sixteen—junior varsity jock, pimples, shiny new driver's license. His only goal at the time was to get laid, and in his mind the way to accomplish that was by taking Sharon Jensen to the prom. Unfortunately, he didn't have the money to rent a tux and buy the tickets, let alone purchase a corsage.

A moment of foolishness—plus one unguarded cash box filled with the weekend's basketball game receipts—might have screwed up his life for good if not for Bo. Matt silently groaned picturing the hubbub over Bo's arrest for vandalism after he broke a window to get inside the building to return the money. The charge was reduced to malicious mischief once Bo's dad had been called, but it still meant five months of community service.

"So," Bo said, walking into the room, a towel tucked about his waist, "are we set, then? You're sure her ultimate destination is eastern Kansas, but you see stops in Wyoming, South Dakota and Minnesota to connect with her siblings."

"Hey, I'm not a soothsayer and I don't want a midnight phone call from you if I'm wrong. You saw how this was done—facts and percentages, not smoke and mirrors. At the moment, with all things considered, this is where your best odds are.''

Bo yanked on jockey shorts and a pair of socks, then slipped on a hideous shirt of greens and gold. "Good Lord," Matt sputtered, "where do you shop? Dumpsters?"

Bo grinned. "No, but I've heard you find some good stuff there. This is a disguise."

"As what? A wino? Hell, I know street people who wouldn't be caught dead in that shirt."

Bo laughed, obviously not put out by his cousin's criticism. "You sound just like Claudie. Maybe I'll let her start picking out my clothes once I convince her to marry me."

Matt rocked back, surprised. "Marriage? She's an ex-hooker, Bo. God, to think about all the—"

Bo reached out and grabbed Matt's shirt right below the neckline. "Don't say it."

Matt swallowed. "Baggage," he managed to choke out. "I started to say I hate to think about all the emotional baggage a person's got to carry around after a job like that." Bo's fingers opened. "Probably right up with cops, don't you imagine?"

Bo looked him straight in the eyes and nodded. "Yeah, you're probably right."

CLAUDIE SHOPPED for her motel with care born of frugality. She found a clean-looking place not far from the mausoleumlike prison perched on a bluff above the Sioux River. The motel manager was a friendly woman with three very loud miniature poodles. The dogs—Mitzy, Fritzy and Poo—cried when Claudie took her room key and started to leave.

"Now, just you hush," the manager told them as Claudie closed the door. "She'll be back here in the morning for her Danish so you can talk to her then."

Claudie shook her head. She'd never owned a dog or cat and she couldn't remember her family ever having pets. Maybe that was something she'd ask Zach when she saw him, she told herself, unlocking the door of her room. *If I see him.*

Claudie hated to think what she'd do if they didn't let her see her brother. Her finances weren't limitless and, although she had a credit card, she hated to use it.

After unpacking a fresh sweater and clean pair of jeans to wear the next day, she decided to go for a walk.

"Excuse me, ma'am," Claudie said, poking her head inside the door of the office. "Is there a grocery store nearby?"

A cacophony of barking almost drowned out the woman's reply. "Sure is. Right down the street about four blocks. Can't miss it," the manager called out brightly, then added more gruffly, "No, Mitzy you can't go along. I promised you a walk later, but only if you're patient."

Claudie closed the door softly. The autumn twilight felt soothing, even with a bite of winter in the air. The long drive eastward from Wall had gone surprisingly fast thanks to a book on tape that she'd found on sale. The story—a romance—had touched her.

Whistling softly under her breath, Claudie thought about Bo. There was no denying it—she missed her

Cookbook Man, which is what she and Keneesha had first named him when they saw him skulking in the cookbook section of Sara's bookstore. She wondered where he was at that moment. *Is he thinking about me?*

As she entered the small, well-lit grocery store, she spotted a pay phone just inside the door. Maybe they call this homesickness, she thought, veering toward the phone. She tried Bo's number but received a busy single. Too impatient to wait and try again, she dialed Sara's number.

Ren answered.

"Hi, Ren. It's me. Is Sara home?"

"No, darn it, and is she going to be mad that she missed you," Ren said, his voice as cheerful and positive as usual.

"Aren't you supposed to be teaching?" Claudie asked.

"My class was canceled. They're painting our building. I'm sitting here grading papers. So, how's everything going with you? We've been worried about you."

"I'm fine. The car's running great. I saw one of my brothers. The other one's in jail...I might get to see him tomorrow." Claudie almost clapped her hand over her mouth, surprised by the amount of personal information she'd just shared.

"Really? Anything I can do to help?"

Claudie had actually considered calling Ren when it sounded like she might have to wait to get visiting privileges but nixed the idea since that would mean broadcasting her location to Bo. "I don't think so. The staff sounded pretty cool on the phone. I'll call you if they give me any grief tomorrow.''

Ren was silent a second. "Monday's the Veteran's Day holiday, you know. Sara wanted to use the long weekend to take Brady to Disneyland for his birthday, but I talked her into going to Half Moon Bay instead. We're leaving in the morning." He sounded almost apologetic.

He was a good man, and Claudie knew Sara had never been happier. She envied them their closeness.

"That ought to be fun. Brady will love the ocean."

"Yeah, we'll probably spend the whole day poking around in tidal pools. I wish you were going with us, but I guess you're doing what you need to do." He hesitated as if he were going to give her some advice, but said instead, "We'll have the cell phone with us if you need anything."

Claudie appreciated the concession because everyone knew how much Ren hated cellular phones. "Thanks, but I'll be fine. Don't worry about me. Have you heard how things are going at One Wish House?"

Ren's soft chortle seemed positive. "Pretty good, I think. Sara was there this morning with Babe. One of the residents…let me see…Maya? Is she Korean?"

"Uh-huh."

"Maya talked them into planning a fund-raiser."

Claudie almost dropped the phone. She'd been praying the place wouldn't fall apart without her; she certainly hadn't expected it to thrive. "What kind of fund-raiser?"

"A dim sum cook-off or something. Sara could tell you more about it. I think it's a ploy to keep the girls from missing you." His voice went a shade deeper.

"We all do, you know. Brady's been so lonely. First, you disappear then Bo."

Claudie had to swallow a funny lump in her throat. "Bo? Where's he? He was due back from Vegas on Monday."

There was a pause. "Umm...he was here, but then he left again. He's...ah...in New York, actually."

"What's he doing in New York?"

Ren cleared his throat. "I...uh, that is we, Sara and me, asked him to find out what's happened to Eve. She kinda fell off the face of the earth."

Claudie remembered Sara mentioning something about not being able to reach Eve, but some quality in Ren's tone made her skeptical. She let it go. "Well, I'd better run. Tell Sara I called and give Brady a big kiss for me. I bought him a dinosaur from the Badlands and two T-shirts—one has a picture of a jackalope on it."

"A what?"

"It's what you get when you cross a jackrabbit with an antelope."

Ren's laugh made her even more homesick. "I hate to tell you this, Claudie, but you sound like a real *tourist*."

"Yep, that's me," she said, fighting to keep from embarrassing herself. "Hey, Ren, it's been good talking to you. If you hear from Bo, tell him I said hi. I hope everything's okay with Eve. Gotta go. Bye."

Claudie hung up, swallowing against the lump in her throat. She grabbed a cart and mindlessly pushed it up and down the rows of the store. "Where are you Bo?" she whispered under her breath.

Looking for me?

She knew the answer. The real question was, what would she do if he found her? Or rather, *when* he found her.

CHAPTER FOUR

THE PENITENTIARY frightened her, and despite the overheated air within the building, she felt chilled to her bones. Waiting for Zach to be admitted to the visitation room, Claudie kept her chin down and concentrated on keeping her lunch in her stomach. Furtively she wiped a bead of sweat from her upper lip then tucked her hands under her butt, tuning out the disharmonious chatter of other inmates and their visitors.

"Claudie?" a voice croaked.

Her chin shot up to see a bald stranger staring at her.

"My God," he softly cried. "It is you. I couldn't believe it when they told me you were coming. Claudie."

Tears filled her eyes, but she blinked them back. She wasn't some weepy little girl. She was tough. Strong. "Zach," she whispered, choking on emotions she hadn't expected to feel. Her arms lifted automatically, but she let them fall to her sides, recalling the warning about appropriate behavior between residents and visitors.

Zach walked to her, a crooked little catch in his step. Yancy's parting words to her had been about Zach's injury. "He messed up his hip pretty bad in the accident,'' he'd called to her as she walked to her car. ''Still has a lot of pain.''

Her gaze was as jumpy as her heart—skittering over the deep creases in his face and the somberness in his eyes that made him look old beyond his years. He eased into an empty chair and after an awkward hesitation took both of her hands in his. Hand-holding was allowed. As was a kiss hello and goodbye. She leaned forward shyly and kissed him lightly on the cheek.

''What are you doing here, Claudie? God, you look terrific. I'd have known you anywhere,'' Zach said with conviction. His voice—deep and kind of scratchy-sounding—was as unfamiliar as his face.

''Really?'' She searched his eyes for a trace of the boy she'd known and loved. ''Yancy nearly keeled over when I showed up at his door. He said you thought I was dead.''

One side of his mouth twitched. Claudie remembered his smile, slow and deliberate when it came—which wasn't often. ''Nah. You're tough. And smart—the smartest of us all. I knew you'd land on your feet.''

Claudie let out a harsh laugh that made the others in the room turn her way. Softly she said, ''On my back, you mean.'' At his puzzled look she added, ''I was a hooker, Zach. Off and on for years. I'd try other jobs—waitressing, I was a clerk in a convenience store for a while, an usher at a wrestling arena and I even parked cars, but somehow I'd always end up working some corner.''

He let out a low epithet.

Claudie shrugged. ''But that's all behind me, now.

I finally passed the GED, and I've got a great job—
two actually. I help run a bookstore and I manage a
halfway house for prostitutes.''

The gladness that filled his eyes made her heart
soar. ''You can't know how good that makes me feel,
Claudie girl. It's like seeing a light at the end of a
long, black tunnel. Maybe some of that glow will
come my way after I get out of this place.''

They talked until Claudie's voice sounded as
parched and scratchy as Zach's. She told him about
Ren and Sara and Brady, the girls at One Wish House,
her interest in old books, her trip so far.

''What about a guy? No boyfriend?'' he asked, ze-
roing in on the part she'd purposely left out.

''There's a guy. A friend. I think he'd like to be
more than a friend, but that won't happen.'' She
sighed softly. ''I guess I'm not made for that kind of
thing.''

Zach's wiry brows bunched together. ''We sure
ended up with some big holes in our souls, didn't
we?''

Claudie nodded, understanding him completely.

''Know what I don't get?'' he asked. She shook her
head. ''I attend a bunch of self-help groups in here—
AA, NA, a Christian ministry. I see guys who really
had it tough growing up—I mean bad. We had it really
good compared to them.''

Claudie's heart twisted peculiarly. ''Garret...''

He didn't let her finish. ''I don't mean after Mom
died. I mean when Dad was working regular and on
the road most of the time. Mom was good to us. She'd
read us books, and we'd take picnics to the park. Hell,
even when the old man was around we had some fun

sometimes. Remember our trip to Pipestone? We saw that play about Hiawatha.''

Claudie frowned, trying to remember. ''Sorta.''

Zach closed his eyes and sighed. ''Things weren't all bad—at least not while Mom was alive.'' He turned his face away. ''I think things started going downhill after Timmy was born, and then Wesley…''

She squeezed his fingers. ''It was an accident, Zach. Whoever heard of a kid choking on a balloon? Cripes, we all used to chew them like gum.''

Claudie always figured Wesley's death hit Zach the hardest because it had happened on his ninth birthday. A party with four or five little boys raising Cain. Everyone too busy to notice Wesley's distress until he dropped flat, blue in the face. By the time the fire truck got there, he was gone.

To distract him, she asked, ''Zach, did we ever have a pet?''

He looked upward as if searching his memories. ''We had bunnies once. Remember? I found a nest of rabbits and Mom helped us feed them with a doll bottle.'' His smile held a look of nostalgia. ''It was your doll bottle, so you said that meant you got to name them.''

She shook her head, dubiously. ''Bunnies?''

He nodded. ''How could you forget Elizabeth?''

Flopsy, Mopsy, Cottontail and Elizabeth. She closed her eyes and pictured herself holding a tiny gray bunny in the palm of her hand. Its heart beat so fast she worried it might explode. ''I do remember,'' she said. ''Garret came home that night and told me Elizabeth was the stupidest name for a rabbit he'd ever heard.''

Zach's smile faded. "He was always hardest on you."

Claudie took a deep breath and straightened her shoulders. "I'm going back to Kansas, Zach. I'm not going to let Garret ruin Sherry's life, too. I'd have gone sooner, but I wasn't ready to face him. I only hope I'm not too late."

Zach didn't try to talk her out of it. Before she left he gave her Valery's address and telephone number, which he had memorized. "She's the manager of a video store. Her stepfolks own two or three in the area. She sent me a flier a few months ago announcing their latest grand opening." His expression turned humorous. "She sent along a picture of herself with her new fancy car. Quite the success story."

Claudie thought she detected a facetious note but let it go. With any luck Val would have enough clout to take off a few days so they could go to Kansas together. As she prepared to leave, Claudie asked, "How much longer do you have?"

"Hard to say. I've got a parole hearing in February." He didn't sound overly optimistic.

"Would it help if I wrote a letter on your behalf? My best friend's husband used to be a judge. Maybe Ren would write something, too."

He squeezed her hand. "I'm doing okay, Claudie. Really. I'm sober. I work with a Christian outreach group in here, and I feel as if I'm making a difference. Like I said, there are a lot of guys who are a whole lot worse off than me."

She leaned over and kissed him goodbye. "I'll write."

"I'll be here." He smiled, and for the first time looked like himself.

Bo REPEATED the address of the prison to Matt. "1600 North Drive." The fact that its street address was the same as that of the White House amused him.

"I heard you the first time," Matt grumbled, steering the rental car along one of Sioux Falls's quiet, tree-lined streets.

It hadn't been easy convincing Matt to accompany him to South Dakota. The lure of a partnership seemed to be the only incentive that worked. Fortunately, Bo wasn't above resorting to bribery. Especially after talking to his mother Friday evening.

"Our mothers seem to think you're suffering from depression," Bo said, hoping his mother and his aunt were exaggerating.

"Yeah, I know," Matt snorted. "Poor sad Matt. First the divorce. Then the awful accident." He shook his head. "My mother calls me daily and Aunt Ruth weekly. They're a sort of intervention tag team."

Bo liked his Aunt Irene, who was a charge nurse at St. Mary's. A no-nonsense woman with a wry view of the world. If she was worried about her son, things had to be worse than Matt let on. And, Bo thought sheepishly, I've been too wrapped up in my problems to give Matt's much thought.

When he'd mentioned the possible partnership idea to his mother, she'd suggested he start by taking Matt with him. His cousin hadn't been overly excited, but Bo was glad for the company.

"Left or right, Mr. Navigator?" Matt asked grouchily. Spending the night on the floor of the airport after a blizzard left them—and a couple of thousand other travelers—stranded hadn't helped either man's temperament.

"Left," Bo gambled noticing the map on his lap was upside down.

A minute later, Matt put on the blinker and turned into the drive leading to the prison.

"Jeez," Bo exclaimed, craning his neck for a better look at the two-story gray stone fortress. "This place looks old."

Matt nosed the car into a parking place. "The information I got off the Internet said it was constructed as a territorial prison in 1881—eight years before South Dakota became a state."

"Wow."

The two men got out of the car and walked toward the imposing stone structure. Even though he told himself it was foolish to get his hopes up, Bo couldn't help scanning the parking lot for a Toyota wagon with California plates. He'd hoped she might stick around to see her brother on Sunday, too.

"Do you think he'll talk to us?" Bo asked.

"You," Matt corrected. "I'll wait in the lobby."

Bo's admittance was expedited by a phone call from Ren. Even a *former* judge had connections. Matt's FBI credentials didn't hurt matters. As Bo waited for Zachary Anders to join him, he debated about how to handle the meeting. He couldn't help wondering if Claudie had mentioned him when she spoke to her brother the day before.

"They said you want to see me," a husky voice said, making Bo look up sharply.

A small, wiry man with a shaved head and stooped

shoulders looked back at him. At first Bo thought he must have the wrong person because Zachary was two years younger than Claudie. Instead of twenty-five, this man looked fifty. But as he studied the haggard face Bo began to detect a hint of Claudie in the eyes. He put out his hand. "Bo Lester. I'm a private investigator, but this isn't work. It's personal. I'm trying to catch up with your sister."

"Claudie," Zach said softly.

Bo nodded. "I know you spoke with her yesterday. I'd have been here sooner, but I got caught in a blizzard in New York."

"I thought you were from California."

He knows who I am. "I went to New York to get my cousin's help locating her. She left without telling anyone where she was going."

Zach's face took on a shuttered look. "Musta had her reasons."

Bo sighed. "The reason is she's stubborn, secretive and ornery as a moose." Zach's mouth twitched as if in agreement.

"She's been on her own a long time," he said loyally.

"I know that. She's also strong, brave and resourceful. And, in all honesty, she probably doesn't need my help, but I'm worried about her and I want to be there when…" He didn't finish what he was going to say. What if Claudie hadn't filled Zach in?

"When she takes on our daddy," Zach finished.

Bo nodded.

Zach was silent a moment, studying Bo. When he spoke, he said, "Tell me why you care what happens to her."

A lump the size of Manhattan formed in Bo's throat. He had to swallow twice before he could say, "Because I love her."

MATT STARED OUT a window at the prison grounds. Autumn had passed, but winter hadn't quite settled in, he decided, noting the crusty patches of grimy snow beneath a knee-high hedge. The grass was a mottled blend of browns and greens. He'd never been to the Midwest and doubted if November was the optimum month to visit, but somehow he'd let Bo talk him into making this trip.

"You don't need me," he'd argued while his cousin stubbornly made the travel arrangements.

"Yes, I do. I know I'm superhuman in certain departments but I haven't figured out how to clone myself so I can be in two places at one time. The weather looks like crap out there. If our plane gets canceled and we miss Claudie in Sioux Falls, then we have a fifty-fifty chance she'll try to find her sister or go straight to Kansas."

Matt tried logic—after all, they knew her ultimate destination so all Bo had to do was go to Kansas and wait, but logic didn't work on people who were in love—and it was crystal clear to Matt *that* was Bo's problem.

Sighing, he walked to the door and exited the building. The bite of the wind felt good on his face and he turned into it, closing his eyes against the sting. *Love.* He and Sonya had been in love once but that died the instant he realized she was having an affair.

"Let's move it and groove it, Cuz."

Matt spun around to find Bo standing less than two feet away. *Damn that man could move softly!*

Bo started toward the car.

"Where to?" Matt asked, following.

"The airport."

Matt had to hustle to catch up with his cousin. "You're giving up?"

"Of course not. We're splitting up. I'm going east. You're going south." He flashed Matt a smug look. "Told you so."

If Matt weren't thirty-six, he would have stuck out his tongue; instead, he flipped him off. Bo laughed outright. "Come on. Let's hustle. I sure as hell don't want to miss her at Valery's."

BO SETTLED BACK in the seat of the chartered airplane—a six-passenger Cessna that his pilot had planned to "take out for a little spin this morning, anyway." Bo was the only passenger. The pilot's wife, who was sitting in the copilot's seat, had told him with a definite gleam in her eye that Shokapee— his destination—was just a stone's throw from some really serious shopping.

The twenty-minute flight would put him less than a stone's throw from Claudie's sister's house.

Bo was glad to have a few minutes to collect his thoughts. Matt was not the most cheerful of traveling companions. Bo guessed he had a right to be sour— life had been pretty perverse lately. Bo's thoughts turned to Claudie's brother. Life hadn't been easy for him either but he'd seemed philosophical about it.

"I figure I'm in here for a reason...and it don't necessarily have to do with paying for my crime,"

Zach had told him. "Nothing I do will ever bring those people back. I was on a downward slide and, unfortunately, I took two other souls with me."

Zach's unexpected candor had taken Bo by surprise. "I gotta admit, I didn't think you'd give me the time of day," he'd told him.

"I wouldn't if Claudie hadn't given me the okay."

Bo's mouth had dropped open. "She what?"

Zach had smiled. "Not in so many words, you understand. But I know my sister, and I know how she feels about you—even if she won't admit it." His eyes had narrowed and he'd added sternly, "But she's been hurt a lot. Our father just had it in for her. Nothing she did was ever good enough for him. One time she brought home a report card with all A's and B's on it and he called her a kiss-ass teacher's pet. She just couldn't win. And there was other shit...." His voice had softened to almost a whisper. "So you'd better not hurt her or I will personally beat the crap out of you when I get out of here."

Sighing, Bo arched his neck against the high-backed seat and took a deep breath. He glanced at the muted squares of color below him punctuated with rivers and gray-looking lakes, but his mind was on Claudie. He had every intention of taking it slow and easy once he made sure she was okay. But first, he had to catch up with her. He'd expressed his fear about missing her at Valery's, but Zach had laughed.

"You don't know Val," he'd said. "Mom always said Val was born late and at the rate she was going she'd be late for her own funeral. Don't worry. Claudie will still be there."

THE SUNLIGHT streaming through the breakfast nook window was almost enough to calm Claudie's nerves. It hadn't taken long after reconnecting with Valery for Claudie to recall the long list of her sister's annoying habits that had always driven her crazy. At the top of the page was her glacierlike start-and-stop pace.

Val had insisted on fixing a fancy breakfast to prepare Claudie for her journey, but it was now almost noon and Claudie's stomach had been growling for hours.

"This is so much fun," Val said, poking through a drawer for something. "I couldn't believe it when I looked up from my desk last night and there you were. Wow. It was eerie. You look just like I remember Mom…except her hair was brown. Like mine."

Claudie studied her half sister as she puttered about the homey, cluttered kitchen. Val, who'd recently turned twenty-two, favored the Anders side of the family—short and dark with broad shoulders, narrow hips and delicate wrists and ankles. She carried an unhealthy spare tire around her middle but otherwise was quite attractive. Her curly auburn hair framed her face in a feminine style.

"Maybe I should grab a bite on the road, Val. I've gotten a little gun-shy about storms since I got stuck in a blizzard in Wyoming," Claudie said, trying to be diplomatic. Val had been a good hostess—taking Claudie out to dinner last night and providing a comfy bed, so Claudie hated to seem ungrateful, but she was anxious to leave.

"I know. This is taking forever. My mom is such a talker, but she's had a rough time of it since Dad passed away." Valery's adoptive mother had called

and talked for almost an hour while Val drifted between chopping chives to making a Hollandaise sauce
from scratch. Claudie would have exploded with frustration if an old photo album hadn't sidetracked her.

The ratty album—held together by peeling masking
tape—was sprinkled with small, square black-and-
white photos that slowly segued to murky color shots.
To her surprise, the sentimental journey hadn't been
as excruciating as she'd expected. Zach was right—
there had been good times, too.

One picture grabbed her and took her straight to the
scene—a skinny six-year-old holding her little
brother's hand as they walked along the shore of Lake
Michigan. Her mother, carrying Yancy in her arms,
and obviously pregnant with Wesley, held her other
hand. What stopped Claudie's heart was the smile on
her mother's face. She looked girlish and carefree.

Years later someone—maybe Val—had pointed out
that the reason Mother had been happy in Wisconsin
was her close proximity to her estranged family.
Maybe she thought they might welcome her back into
the fold. But that had never happened because Garret
got yet another new job and they'd moved to Dav-
enport, Iowa the next spring and Claudie didn't recall
ever meeting anyone she could call Grandma.

"Do you prefer ham or Canadian bacon?" Val
asked, squatting in front of her refrigerator. "I have
both."

Both? Aren't they the same? "Umm, either is fine,
thanks. I'm not much of a gourmet."

"I love to cook," Val said with passion. "I plan to
open a restaurant after Mom's gone. I'd never sell the
video stores as long as she's alive—she likes to come

in and throw her weight around once in a while, but commercial retail is not my thing. I'm good at it, but I'd rather be in a kitchen.''

As far as Claudie could surmise, Val *was* very good at what she did. Not only was there a new Mercedes in the driveway of her charming older home, but when Claudie had walked into the video shop the previous evening, she'd had a chance to watch Val in action.

''You *will* have my order here tomorrow,'' Val had barked into the mouthpiece of the telephone headset. Her back was to the doorway where Claudie was standing. ''I can't *sell* excuses.''

Her strident tone had been loud enough to make several shoppers turn around and look.

''What kind of food would you cook in your restaurant?'' Claudie asked, relieved to see Val pull out a frying pan.

Val set it on a burner then refilled her coffee cup. She offered Claudie some, too, but Claudie declined— certain her eyeballs might begin to float if she didn't get some food in her stomach soon. ''I haven't narrowed that down, yet,'' Val said, taking a sip from her cup. ''Maybe French. Maybe Scandinavian. There are a lot of folks around here who go for that good Norwegian food,'' she said, faking an accent that made Claudie smile.

In all honesty, Claudie had enjoyed her visit with her sister more than she thought possible. They had absolutely nothing in common but somehow that didn't matter. The novelty of the feeling made her smile.

''I'm surprised you didn't make more money as a hooker, Claudie,'' Val said, apropos of nothing. ''I mean, you're pretty and thin. Guys go for girls who look like you.''

Val's bluntness didn't shock her. It was the Val she remembered. ''Prostitution doesn't have a lot of benefits or job security. It's like any other sales job—if you're not out selling, you don't get paid. I got real sick of sellin'.'' My *soul,* she added silently.

Val nodded sagely as she began cracking eggs into a bowl. ''Yeah, I know how that goes. Some days it's all I can do to make myself go to the video store. If it weren't for Mom...''

She didn't complete the thought, so Claudie asked, ''Is she demanding?''

Val's shoulder's stiffened. ''I prefer to call it high maintenance. The more I encourage her to go out and reconnect with the world, the more she pesters me about settling down and having kids.'' She gave a derisive snort. ''Like kids would be on either of our lists.''

Claudie was taken aback by her sister's vehemence. An image of Brady flashed in her mind. ''I think I might like to have kids someday,'' she admitted softly—as much to herself as Val.

Val looked dumbfounded. ''How could you even think about it after what our mother went through? Do you remember how she looked at the end? I was only twelve but I can still picture her in the hospital. Her skin looked like waxed paper. Do you know I can't stand to touch the stuff even today?'' A shudder passed through her body. ''She was as depleted as an empty corn husk.''

Claudie didn't argue the point. She'd been with her

mother right up to end. She'd watched her waste away like a stream drying up in the summer heat.

Val spun back to the counter. "Nope," she said with conviction, "not me. I don't plan to be anybody's baby factory."

Claudie didn't say anything. The only sound was the snap and crunch of Val breaking eggs into a bowl. Both women jumped when the doorbell rang. "Would you get that, Claud? It's probably Mom. She usually stops over once or twice a day on weekends."

I should have left an hour ago, Claudie thought stifling a sigh. She trudged down the short hallway to the foyer. Plastering a fake smile on her face, she opened the door. "Bo." His name came out as a strangled yelp of shock that brought her sister running.

"Hi, Claudie, long time no see," he said, his voice dangerously soft, deceivingly calm. His eyes burned, a muscle in his cheek twitched, his left hand gripped the threshold as if to block her escape.

What he couldn't know was how glad she was to see him. It was on the tip of her tongue to tell him so when he glanced at Val and said, "You must be Valery. I'm Bo." He reached around Claudie to give Val a quick handshake then said, "Excuse us a minute, but this is long overdue."

Before Claudie could react, his right arm shot out and he hauled her up against his chest and kissed her. Hard. A kiss unlike any she'd ever known. Possessive. Passionate. And, above all, welcome.

CHAPTER FIVE

THEY'D KISSED BEFORE—friendly pecks, one or two tentative investigations. But this kiss was different. Bo was in zero gravity before he knew what hit him. Her arms were around his neck. Her tongue touched his. *Her tongue.* Her sweet, wonderful tongue.

A fake cough blew him right out of orbit. He jumped back like a kid on his first date. When he realized he was looking at an amused sister not an angry dad, he blushed with chagrin. "There," he said, with as much bluster as he could fake, "that'll teach you to run away without telling anybody."

Valery laughed. Claudie looked too stunned to move. *I freaked her out. Damn. Way to go, Lester.*

Bo hadn't planned to kiss her. He'd promised Zach to take things slow and easy with Claudie, but something had come over him the minute he'd seen her standing there looking bright and chipper. He'd had to touch her just to reassure himself she was real.

And she was real all right—real pissed off. He could tell by the way her shoulders stiffened and her eyes narrowed. He'd learned long ago the best defense was to hold his ground.

"Let's get it over with. Do you want to yell at me? Fine. I want to yell, too. But I'm willing to let you go first."

"This sounds like fun. Can I watch?" Valery asked, smiling mischievously.

"No," Claudie snapped. "There won't be any yelling because Bo isn't staying. He can just jump back on whatever white horse he rode into town on and go home."

"They didn't have any white horses at the car rental agency. I got the last thing on the lot, but I'm altogether sure it's a car," he said, looking over his shoulder. "It was the best they had on a Sunday. I guess there's a whole slew of veterans in town for the holiday."

Her lips pursed as if to scold him, so he continued his nonsense before she could speak. Odd, he thought, all this time to think about what he wanted to say and it had never crossed his mind to prepare a speech. "Listen, Claudie, I know you don't want me here, but I'm not leaving. If you and Val are heading to Kansas…" She made a surprised sound and covered her lips with her hand. Bo explained, "My cousin's with the FBI. He helped me put all the pieces together."

She shrank back. "You know? Everything?"

His heart squeezed at the vulnerability in her tone. "Just the basics. Name, date of birth, vaccinations," he said, trying to lighten the mood. "We found bits and pieces and kind of put them together the best we could. The Internet helped."

Claudie looked from him to Valery and back. "Why?"

Now was not the time to blurt out the answer he'd given Zach so he said, "I was worried about you. You're not the kind of person who just takes off without a reason, and I was afraid your reason might have to do with the past—the past that put you on the street.''

Her brow shot up. "You thought I'd go back to hooking?''

"Of course not. But whatever made you run away from home had to hurt a lot—I wasn't about to let it hurt you again.''

Valery suddenly lifted her chin and sniffed. "Oh, hell,'' she exclaimed. "My butter's burning.'' She spun around and sprinted down the hall.

Bo shifted from one foot to the other, waiting for some kind of sign. Claudie was looking at the ground. Bo's jacket felt insufferably warm, despite the chilly breeze whistling through the two tall pines in Val's front yard. Claudie wrapped her arms around her chest and slowly lifted her chin. "I should be mad, but I guess I'm not too surprised. Ren said you'd gone to New York to look for Eve. I think in the back of my mind I knew you might come.''

His heart started pumping normally, and he let out the breath he'd been holding. "Does that mean I can hang out with you and your sister or do I have to tail you all the way to Kansas?''

She looked around his shoulder at his humble little two-door hatchback parked behind her station wagon. "Val isn't going with me, so I guess you can tag along.''

Bo had to work to keep his jubilation from showing, but she scowled as if sensing it. "I don't know what you're doing here or why you want to come with me, but this is *my* trip and I'm boss. If you don't like it, tough.''

He saluted her briskly. "Can I come in? I doubt if Val wants to heat up the outside with her electricity."

Claudie stepped aside so he could enter. Her scent enveloped him the minute she closed the door. It was warmer, more welcoming than the smells emanating from the kitchen. Bo shrugged off the parka he'd bummed from Matt and laid it across the back of a sofa as she led him down the hallway.

"I hope you're hungry, Bo," Val called. "I always make enough for thrashers, as my mother likes to say," Val said when they reached the kitchen.

"Starved," he said. And he was—for Claudie. Her rare and wonderful smile. Her hard-knock sense of humor. Her touch.

Without words she offered him a cup of coffee. He nodded. Their fingers met during the exchange and Bo felt a jolt.

He'd promised Zach to take things slow and easy with Claudie, but that might prove tougher than he'd thought—especially when she smiled that impish grin when she thought he wasn't looking.

CLAUDIE GRINNED. It was hard to keep from grinning when a white knight charged up on his trusty steed to rescue you. Granted the steed was a hunk of junk blocking the driveway, but the knight was hers. Bo. She had to keep staring at him for fear he'd disappear.

Thankfully Val never stopped talking long enough for Claudie's overt attention to become noticeable.

"Claudie was like the big mean sister from hell growing up, weren't you, Claud?" Val asked, her voice retaining a hint of the childhood whine that used to drive Claudie crazy. "I always thought she was picking on me. It wasn't until I got older that I realized she was filling in for our mother."

She paused, her lips pursed pensively. "Mom was sick a lot. One thing after another. Then, the day after Christmas, Dad took her to the hospital and she never came home." She looked at Claudie. "I remember you wouldn't let anybody take down the Christmas tree because you said Mom had a special way of wrapping up the ornaments and nobody else could do it. Remember?"

Claudie gripped her cup a little tighter. "No," she lied, picturing her stepfather standing in the midst of shattered ornaments—green and red shards littering the hardwood floor beneath the scraggy pine. It was early morning, still dark enough that the lights from the Christmas tree filled the room with color. When he'd lifted a shiny silver ball to his face, she'd seen tears, and Claudie had known her mother was dead.

Val frowned as if trying to remember some detail. "Sure you do. Because after Dad woke us up to tell us, I ran into the living room and the tree was gone and you were sweeping up needles. You were crying. I'd never seen you cry before. I think that scared me more than losing Mom."

She turned back to her cooking. Bo reached out to cover Claudie's hand with his own, but she picked up her cup and walked to the sink. "How much longer, Val? I think I'll run and close up my suitcase."

Val took a plate from the cupboard. "I'll serve Bo first. Yours will be done in a minute." Claudie watched her carefully arrange a sprig of parsley atop the creation then place it before Bo.

He studied it a moment. "This looks better than

what they serve in restaurants." He took a bite and groaned in pleasure. "Oh, baby, this...is...sinful."

Claudie pivoted on her heel and marched away. Her heart was beating much faster than it should have been and she tried to tell herself she was just nervous about getting a late start, but she knew that was a lie. She stuffed her nightgown in her backpack as if it were a rag and yanked the zipper closed.

"Yours is ready, sis," Valery called as Claudie plunked her travel-size tube of toothpaste into her cosmetics bag.

Claudie glanced in the mirror and practiced a fake smile. It was pathetic enough to make her smile for real.

Claudie slid into the chair across from Bo, meeting his quizzical look with a nod. Aromatic steam from the plate Val set before her made Claudie inhale deeply. "Umm," she said, her mouth watering.

Oddly put out by its perfection, Claudie hacked down on the three-inch stack of eggs, ham and English muffin with her fork. Hot yolk squirted sideways sending a yellow stream across her left hand.

"Oops," Val said, turning away. "I forgot napkins."

Before Claudie could react, Bo reached out and lifted her hand, bending down as if to gallantly kiss the back of it. Instead, he sucked the egg from her skin, adding a last little lick before her sister returned.

Claudie gaped in shock. She couldn't decide whether to be angry or amused. Bo's roguish wink sealed her fate. She laughed. "You are one sick puppy, Bo Lester," she said.

Val looked between them, a frown on her face. "What'd I miss?"

Claudie took the pretty print napkin from her sister's hand. "Nothing important. I've just agreed to travel with a madman. That's all."

Obviously, upset to be out of the loop, Val turned back to the stove to dish her own plate. Inwardly, Claudie groaned. She didn't want to upset her sister after coming all this way to visit. To her surprise, Bo soon had Val smiling as he regaled them with the horror story of his trip from hell with his cousin Matt.

"First, I swear, there's nothing like four feet of snow to bring out the crazies in New York. The bridges were like skating rinks and every taxi driver thought he was Wayne Gretzky. We were lucky to make it to the airport alive. Unfortunately, our flight was canceled—along with everybody else's, so we ended up sleeping on the floor."

Claudie shuddered. "That's disgusting."

"That's not the worst of it," he said, pausing dramatically. "The woman who was sitting beside Matt had a little dog in one of those plastic carriers. Turns out the dog had the worst halitosis imaginable…and it spent the whole night trying to lick Matt's nose."

Val hooted with laughter. "What'd he do?"

Bo shrugged. "He was asleep. He didn't realize it until he woke up, then he nearly gagged." He gave Claudie a wink. "He told me he'd been dreaming his ex-wife was trying to seduce him."

"Where's Matt now?" Claudie asked, trying hard not to be charmed.

Bo took a swallow of coffee. "On his way to Kansas—in case you headed there instead of here."

Claudie frowned. She wasn't sure how she felt about the idea of having two men track her movements—one was bad enough.

"What will he do until we get there?"

"Scope things out. He was in law enforcement. He knows the routine."

Claudie rose and carried her plate to the sink. After scraping the leftovers into the garbage can, she reached for the handle of the faucet, but Val said, "Just leave it on the counter, Claudie. You cleaned up after all of us for years. I'll do the dishes later, after you're gone."

"Are you sure you don't want to come along?" Claudie asked, trying not to sound pathetically hopeful.

Val let out a long, heartfelt sigh. "Like I told you last night—Otter Creek is the last place on Earth I'd go to voluntarily. I put that life behind me when I got adopted. And it sounds like you've got a nice life back in Sacramento, Claudie. I really don't understand why you're doing this."

"I told you last night. I don't want the same thing to happen to Sherry that happened to me."

"But why do you care? You haven't seen her in ten years—she probably doesn't even remember you, or any of us for that matter."

"Then she has a right to know. We're her family."

Val's groan twisted Bo's stomach in a knot. "Big whoop. A brother in prison, a sister who's an ex-hooker, another brother who drives a big truck and chases women other than his wife." Claudie's brows shot up in surprise, which prompted Val to add,

"That's what Zach told me. Seems Yancy can't quite get his first wife out of his system."

Claudie frowned. "No family is perfect, but she still has a right to know us."

Val's eyes took on a speculative glint. "Are you sure this isn't more about your revenge on Dad? If that Web page you showed me is right, he might have cleaned up his act and your coming along will open a big ugly can of worms that could ruin his life." She smiled serenely. "Not that he doesn't have it coming for what he did to you, but I'm just curious about your motivation."

Rather than answer her sister's question, Claudie started clearing the table, but Val had given Bo a smug look as if she had her answer.

BO TRANSFERRED his bag from the trunk of the rental car to the back of the station wagon, which was idling with the heater blasting in an effort to defrost the windows. He hadn't decided if he truly trusted Claudie to follow him back to the rental lot, but he figured she was too softhearted to take off with his luggage.

He looked toward the small white bungalow where the two sisters were standing on the stoop. Claudie turned to leave, but Val stopped her, then dashed back inside. Claudie looked at Bo and threw up her hands in frustration. Dressed in a purple-and-white ski sweater and black leggings—her blond hair its usual "bed-head" style, she looked like a teenager ready for a day on the slopes.

Seeing the sunlight pick up streaks of white gold in her mop of waves, Bo was struck by how angelic she looked, as if the tragedy and ugliness of her past had bounced off. Bo had defended her without hesitation, but now his trepidation returned. What was she seeking? Revenge? Redemption? Maybe just a simple "I'm sorry"?

Bo wished he had a clear-cut answer, but he doubted if Claudie knew herself. They looked at each other from across the distance. A quick smile touched her lips then disappeared. Bo's heart turned over as giddy as a kid with his first crush. He slammed the rear door of the wagon with more force than necessary. Claudie's chin tilted questioningly, but only for a second. Val returned and Claudie turned to face her.

Bo couldn't hear their conversation, but he headed in that direction when he saw Val hand Claudie a white box the size of a toaster oven. As he approached, he heard Claudie ask, "How'd you get it?"

"Dad sent it to me when I graduated from high school. I don't know how he knew where I lived. We'd moved up here shortly after my adoption was final—Mom wanted us to make a fresh start, and I'd never had any contact with him or the boys after we left town. There wasn't a card or anything, but his name was on the return address. Mom said maybe it was his way of apologizing for everything that went wrong."

Bo joined Claudie on the stoop in time to see her lift the lid of the box, which on closer look appeared to be a cheap jewelry box covered in white watered silk slightly yellowed with age.

"It's Mom's stuff," Claudie said, her voice hoarse with unshed tears.

Bo looked at Valery who lifted one shoulder as if to say, "Whatever."

"Don't you want to keep any of it?" Claudie asked. "You might want to give something to your kids some day...."

Val cut in. "Like I told you before. I'm not going to have kids. Kids make your life miserable. No thanks."

"But, don't you even want something to remember Mom by?"

Bo's heart split down the middle at the little-girl quality in her voice.

Val shook her head. "No. It's *your* mother's stuff, Claudie. My mother lives three blocks away, and, believe me, she wouldn't be caught dead in any of that junk."

The put-down made Bo start to snarl, but Claudie seemed too moved by the unexpected gift to be offended. Bo looked at Val over Claudie's head. *Brat.* She batted her lashes innocently.

"We gotta hit the road, kiddo," he said, taking Claudie's elbow. She was so engrossed by the treasure chest, she didn't even flinch when he put his arm around her shoulders and guided her to the driver's side door. "Aren't you going to tell your sister goodbye?"

Claudie looked up as if coming back to reality. "Oh," she said with a gulp. She shoved the box into Bo's hands and dashed back to hug Val. "I'll let you know what happens," she called over her shoulder as she sprinted to the car. "Thanks for everything."

Bo placed the box in the back seat, fearful she'd be too distracted to drive safely. "You can go through it once I'm driving. Not before," he said sternly.

She gave him a goofy salute and got in the car.

"Then let's get going. It's a long way to Kansas, you know."

Her impish grin stayed with him all the way to the rental shop. He and Matt had mapped out the trip before leaving New York. Two days on the road. One night. It wasn't the days that worried him.

"CAN YOU believe this traffic?" Bo said for the second time in ten miles.

The sense of wonder in his tone made Claudie smile. They'd had a brief argument over whether to drive east and catch the interstate or take the same road Claudie had driven. Since Bo had insisted on driving, Claudie had acquiesced to his preference, and she was glad since he seemed so bemused by the lack of cars on the spacious, nicely groomed four-lane highway.

"I'm sure it gets busy on weekdays. And tomorrow's a holiday, don't forget," she reminded him.

"Yeah, I suppose you're right." He was quiet a moment then he swore and slapped his palm against the steering wheel, making Claudie jump.

"What?"

"Today's the little guy's birthday. I forgot to get him a present."

Claudie had to bite her lip to keep from laughing at Bo's tormented tone. "I sent him two T-shirts and a dinosaur from the Black Hills, but I doubt if he got them in time. Ren and Sara were taking him to the coast for the long weekend."

Bo reached between the seats for the navy-blue parka he'd thrown to the back. He handed it to Claudie. ''Get my cell phone out of the pocket would you?''

She had to try three different pockets before she found it. Each pocket was an adventure. One was stuffed with bags of airline peanuts, the second with sugar packets—one of which had broken open. She got sticky grains under her fingernails. Sucking her fingers to remove the sugar, she held the small black phone in her other hand. ''How do you know where to call? You know Ren won't have his phone on.''

When Bo didn't answer, she looked up. He was staring at her fingers in her mouth. Her heart began to race, and she immediately shoved her hand under her butt. His gaze went straight back to the road, but Claudie could tell by his ruddy color he knew she'd guessed what he was thinking.

''If we can't get them on the cell, you can try Babe. She ought to know where they're staying.''

Claudie silently groaned. She wasn't ready to talk to Babe Bishop. Although the woman had been nothing but supportive of Claudie recently, she still felt shy around her. And Claudie certainly didn't want to explain this trip.

Holding her breath, she punched in the phone number then listened to the ringing tone. Two rings. Three…

''Hello.''

''Ren?''

''Claudie?''

From the background came a loud, shrill cry followed by a muffled curse and thumping sound. ''Claudie,'' Sara cried, the joy in her voice causing tears to fill Claudie's eyes. "It's so good to hear your voice. How are you?"

Claudie wasn't sure she could speak without embarrassing herself so she said, "Bo wants to talk to you," and passed the phone to her left.

Obviously surprised and unprepared, he shifted slightly and took the phone. "Hi, Sara. I found her."

Claudie stared out the passenger window at the rolling farmland now sitting fallow. She'd passed through this country once or twice in her family's many moves, and it felt comforting—like greeting an old friend. But, in reality, Claudie only had two friends: Sara and Keneesha. And she missed them both more than she thought possible.

"I just remembered Brady's birthday and we called to wish him happy birthday," Bo was saying. "Put him on."

Bo leaned toward Claudie and motioned her closer with a nod of his head. She inched sideways until their shoulders touched. She felt the connection all the way to the soles of her hiking boots.

He held the phone so they both could hear Brady's excited jabber. Since Bo was trying to talk and steer, Claudie reached between them and took the phone from his fingers. A jolt of awareness overrode all incoming messages.

"Slow down, honey boy, I can't understand you. You touched a what?"

"'Tar fish," he cried. "Orange 'tar fish."

Claudie and Bo exchanged a look. "A star fish," he mouthed.

Her mouth went bone dry. *What is wrong with me?*

Sara came on the line and Claudie sat back, giving

herself some much needed space. This wasn't like her at all. She'd been with Bo in the car dozens of time and nothing like this had ever happened.

"What, Sara? I'm sorry. My mind's a little out there."

"Understandable. It was probably quite a shock to see Bo. We were afraid you wouldn't be too happy about him joining you." *Happy?* Claudie wasn't sure how she felt, but happy might actually be part of it, she thought. "But, you know Bo, once he made up his mind, there was no talking him out of finding you."

"It's okay for now," Claudie said, aware he was listening to her conversation. "I won't kill him before we get to Kansas. Just in case the car breaks down again."

Bo's lips pursed in a mock scowl.

Sara's voice dropped. "You're not really going to kill anybody are you, honey?"

Claudie started to laugh, but suddenly she understood Sara was serious. In a flash she realized her friend might have thought her intention was revenge. It crossed her mind to be mad, but only for a second.

"Don't worry, Sara. I'm not going to do anything stupid. I already have a brother in prison for vehicular manslaughter. I stopped to see him on my way, and believe me, I'm not in a hurry to go back there."

Sara's sigh seemed mixed with tears. Ren came on the line. "I'm glad to hear you're okay, kiddo," he said. "Put that doofus friend of mine back on the line."

Claudie passed the phone to Bo. She tuned out the conversation, still thinking about Sara's doubt. Did this mean her best friend in the world knew so little about her that she believed her capable of murder? *Bo says I'm like a clam. Maybe it's true.*

When the phone landed in her lap, she looked at Bo. He had a serious frown on his face that made her stomach contract. "Is something wrong?"

He sighed.

"Ren said Eve's old agent called him. Apparently she heard about Eve leaving the network—"

Claudie interrupted him. "She quit her job?"

Bo nodded. "Looks that way."

Claudie shook her head. "I don't believe it. Network was her dream job. She told me so herself when she was back for the wedding."

Bo shrugged. "Sounds like some guy came in and swept her off her feet. The only weird thing is, nobody's heard from her since."

"Do you think something happened to her?"

"Nah," he said, shaking his head. "She's probably shacked up in some tropical love nest."

Claudie frowned. She couldn't picture anyone less likely to succumb to a sweet-talking man than Eve— except herself. "Men always think that, don't they?"

"Think what?"

She started to let it go—after all she was no fan of Eve Masterson's even if Sara was willing to forget the woman had once been engaged to Ren, but instead she turned sideways in her seat to face him. "Men always think women are ready to give up their lives, their careers, their identity for a wedding ring and regular sex. Right?"

"As opposed to no wedding ring and irregular sex?" he asked, shooting a quick glance her way.

She stuck out her tongue. "You know what I mean."

"Not really."

She threw up her hands. "Isn't that what normal people do? They grow up, go to school, meet someone then settle down for a nice, safe life."

"Didn't you leave out the word *boring?*"

She scowled at him even though he wasn't looking at her.

"Claudie, I know you well enough to figure out when you're trying to pick a fight. If you want to yell at me for tracking you down and nosing in on your business, then go ahead and yell. But don't try to confuse me by arguing about normal people. Frankly, I don't give a damn about the normal people of the world. I do care about you."

"And I'm not normal. Is that what you're saying?" She kept her tone even so he wouldn't hear the little kid inside her who'd known from the earliest memory she was somehow different from her brothers and sisters. Different in a bad way.

Instead of answering he hit the blinker.

Claudie looked up surprised to see a rest area sign. She held her breath as the car decelerated and pulled to a stop well away from the other vehicles.

Bo shut off the motor and turned to face her. "Claudie, you know you're not like other people. Neither am I. Frankly, I don't see that as a bad thing. We are who we are, and it gives us character." He took a deep breath and let it out. "Maybe I would have liked things to be different growing up. My dad was a horse's butt as fathers went, and yours was no prize winner, either."

Claudie leaned back against the door. The coolness of the window seeped through her sweater giving her a chill. "My father committed suicide," she said.

Bo's bushy brows collided. "I beg your pardon?"

"My real father. My mother fell in love with the minister's son back in the town where she grew up. It was a small, mostly Scandinavian town in Wisconsin. They were both seventeen. When she found out she was pregnant, he offered to marry her, but his father wouldn't hear of it. He claimed my mother seduced his boy. He sent my father away to a boarding school back east. It was very hush-hush. My mother was left to do the right thing, which in those days meant giving me up for adoption."

He ran his thumbnail along the seam of her leggings. The touch sent squiggly tendrils up and down her legs. "But she didn't," he said, prompting her to go on.

"She was going to, but at the last minute she backed out. Her parents were furious. They told her she couldn't bring me home because they had her two younger sisters to worry about and they didn't want them contaminated by her loose morals."

Bo made a sound of disgust.

Claudie shrugged. "Mother had a hundred dollars. She moved in with one of the nurses from the hospital. The *St. James* School for Unwed Mothers," she added softly.

He opened his mouth but didn't say anything.

"She was working as a waitress when she met my stepdad. Mom once told me Garret asked her to marry him before she could ask, 'What'll it be today?'"

Bo leaned forward. "So she said yes, and your real father heard about it and committed suicide?"

"Who's telling this story? You're as bad as Brady," she scolded. "Actually, Garret, my stepfather, asked her to marry him once a week for four months—he only passed through town on his sales route once a week. She always turned him down. Until the day she talked to an old friend of hers back in Wisconsin and she found out my father had committed suicide in his dorm."

Bo sat back. "Wow. I didn't know any of that."

"I don't suppose it's the kind of thing that shows up on a computer search."

"Did she ever reconcile with her parents?" he asked.

Claudie shook her head. "Not that I know of, but she never blamed them for putting her out. She told me they were doing what they thought best, and as a parent sometimes you make tough decisions for the good of the children." She didn't bother trying to disguise her bitterness.

"You think she was wrong?"

"I think she was weak and selfish. Maybe if she'd given me up for adoption I'd have had a normal life— like Val. Instead I grew up watching her pump out babies like there was some kind of competition to make the most. She was pregnant something like ten times in twelve years. Three were miscarriages, and my little brother Timothy died at birth, but still she had six kids before she was thirty-five."

"Why do you think she wanted so many kids?"

Claudie glanced in the back seat where her mother's jewelry box sat. She felt slightly disloyal sharing her mother's secret with Bo, but she figured it didn't matter any more. "She told me that was the only way she could make it up to him."

At Bo's puzzled look, she explained, "Mom felt she owed something to Garret because he loved her, but she never loved him. Even after giving Garret six kids, she still loved my father." Claudie looked into his eyes and read the compassion she'd never known from another man. "That's why he hated me. I reminded her of my father. Every day he had to live with that reminder." She broke the contact and looked away. "I guess, you can kinda understand why he raped me."

"No," Bo barked, startling Claudie with both the volume and the passion. "I can't understand it, and I can't wait to meet the bastard."

Claudie peeked around to see if anyone was looking. She wasn't used to having someone defend her—it made her nervous. "Listen, Bo, I said you could come along with me because I knew you'd follow anyway, but I don't want you sticking your nose into my business once we get there."

He rocked back, his face still flushed from anger. "Tough."

She blinked. "What did you say?"

"I said tough. I'm here and I'm in it all the way."

"Not if I don't want you there."

"Wrong."

Speechless, her mouth dropped open.

He leaned forward, crowding her space. His breath was warm and smelled of coffee. "I'm here, Claudie, and I'm not about to let you face this jerk alone, even if you throw a hissy fit. People like your stepdad know only one way to operate—they tear you down. They find a way around your good, fine, logical arguments until they make you feel stupid and small and deserving of all the crap they gave you. He raped your spirit, your self-esteem, long before he ever physically touched you. And I plan to make damn sure he doesn't get the chance to do it again.''

Claudie couldn't breathe. She couldn't move without crumpling into a ball and weeping, so she sat very still and waited for him to move back. When he did, she opened the door. "I need to use the bathroom," she said, after gulping in a deep breath of chilled air. "I'll be right back."

She got out and closed the door. She walked briskly praying she could make it to the low brick building before she broke down completely.

He caught up with her halfway there. His hand closed over her shoulder. She froze. "Claudie," he said softly. He gently squeezed his fingers. "I'm sorry. That was—"

Without thinking she spun around and threw herself sobbing into his arms. She didn't want his apologies— she wanted something else. Something she couldn't have—an ordinary life with an ordinary past. And with any luck...an ordinary future.

CHAPTER SIX

BO GLANCED to his right. Claudie had reclined the seat as far as it would go and was fast asleep, her head resting on his bunched-up coat just inches from his elbow. They'd stopped for gas and a couple of sodas in the town of Faribault, Minnesota. She'd tried reading the newspaper for a few miles but was obviously having a hard time staying awake so he'd suggested she nap.

"Hey, you're the one who slept on the floor last night. I should be driving so you can sleep," she'd argued.

Bo had insisted he wasn't tired, and he hadn't lied. For some reason, being around Claudie energized him. In New York, he'd had to force himself to trudge through the motions of looking for Eve and conducting his company's business from Matt's apartment. Last week on his trip to Las Vegas, he'd lacked the initiative to check out even one of the fancy new casinos. Life seemed to lack any purpose when Claudie was gone.

That's how Bo knew he was in love with her. He'd known since Vegas but hadn't been ready to admit it until Zach called him on it. But there was no denying it now. The second she'd melted into his arms, her tears soaking his shirt, he was lost. Too far gone to

even give a damn. His only problem was how to tell
Claudie without totally freaking her out.

His cell phone trilled just as they passed a sign announcing the Iowa border.

"Is this my Welcome-to-Iowa call?"

A familiar chuckle answered. "No, it's the I-don't-
give-a-damn-where-you-are call."

"Sure you do. You're my cousin. And my business
partner."

"Maybe. We only have our mothers' word on the
first and I'm rethinking the second. So far this P.I.
business is nothing more than racing around like a
headless chicken."

Bo grinned. He checked his speed and eased his
foot off the accelerator. "I disagree. I've had an ex-
cellent day. Not only was I treated to an aerial view
of Minnesota, I found the woman of my dreams and
even managed to scarf down eggs Benedict."

"Hey, that's what I had for breakfast, too—mine
came in a sack with a little toy. Bet yours didn't."

Chuckling, Bo asked, "So, where are you?"

"I'm at a rest area just past St. Joseph, Missouri,"
Matt said, the connection fading like a long echo.
When it surged back in, Bo heard him say, "...a motel in Kansas City tonight, then head to Otter Creek
tomorrow." He made a snorting sound. "I can't believe I'm on my way to a town called Otter Creek. I
bet you dollars to doughnuts it has neither."

"If Claudie were awake I'd ask her, but you'll just
have to check that out for yourself."

"I can't wait," Matt said, facetiously. He added
more seriously, "How she'd take it—your jumping
into her life with both feet?"

"She was thrilled to see me."

"Yeah, I bet."

"No, really." Bo noticed her peeking up at him, so he added, "Claudie agreed she needed me along for all the really important things—like pumping gas and washing the windshield. You know, you can't get that kind of service at a lot of places anymore."

Her soft chuckle made his insides percolate. "And neck rubs," she added so softly he almost missed it.

"How far do you think you'll make it tonight?" Matt asked.

"How far will I get tonight? As far as she lets me," Bo quipped, bracing for the slug that was sure to follow. "Ouch!" he yelped. "She pinched me."

Matt's chuckle hummed across the line. "She sounds like a pistol. Speaking of which—she isn't carrying, is she?"

Bo held the phone away from his ear and asked loudly, "Claudie, Matt wants to know if you have a gun?"

She shot upright. "What is it with you people?" she shouted. "You watch too much television, right? No. I don't have a gun and I don't plan to shoot anybody. Jeez." She plopped down turning her back to him.

Bo returned the phone to his ear. "Did you get that?"

Matt was still laughing. "I got it. Boy, Cuz, can you pick 'em. She makes Sonya look like a soft touch."

"But her breath is better," Bo replied.

Matt's hoot echoed in the car. "I'll be sure to tell Sonya you said so when I call home tonight. In the meantime, I'd better hit the road. I'll talk to you to-morrow—unless you want me to check in tonight when I get to my motel."

"Nah," Bo said, "Call me in the morning so we can set up where to meet. Give Ashley my love."

He pushed the disconnect button and dropped the phone into the breast pocket of his flannel shirt. He glanced over his shoulder and saw Claudie looking at him over her shoulder.

"Who's Ashley?" she asked.

"Matt's daughter. She's twelve, I think. A real sweetie pie and Matt loves her to pieces, but he doesn't get to spend a lot of time with her thanks to his ex-wife." He frowned, switching lanes to avoid a convoy of tractor-trailers. "Ashley's the reason we were late following you to Sioux Falls. Matt had the information for me on Friday, but he couldn't leave because Ashley was in some play at school. If we'd have left earlier, we'd have missed the storm."

"Why did you want him to come along?" she asked, her tone puzzled.

Bo sighed. "Matt's mom and my mom are not only sisters-in-law, they're really close friends. And they're both worried about Matt. They think he's sinking into some kind of depression. He was in a bad accident awhile back and can't work on the street anymore. His precinct gave him a desk job—and even loaned him to the FBI because he's so good at what he does, but he feels inadequate not doing what he loves."

"What's wrong with him?"

"His leg got crushed and they had to build him a new knee. He barely limps at all any more, but he's not a hundred percent and never will be."

"That sucks."

"Hey, it's a good break for me. I could really use his help in my business. I've offered him a partnership, which is partly why I wanted him along. He needs to see what the job involves. But like my mom said, he needed someone to shake him out of his rut, too."

She was silent a minute then said, "I liked your mother. We spent a little time together at the wedding. She's smart, but she doesn't rub your nose in it like some smart people do."

"You mean like me?" he teased.

"You're not that smart, Bo."

He pretended to be offended. "I beg your pardon."

Snickering, she repositioned herself so she could draw her knees up and wrap her arms around them. "Okay, you're street smart—like me, but you've got a ways to go to catch up with your mom when it comes to reading books."

He blew out a sigh. "You've got that right." He hesitated a moment then said, "When I was a kid, I resented her books. I was jealous of them."

"How can you be jealous of a book?"

"Easy, when your mom's busy reading instead of playing with you."

"Oh," she said reflectively. "I see what you mean. My mom never had time to read because there were always three or four kids whining for something, but it was kinda the same thing. She wasn't giving *me* her attention."

"Exactly. I think that was one of the reasons I didn't read for years."

"Ren said you never opened a book in college. He

said the only way you graduated was because you were naturally intelligent and you soaked up information like a sponge.''

Bo sat up a little straighter. ''He told you that?''

She nodded. ''Me and Sara. One night when we were sitting around the pool. I don't know where you were.''

''Hmm…well, he got the part about not opening a book right. I really regret that now. What a waste! Between the parties and the hangovers I don't know how I ever learned a thing.''

Neither of them spoke for several minutes, then Claudie asked, ''Where does Matt's daughter live?''

''With her mother and stepfather. He's a plastic surgeon and they have a big, fancy house on Long Island. I think that's another reason Matt isn't feeling too good about himself. He hates it that Ashley has to choose between spending time in his rinky-dink apartment or hanging out in upper-class suburbia.''

''It's the pits when kids get caught in the middle,'' Claudie said. ''My brother Yancy told me he has a daughter by his first wife, but he hardly ever sees her. At least your cousin makes the effort to stay connected.''

''Matt's a good father, and he was a damn fine husband until Sonya had an affair with the nose doctor. Of course, she blamed Matt because he was never home. She said she wanted more out of life than being a cop's wife.''

''You sound like she was unfaithful to you,'' Claudie said, hearing more than he wanted to say.

''It pissed me off that Matt's job wasn't good

enough for her. The same thing happened to a friend of mine when I was on the force.''

"Is that why you never married?" she asked in a soft voice.

He kept his eyes on the road—amazed by how easy it was to talk about things he never shared with anyone. "I dated one woman for almost four years. We talked marriage but never got around to setting a date. She worked for a dentist, and she was…" He didn't know how to describe the lack of emotional involvement he'd felt toward Janelle. He'd liked her. They'd had a good sex life. They'd had fun together. But that was as far as it went.

"What?" Claudie probed. "Was she too pushy? Too chubby? Too short? She snored? Her breasts were too big? Her feet were too small?"

Bo flashed her a droll sneer. "I liked her a lot, but I didn't love her."

"Oh," she said softly. "Did she love you?"

"Yes," Bo said with a sigh. "That's why I haven't dated for a long, long time. I hurt her—without meaning to, and I didn't like the way that made me feel."

She pushed the lever to bring her seat into the upright position. It made a clicking sound until it reached the angle she wanted. She turned slightly, her seat belt crossing at her shoulder. "You're a good man, Bo Lester. I guess I always knew that about you."

Bo's heart swelled. "Thanks." His voice sounded gruff and the fabric of his flannel shirt felt as though it were scraping his neck.

"You're welcome." She took a breath and let it out. "Can we eat soon? I'm hungry."

"DECISIONS. DECISIONS. Apple pie or cheesecake?" Bo said, studying a laminated dessert menu that had been left on their table by their harried waitress. "What are you ordering?"

Claudie's appetite had disappeared the instant he suggested getting a motel instead of traveling on. "Neither."

His left eyebrow quirked. "Are you sure?"

"I think we should hit the road," she said glancing out the window at the black sky. Deep down she know Bo was right—it was foolish to drive any farther when they were both exhausted. But to agree would mean she'd have to voice her request for separate rooms. Bo might think it pretty silly coming from a woman who used to sleep with men for a living.

"Claudie, you told me you didn't sleep well last night and, frankly, I'm shot," he said, his voice reflecting fatigue. "If you're worried about the money, don't be. I'll pay for the motel since I know you're on a budget and I want a good one."

She tried to cover her nervousness with attitude. "Two drivers means one person drives while the other sleeps. I'll take the first shift."

His mouth fell open. "You mean drive all night?"

Nodding with more enthusiasm than she felt, she took another drink of iced tea. Maybe a shot of caffeine would give her the jolt she needed to stay awake.

After a few seconds of stiff silence he let out a big, "Ohhh…I get it. You think if we get a motel I'll expect you to sleep with me. Right?"

Claudie looked away, wishing she could disappear. "No," she lied. "I don't have much time off from the bookstore, and I need to get this over with. We're still in Iowa and the sooner we get to Kansas, the sooner I can go home.''

When she braved a look, his gaze scrutinized her, making her squirm. ''Well, you won't save any time if we wind up in a wreck.''

He picked up the bill and slid out of the booth. ''Here's the plan. We're checking into the motel across the road. I've stayed in that chain before and they honor my business club discount card, which means I save enough money to afford *two* rooms.'' He wiggled two fingers. ''Okay?''

Unable to look him in the eye, she nodded.

By the time they pulled into the parking lot of the motel she was tempted to tell him one room with two beds would be okay. He was right, of course. They were adults, friends. He'd come all this way to help her. She was an idiot.

But before she could voice her change of heart, he was standing at the registration desk. In a blink he returned with two plastic credit-card type keys and a map with two red circles on it.

''We're right across the hall from each other,'' he said, looking over his shoulder to back up the car.

He drove around the far side of the building and parked. They unloaded their suitcases in silence. Bo used his key to unlock the outside door. As they headed down the hallway, he stopped to sniff the air.

Claudie recognized the smell. *Chlorine.*

''The desk clerk said they have a heated pool,'' he said, waiting for Claudie to open her door. ''And a spa, too.'' The childlike excitement in his tone made her feel even more foolish.

''I didn't bring a suit,'' Claudie said, carrying her

suitcase into the spacious, handsomely appointed room.

"Didn't I see a mall down the road?" he asked, his tone too innocent to be real. "It's off season. You could probably get a good deal, if you wanted one."

Sometimes Claudie felt as though arguing with Bo was as futile as trying to change the past. With a sigh, she held out her hand. "Gimme the keys," she muttered. The least she could do was be a good sport.

BO'S NOSE CRINKLED at the strong odor of chlorine. Paradoxically, it made him homesick for his houseboat. His life had been so hectic lately he hadn't had much time to spend on his funky vessel, but he loved the peace it brought him. Water was his retreat—his oasis. Any kind of water—even an Olympic-size aqua-blue rectangle surrounded by white plastic chairs beneath a huge Plexiglas dome. The steamy room reflected the loud chatter of a group of teens laughing and splashing in the far corner of the facility where a sunken spa occupied a raised dais. Surrounded by potted palms, it resembled a small oasis.

He grabbed a towel from a rack and walked to a spot visible from the entrance, in case Claudie came looking for him. Yeah, right, he thought frowning. They'd been getting along fine until he brought up the idea of the motel. It had seemed natural. No sane person drove all night unless it was a matter of life or death. The rationale behind her reaction had been transparently obvious.

Bo dropped his towel and room key on a chaise then yanked off his T-shirt. He dove into the water without hesitation. Its initial coolness startled him but as he lengthened his stroke toward the far end of the pool the water felt pleasantly soothing.

You gotta give her space, man, he told himself as he swam. Given her past, she may never want to be with a man, he thought despondently. He didn't blame her. What good had men done her?

When his fingers touched the wall at the shallow end, he stopped. Standing, he shook the water from his hair and face then sank up to his shoulders back into the now too warm water. With elbows resting on the tiled step he swirled the water with his feet. A sudden thought made him flinch. *What if she just kept going?* It hadn't occurred to him before, but she could have gone back to her room for her bag and taken off without him.

The idea made his stomach churn. He was just about to leave the pool when the door opened and Claudie walked in. "Holy sh—" he softly swore, taking in the cobalt suit, the dazzling expanse of skin and a sinfully provocative wisp of material encasing her hips.

Forgetting to breathe he sank lower until chlorinated water filled his open mouth. Choking, he stood up and waded toward her. "Nice suit," he said, mortified that his vocal cords chose that minute to act like a horny teenage boy's.

She clutched a towel to her chest as if to hide behind it. "It was the only one they had," she said. "How's the water?"

"What water?" He couldn't get over how beautiful she was. Perfect, really.

She gave him an arch look and pointed to the pool. "Oh," he said, feeling his face heat up. "Great.

The water's great. I haven't tried the spa yet. I was waiting for the kids to leave.''

As if on cue, the noisy group gathered their things and walked toward the door. As they passed, Bo saw the three young studs check out Claudie. Their girlfriends quickly hustled them off. Claudie's gaze followed them until they were out of sight.

"Swimming sounds good," she said, more to herself than Bo. "Work out a few kinks."

Bo gave her space, ordering himself to return to his laps. It took every bit of self-discipline to stay focused on his stroke. And it worked—until he accidentally bumped into her.

CLAUDIE LOVED WATER. As a child, the local swimming pool had been her favorite retreat. The underwater world was one of muted quiet and shimmering beauty—very different from her normal life. She knew Bo liked the water, too, but she'd never seen him attack it quite so relentlessly.

She casually drifted to his side of the pool and *accidentally* bumped his shoulder.

"Oops. Sorry," he said, jerking back in the chest-deep water.

"Are you in training or what?" she asked.

He looked confused.

"That's how Ren swims when he's upset about something. Sara said he put in about three miles a day before he decided to quit the judiciary."

Bo rolled his shoulders. Squarish. Solid. Such fine shoulders, Claudie thought before she could stop herself. She liked the nice even coat of reddish-blond curls on his chest, too.

Bo backed up a step and sank down until the water was up to his chin. "I was in the zone—mindless repetition," he told her, the look in his eye cautious.

She didn't blame him for being suspicious of her new mellower mood. "I'm sorry I was so cranky before. You were right. I was a little freaked about the room situation." She made a face. "You probably think it's stupid for someone like me to worry about where I sleep and who I sleep—"

He stopped her with a hand to her upper arm. A light touch, but it made her gulp. "Claudie, I've been worried about *where* you were sleeping ever since you left. I know how tight money is and I was afraid you might spend the night in your car. That's dangerous," he said sternly. "But it never crossed my mind to wonder *who* you might be sleeping with." He stepped closer and lowered his voice even though they were the only two in the place. "I *know* you, Claudie. I also know that performing sex for money is not the same as making love with someone. When it comes to that, you're practically a virgin."

Claudie's involuntary bark of laughter hid a deeper emotion that ripped through her middle. She backpedaled for breathing space. A tingling sensation under her arms made her want to race away. "That's the stupidest thing I've ever heard, Lester," she said, forcing herself to stand her ground.

"No, it's not. It's the truth."

She snorted her opinion. "I've done things that would make you blush."

"I was a cop for nine years, Claudie. I don't blush easily."

She took another step back but encountered the

solid wall of the pool. "I bet you never saw—" He didn't let her finish.

"Forget it, Claudie. You can't scandalize me, or freak me out by telling me some horror story about life on the street. I've been there. It's ugly. Enough said." Claudie's heart was beating so fast she could barely breathe. "If you need to unload some of that baggage you're carrying, I'd be glad to listen, but don't tell me that stuff if you're trying to scare me off. It won't work."

He looked so serious, so intent she almost turned around and fled.

"You know what this is about, Claudie," he said softly.

She shook her head. "No, I don't. It's not about nothin'."

His gaze pinned her to the wall. "It's about love, Claudie," he said slowly. "I...love...you." He said each word distinctly as if speaking to a person who didn't understand the language.

"No," she cried, spinning away. She stumbled up the slippery steps and practically clawed her way to the chair where her towel was. She wrapped it around herself, trying to hide from view. When she glanced over her shoulder, Bo hadn't moved.

With a faltering breath, she sat down in the plastic chair, her knees too shaky to support her. Neither said anything for a few minutes, then Bo waded to the side of the pool and hoisted himself out of the water. Dripping, he sat with his back to her a full minute then he said, still not looking at her, "I'm sorry that came as such a shock to you. I thought it might have been apparent when I raced from one coast to the other and halfway back trying to find you.''

She closed her eyes against the tears that wanted to escape. "We're friends, Bo. That means more to me than you could possibly know. Let's not screw things up by making it more than it can be.''

He turned and looked into her eyes. "Why can't it be more than that?''

She gaped, momentarily speechless. "Because of who I am. What I did for a living.'' She let out an epithet she'd promised Sara to banish from her vocabulary.

He held up his hand. "I get the picture. You have your past. I have mine. I was a drunk. Not a classy, pleasantly inebriated sot. An in-the-gutter, can't-remember-my-name barfly.''

"Don't, Bo.'' Claudie covered her face with her hands. She didn't want to hear his confession. It hurt too much.

She heard him stand and walk to her side. He placed his hand on her bare shoulder and the touch went clear through to her heart. "The point is we're perfect for each other,'' he said, his tone gentle and slightly mocking. "But I'm not telling you anything you don't already know. You're just not ready to admit it, yet.'' He took his hand away. "That's okay. I can wait.''

She wanted to deny his words, tell him to go to hell, but her throat was too tight to speak. When she looked at him, he smiled—his easygoing Bo smile. "Let's hit the hot tub before bed. I don't know about you, but I'm a little tense.''

Claudie followed, but she was pretty sure she was

already in hot water where Bo was concerned, and probably in over her head as well.

"I BROUGHT a couple of bottles of white wine from the minibar, if you want them," Bo said, carrying two small bottles and one water glass in his hand as he approached the spa. He'd returned to the room ostensibly to call Ren, but in truth he needed to give his libido a break. If he was still drinking, he'd have cracked open a whole row of tiny bottles just to numb his mind.

Claudie, who was already sitting amidst the noisy cauldron of bubbles, gave him a suspicious look. "Why? Are you trying to get me drunk?"

He set the bottles on the green plastic lawn an arm's length from the spa and shrugged off his shirt. Despite the towel he'd wrapped around his middle, the bottom of the shirt was damp. He tossed it over a nearby chair. "No," he told her, stepping down into the near-scalding water. "I thought you might like some wine but wouldn't feel comfortable taking something from the minibar in your room since it might obligate you to be nice to me."

He meant his tone to be light and teasing but she winced as though he'd caught her in a lie. "You don't have to drink it. I just thought it might help you sleep."

She glanced at the wine bottles a second then sighed. "Thank you," she said in a small voice. Drawing her feet up to the concrete bench, she moved incrementally—as if each inch sealed a bargain with the devil. Squatting to keep as much of her body underwater as possible, she reached out, her back to Bo.

Bo couldn't help but stare. Water cascaded down her long, delicate neck to stream over her shoulders. A summer tan line was dissected by the skinny blue tie of her bikini. Her shapely hips and creamy skin invited touch. He sank down immersing his head underwater.

He held his breath as long as possible. When he resurfaced, Claudie was looking at him, glass in hand. "Thanks," she said gesturing in a toast. "You're right. I'd never have opened the bar—even knowing you wouldn't have minded. I learned a long time ago there's no such thing as a freebie."

Bo kept his sigh to himself. He watched her sip her wine and slowly melt in place, head back in pleasure.

He stretched his legs, resting them on the bench beside her. A jet of water pummeled the tense muscles between his shoulder blades. "This feels great, doesn't it?"

"What did Ren say?" she asked, her gaze studying him in a way he wasn't used to.

"He didn't answer. Must have turned the phone off." Bo shrugged. "No big deal."

Neither of them spoke for some time, then Claudie asked, "Will you and Matt room together tomorrow night?"

Bo didn't know what to read into her tone. Was it at all wistful or was that just his imagination? "I told him to try to book three rooms if he could. I can sleep almost anywhere when I have to, but since this trip is more like a vacation than work I figure we should get something nice."

She snorted. "In Topeka maybe, but there's not a lot to choose from in Otter Creek. Val told me last night she went back once to bury her stepfather's ashes and couldn't believe how small it seemed. The only motel had closed up. She and her mom stayed in a bed-and-breakfast that some lady from Boston set up.''

As wrapped up as he'd been in the search for her, Bo hadn't really given their destination much thought. ''Well, if it's not available, we'll get a motel in Topeka and commute. You don't have any other relatives around that you could stay with, do you?''

She shook her head. ''I never knew my mother's family. She had two younger sisters but we never met them. My stepfather told us he tried calling Mom's parents in Michigan after she died, but whoever he talked to said my grandparents had died and her sisters had moved. I don't know if that's true, but I believed it at the time.''

''What about your stepdad's family?''

''He claimed to be an orphan. Mom used to say that was why he wasn't much of a father—he'd never had a good role model.'' She polished off her wine with a gulp and set the glass behind her.

She looked at him with a peculiar, speculative glint in her eye and Bo's heart missed a beat. ''Want a foot rub?'' she asked.

His feet immediately started itching. ''I beg your pardon?''

''You heard me,'' she muttered, grabbing his left foot so sharply he almost lost his seating. He jammed his hands to the bench.

''Sure,'' he said, trying to be casual—although there was nothing casual about his reaction to her.

Holding his breath, he closed his eyes and savored

the rich, provocative sensations emanating from her touch. Her thumbs plied the sole of his foot. Her nails zigzagged across his instep in a way that made his groin tighten.

"That's nice," he said, gratified by the control he was able to achieve.

She nodded, seemingly lost in her task. "I knew a girl who went to massage school. She said massaging the foot is like giving a minimassage to the whole body because all the nerves wind up there."

"I believe it," he said gruffly.

She looked up. Whatever she saw in his face must have unnerved her because she let his foot drop with a splash and she reached behind her to crack open the second wine. "Just a sec," she said, taking a big sip. She took a second for good measure then picked up his other foot.

"You have nice feet," she said.

"I do?" Bo asked, snorting skeptically. "I don't think anybody's ever told me that."

"You do. I used to be able to tell a lot about a man by his feet. Men who wore ratty shoes and bad socks usually had smelly feet with corns and blisters and calluses. Men who wore good shoes took better care of themselves overall and they had nicer feet."

"Did that make them better men?"

"How could it? They were with me, weren't they?"

Bo sighed. He hated it when she put herself down. "You know, Claudie, there were two schools of thought among policemen when it came to prostitution. One believed hookers were low-life scum out to rip off innocent men." He snorted and shook his head. He'd clashed more than once with the group he considered narrow-minded hypocrites. "The rest of us saw working girls as the victims, doing what it took to get by. The problem came with drugs. There are a lot of junkies out there who sell their bodies to get a fix and if they get desperate, things can get ugly."

She stopped massaging. "I saw a girl overdose once. It scared the living crap right out of me." She shuddered.

She looked so remorseful he automatically reached out and pulled her to him. That she came without resistance spoke volumes. He moved slightly so her body was aligned beside his, but separated by the forceful wash of the jet. She kept her chin down.

"Relax, Claudie," he told her, trying to lighten the mood. "I promise not to make a move on you." He turned sideways. "Here. Let me rub your shoulders. It's hard to get the jets up high enough without drowning."

She took the deep breath of a person facing a firing squad.

The water added a novel dimension to the sensation of touching her. Those rare times she'd tolerated his touch, Bo had been struck by her skin's soft, chamoislike feel. Moisture turned it as fluid as satin.

"You have pretty skin," he told her, his voice husky.

She stilled his hands by placing her fingers atop his.

"Does that hurt?" he asked.

After a minute of silence, she shifted slightly and looked over her shoulder at him. "Would you kiss me? Just once?"

Bo wanted that more than anything, but he'd never in his life been more terrified of the outcome.

What a stupid thing to ask! Claudie silently berated herself.

Even though Bo didn't answer immediately, Claudie sensed his reluctance. She would have jumped out of the hot tub to hide her mortification, but his hands gripped her shoulders, as if suddenly fearful of something. When she looked into his eyes, she caught a glimpse of anxiety. *Bo's afraid? Of what? Me?*

"There's nothing in the world I want more," Bo said, his voice weaving itself into the very fiber of her being. "But I don't want to blow it."

Claudie suddenly felt brave. She turned, balancing one hip on the concrete step. "It doesn't have to be a big deal," she told him, pleased by how normal her voice sounded. "Just a little—"

He cut her off by leaning forward and placing his lips on hers. At the same time his hand went around her back, gently cupping her rib cage. He didn't pull or grasp. His mouth was warm and sweet, tender in a way she'd never known. That tenderness was more seductive than any words or promises—it gave her permission to explore her own reactions and test new boundaries.

She opened her mouth and touched her tongue to his lips and teeth. He tilted his head to give her freer access but didn't engage his tongue with hers. She leaned closer, reveling in the adventure. She'd never liked kissing. This was not only joyful it was sexy. She felt a moist heat between her legs that had nothing to do with the hot tub.

Startled by the intensity of her reaction, she jerked back. Bo's hand kept her from falling off the bench. He opened his eyes. "Are you okay?" he asked.

She nodded, not trusting her voice. It was a lie, of course. She was in bad shape—longing for something she couldn't have and she wasn't doing Bo any favor by leading him on.

"Bo..." she began, but he interrupted her.

"Can we talk about this tomorrow? I'm beat."

Claudie shrugged. A reprieve. She vowed to spell things out in the morning. Bo couldn't love her and she couldn't love him—even if his kiss was the most tantalizing sensation she'd ever known.

CHAPTER SEVEN

CLAUDIE STALLED for as long as she dared. She'd agreed to meet Bo at eight-thirty in the lobby where a continental breakfast was being served. Last night, after that stupid kiss, she would have agreed to anything that got her out of his sight, but now she was sweating their upcoming face-to-face.

The morning after, she thought grimly, *and nothing even happened.*

But it could have. Claudie had to admit she'd been tempted in a way that wasn't good. In fact, it was scary. Lying awake before dawn she'd asked herself if she ought to run away, try starting over where no one knew of her past. She'd done it before; she could do it again. Maybe she'd find a man—someone who didn't know the grim reality of her past. Maybe with a stranger, she could make a life that included sex.

Unfortunately, she thought, he'd have to be someone she didn't care for as deeply as she did Bo. No way could she bring herself to share her used and damaged body with anyone as wonderful as Bo.

But how could she make Bo understand that? How could she get it through his thick head she was doing him a favor by rejecting his declaration of love?

Love. She paced to the window and gazed at the cars in the parking lot. Love was for people like Ren and Sara, not someone like her. Stifling a sigh, Claudie bent down and picked up her bag. She started out the door. No more pussyfooting around, she decided. We're going to settle this once and for all.

She followed her nose to the motel's dining area where Bo sat—a newspaper in one hand, a forkful of scrambled eggs in the other. Claudie ignored the twelve-foot long buffet and marched directly to his table.

"Bo, we're friends. You think you want to be *more* than friends but trust me, it isn't gonna happen," she said, speaking in a strident tone.

Bo lowered his newspaper but finished lifting the forkful of eggs to his mouth. He chewed and swallowed with irritating slowness then flashed her his most heart-stopping grin. "Good morning, Claudie," he said, reaching for his coffee cup. "How'd you sleep? I slept great. Must have been the hot tub."

She frowned. "I'm serious, Bo. You can't pretend you didn't say what you said."

One brow shot up. "Who's pretending? I meant every word. Want me to say it again in front of witnesses?" He started to rise, as if intending to announce his feelings to the neighboring tables.

Claudie rushed forward and put a hand on his shoulder to push him back down. He seemed startled and gave in without resistance. She quickly fell into the closest chair. Leaning forward, she pleaded, "Bo, quit. Just quit."

He cocked his head. "Quit what?"

"Everything." Her heart was beating too hard to think clearly. If only he wouldn't wear that hurt puppy dog look. It got to her every time.

"Bo," she said, wishing his cowlick didn't tweak the hair at the crown of his head in that Little Rascal way. She could hardly resist reaching out to pat it back down. "You know me, Bo. I don't do the boyfriend-girlfriend thing. I can't. Even if I did, I wouldn't be any good at it. Trust me. The only guy I ever dated dumped me at a truck stop in Oklahoma without even saying goodbye."

She couldn't prevent the twinge of pain that always accompanied the memory of seeing Darren Blains—her first love—hunkered down like a convict at the window of a northbound bus. A sympathetic ticket agent told her he'd confessed that he sold his Chevy Malibu to the garage owner who was supposed to be replacing its fuel pump. "Believe me, honey," the clerk had told her, "you're better off without a weenie like that."

Bo's sudden smile caught her off guard. "What?" she asked, mesmerized by the understanding look in his eyes.

"I just got it. The reason you back away any time I get close is that you're afraid I'll love you and leave you."

Her stomach turned over. "What kind of dumb mumbo jumbo is that?"

He took a sip from his cup. "Not only did I take a psychology course in college, I knew a girl who was a head case. She dated like mad but never stuck with the same guy for more than two months."

"Were you one of 'em?" Claudie asked, despite herself.

Bo shook his head. "Nah. We just frequented the same bars. One night, she spilled out her life story.

Classic abandonment issues. Her father killed her mother when she was a baby and she was raised by her elderly grandparents who died before she was out of high school. Her shrink said the reason she couldn't keep a boyfriend was *subconsciously* she didn't trust anyone to love her without leaving, so she left first to avoid being hurt.''

Claudie frowned. ''What's that got to do with me?''

''You're so sure I'm like every other guy you've ever known, you're afraid to give me a chance.''

She sat up straighter. ''I'm not afraid of anything.''

He looked at her over the rim of his cup. ''Sure you are. We all are. When it comes to love it's the nature of the game, but you gotta play.''

''Who says?''

He looked momentarily abashed then threw back his head and laughed. ''Matt's right. You are a pistol.''

His joy was even harder to swallow than his hurt. ''Let's go.''

''I'm not done with my coffee.''

She took the cup from his fingers and finished off the inch of lukewarm liquid in one gulp. Its insipid sweetness nearly choked her. ''Good Lord, that's disgusting,'' she sputtered.

''I like it sweet.''

She made a face and shuddered. ''Nobody likes it *that* sweet.''

He grinned as though she'd just awarded him a medal. ''Exactly my point. I'm unique. Which means I'm the one person in the world you *should* date.''

He looked so smug she had to laugh—which, for some reason, seemed to be the impetus he needed to move. He picked up the suitcase beside his chair then grabbed hers and started out the door.

Shaking her head, Claudie followed. He had one thing right—there was nobody like Bo.

BO FIGURED they'd make Kansas before dark—well within the time frame he'd given Matt when they talked that morning. Matt planned to spend the day in Topeka putting together a dossier on Garret Anders then he'd get rooms for them in Otter Creek.

Bo glanced at the clock on the dash. He'd offered to buy lunch in Des Moines but Claudie had waved off the suggestion, totally engrossed in exploring her mother's jewelry box. Every once in a while she would exclaim over some bauble with a bittersweet "I remember this!" or an amused "Major ugly!" Twice she'd held up a glittery piece and given Bo a history of its significance in her mother's life.

Bo was actually beginning to feel as though he knew Peggy Anders through her collection of costume jewelry.

"Are you ready for lunch?" Bo asked.

Claudie set aside the box's removable tray and poked her finger into the cluttered jumble below. "Huh?" She glanced up.

Bo made a rubbing motion on his belly. "Feed me."

Her eyes went wide. "Oh!" She looked around. "Sure. Stop anywhere you want."

Her chin dropped and she went back to her mining. "Ooh, what's this?" she said holding up a tattered, dollar-bill sized manila envelope. "Look. It says Claudine on it."

Bo's stomach rumbled but not from hunger. He noticed Claudie's fingers were shaking as they flipped up the metal clasp.

She held open her left hand and poured the contents into her palm. A thin gold necklace spilled between her fingers before a golden heart about the size of a fifty-cent piece landed with a hollow clink.

"It's beautiful," Bo said. "It looks old."

"It's lovely, but I don't remember ever seeing my mother wear it." She held it up to the light. "It's engraved. M.A.R. and J.L.S." She gave him a pensive frown. "M.A.R. Margaret Ann Robertson. My mother's maiden name, but the other isn't Garret."

"Maybe it's your father's," Bo said softly.

Claudie shrugged as if it didn't matter. Using her nail, she had to pry open the stubborn latch. A slight peep escaped from her lips when a gossamer lock of hair fell out.

"Your baby hair, I bet," Bo said. "My mother has a hunk of my hair pasted in my baby book."

"I never had a baby book," Claudie said in a small voice.

Bo would have given anything to pull off the road and hug her, but after her speech at breakfast he didn't think she'd appreciate it. She didn't want their relationship to get any more complicated, and he'd promised her brother he wouldn't do anything to hurt her.

"Is there a picture of you?" Bo asked, craning his neck to peek.

Claudie shook her head and held it up for him to see. A young man's face stared back. Unsmiling. Black and white. Obviously snipped from a yearbook.

"Wow," he said. "Your dad. He's handsome."

Claudie didn't say anything. She hastily pressed the small golden curl back into the heart and snapped it shut. She held it a moment as if trying to decide what to do next.

Bo was about to suggest she put it on when Claudie exclaimed, "Oh, my gosh, look at that!"

Out of the corner of his eye, Bo saw a billboard but he couldn't read the print. "What'd it say?"

"This is where they filmed that movie, *The Bridges of Madison County*. Sara and I read the book." She looked around as if expecting to see one materialize over the highway. When none appeared, she reassembled the jewelry box and dumped it on the back seat. Almost as an afterthought she slipped the golden locket over her head. "Bo, I wouldn't mind seeing the bridge. Sara would really get a kick out of this. I think the sign said something about a park. Maybe it's on the map." She reached under the seat for the atlas.

"You know we're a little pressed for time...." Bo began, but her delighted squeal cut him off.

"It's close, Bo. Really close. Ten or fifteen miles off the highway. I'm sure we could eat there, too. Can we stop?"

Bo couldn't resist the glimmer of anticipation in her eyes. He followed her directions to Winterset, Iowa.

The detour itself wasn't long or even too far out of the way, but once she got there, Claudie didn't seem to want to leave. Bo wasn't sure what was going on in her head.

"Seen enough yet?" he asked two hours later as he followed her toward the red, hundred-foot bridge that somehow seemed vaguely familiar even though he knew he'd never seen it before.

This bridge, the Roseman Covered Bridge, was their second stop. The first had been the eighty-foot Cutler-Donahoe Bridge in Winterset's municipal park where Bo had polished off two hot dogs and one chocolate malt while Claudie explored. Just when he thought they were done sightseeing, Claudie announced her desire to visit the bridge where Francesca, the heroine of the book, left a note for Robert Kincaid, the hero.

They found it without a problem, but the bridge itself didn't seem all that romantic to Bo. However, he decided it was worth the stop to see Claudie strolling toward the weathered red structure, its yawning mouth welcoming her in an oddly benevolent way. In hiking boots, snug jeans and a turquoise sweater, she looked every bit the country girl, fresh and vibrant—and very appealing.

"Will you take my picture?" she asked, glancing over her shoulder.

He held up the small disposable camera.

"This place is wonderful. Just like in the book. Did you read—" she stopped midsentence, realizing her mistake.

He snickered. "Even if I *read,* I wouldn't have picked up that one."

"The Unturned Gentlemen read it," she told him, naming Sara's reading group of which Bo was a fairly recent member.

Bo gaped. "You're kidding. The guys actually read that?"

Her serious nod was negated by a playful grin that gave her away and he came close to scooping her up in his arms and kissing the daylights out of her.

"No, but Ren did," she said, leaning over the white railing to study the autumn grasses below. "He and Sara got in a big argument over it one night. Don't you remember?"

How can I be expected to remember anything when she looks so damn cute?

"Bo?" Frowning, she waited for his answer.

He tried to focus. "Yeah, I kinda remember. Ren called it sappy mush, and Sara thought it was tragically romantic, right?"

She tilted her face upward, squinting into the rafters as if checking for ghosts. "Pretty much."

A thought hit him a moment later. "It seems to me you backed Ren." She turned away, but Bo caught her telltale blush. "In fact, you said they were fools who deserved to die alone because they weren't brave enough to fight for what they had."

She started to step away into the dim interior, but Bo stopped her with a hand to her elbow. "Didn't you?"

She frowned. "Maybe. Something like that."

Bo waited for her to meet his gaze. "Why are we here, Claudie?"

Claudie sighed. "I don't know… Sara liked the book and I thought…" She didn't finish.

He looked at the locket hanging so innocently between her breasts. "Maybe it has to do with your mom," he suggested.

Claudie fingered the locket. "It wasn't the same. My mom and dad were young. The people in the book were adults. And Robert Kincaid didn't commit suicide."

Bo shrugged. "Living the rest of your life without the woman you love sounds like suicide to me."

She looked momentarily stricken then pivoted and stomped away beneath the famed canopy. "That is such bull, Bo Lester," she yelled. Her voice echoed in an eerie way.

"How am I supposed to know?" he muttered, walking in the other direction. "I didn't even read the book." Of course, a part of him knew neither of them was talking about a book, but he wasn't ready to consider what his life might look like if he couldn't convince her to return his love.

She didn't join him at the car for a good twenty minutes. Bo would have been worried if this were anywhere but peaceful, idyllic Iowa. He looked up when he heard her coming. Her walk was slow and lazy but the way she had her arms wrapped around her middle suggested she was cold.

"Too bad we lost our sun," he said, conversationally. "I hope that doesn't mean we're going to get hit with a snowstorm."

She looked skyward. "God, I hope not. I already lost a day to snow. I guess we'd better get going, huh?"

Bo opened the passenger door for her. "The lady at the hot dog stand said there are five more bridges."

She shook her head. "No thanks. This is just about all the romance I can handle," she said with a self-deprecating chuckle.

"I wouldn't beat myself up about it if I were you. I figured out the real reason you wanted to come here."

She looked up, her chin tilted in a questioning look.

"To put off the inevitable."

Her color rose. "You mean..."

Bo squatted beside the door. He placed her camera in her lap then reached out to touch her chin. She trembled but didn't pull back. "Claudie, let's just drop this stuff about us for the time being. It was stupid of me to bring it up. I told you how I feel and I meant it, but this isn't the right time to get into it. You came all this way to do something important, and you don't need anything else to worry about. Okay?"

She nodded. "But—"

Her reply was so Claudie he couldn't stop himself. He leaned in and kissed her. Just a soft, sweet peck. At least, that was what he intended. And he'd have managed to keep it platonic if she hadn't let out a small cry and put her arms around his neck.

He sensed her need even if he didn't understand it. He tried to give her what she wanted without taking anything for himself but the sweetness of her taste, the softness of her lips and the low moan trapped in her throat made him deepen the kiss. His fingers toyed with a lock of hair at the nape of her neck. "Maybe this place is more romantic than I realized," he whispered. "But," he sighed. "We'd better hit the road or we'll never find the B-and-B Matt booked." Matt had called while Claudie was on the bridge. The Apple Blossom Inn was just off Main Street in Otter Creek, Kansas. Three of the inn's five rooms belonged to them for as long as needed.

He could hear Claudie's chortle as he dashed around the car and hopped in the driver's seat. "What's so funny about that?"

"You've obviously never seen Otter Creek. You

couldn't get lost if you tried. Believe me, I know. I tried.''

He started the car and backed around. They weren't far from the highway. With any luck they'd catch up with Matt in time for dinner. As much as he enjoyed spending time with Claudie, he was looking forward to having another person around to run interference.

Maybe that was how he'd been able to sublimate his feelings for her all these months, Bo thought. The two of them had almost never been alone. Between Brady and his parents and the girls at One Wish House, Bo and Claudie had nonstop chaperons. Maybe, deep down, he told himself, that was why he'd insisted Matt join him on this trip. *So much for Mr. Altruism,* he thought dryly.

CLAUDIE HATED to wake Bo, but her purse was on the floor behind his seat and she needed money for the toll. Taking her foot off the accelerator, she leaned to the right, reaching behind the seat. The movement brought her practically face-to-face with him.

He moved—a catlike, lazy stretch that made her smile. She'd once awakened him accidentally on his houseboat when they'd been baby-sitting Brady. She'd inched close enough to study his face—something she'd never dared do if he were awake. Even asleep, she felt as though he might know what she was doing, how she felt about him.

"Hi," Bo said, yawning. "I fell asleep, huh?"

"Twenty miles ago," she told him, moving back to her side of the car. "Can you reach behind the seat and grab my purse? We need change for the toll."

His brow shot up. "We're crossing the river?"

"We will eventually. This is a toll road."

He sat up. "You gotta pay to drive on it?"

She nodded.

"How much?"

"I don't know. Just get some money out, will you?"

The tollbooth was designed for speed. She paid the fee and off they went. "That wasn't so bad."

"Totally un-American," he grouched.

She chuckled. "Like you don't pay taxes."

"I pay my share and half of everybody else's, which is why I don't think I should have to pay to drive on my own roads."

"Yeah, but you're not in California anymore. This is Kansas." Saying the word aloud hit her in a way she wasn't expecting. A rush of memories took her breath away.

Bo sat up suddenly and leaned close. "Claudie. Are you okay? What's the matter, love?"

She hauled in a ragged breath, tightening her grip on the steering wheel. "I'm fine. Just a little reality check."

Bo pointed to the side of the road. "Pull over. I'll drive the rest of the way."

Claudie started to protest. She knew the way, she was the one who should drive, but her arguments never made it to her lips. Stifling a groan, she eased the car to the shoulder. Bo was out and around to her door before she could change her mind.

"This is silly," she said, climbing out.

He pulled her into a quick hug that set her heart racing. "No. It's what I'm here for. Now, you concentrate on telling me where to go—isn't that what you dream of?''

His grin was too infectious to resist. She smiled back then dashed around to the passenger side. She knew at that moment just how glad she was to have him with her. Maybe she'd survive this after all.

AT THE SOUND of a soft knock, Matt looked up from Bo's laptop. ''Your other folks just got here, Mr. Ross. I seen the car lights,'' Mrs. Green said.

The fifty-something owner of the Apple Blossom Inn was a dynamo who'd been running Otter Creek's lone bed-and-breakfast single-handedly since her husband's stroke. Mr. Green, a docile figure with a distant look, followed her around like a puppy.

''Thank you,'' Matt said. ''I'll be right there.''

At his inquiry about a local library, the friendly innkeeper had offered him the use of the desk in the study as well as a phone line for his modem. From that spot Matt had been able to amass most of what Bo wanted to know.

He saved his files and exited the program.

Strolling to the foyer, he braced himself for his first glimpse of the infamous Claudie St. James. Matt didn't consider himself a prude, but he couldn't quite fathom how his cousin could be in love with a woman with her kind of past. He'd formulated a mental image of her—and, frankly, it wasn't too flattering.

Matt opened the door and walked outside. The brisk night air was an eye-opener—as was the woman gracefully stepping from the passenger side of the small station wagon. Petite, young and vulnerable were Matt's first impressions.

"Yo, Cuz, we finally made it," Bo called, hauling himself out of the car. Matt thought the joviality in his voice sounded a bit forced.

"'Bout time. Mrs. Green was going to rent your room to someone else," Matt teased.

"Room?" Claudie questioned, her eyes saucerlike in the light from the porch.

Matt heard a tremor in that single word that spoke multitudes.

Bo hurried around the car and stood at her side without touching her. "Rooms," he said, looking to Matt to confirm.

Claudie's apprehension was further broadcast in the look she gave Matt. He walked down the steps, stopping at the gravel driveway. "Your room is on the top floor, Claudie," he said, pointing over his shoulder.

The turn-of-the-century home featured a third story built into the roofline. Three dormer windows were backlit in a soft amber glow; lace curtains added an old-world charm. "Mrs. Green says it's the nicest room in the house in winter."

Claudie stared upward. "Two old maids owned this house when I lived here. My brothers said they kept the dried-up remains of their folks in that room."

Bo hooted. "Bet that's not a rumor the owners want circulated."

Matt couldn't quite get over the fragility he sensed in her. He was expecting brash and brazen, not sad and reserved. "Your room is called the Golden Delicious suite. Bo's in Jonathan, and I'm in Winesap."

Her face—pretty, but certainly not provocative—screwed up as if certain he were pulling her leg.

"No, seriously," he said. "Mine's Winesap. My

other option was the Pink Lady. The Fuji was already rented.''

She smiled, and for the first time met his gaze. *Oh,* Matt silently acknowledged. He glanced at his cousin who grinned as if reading Matt's mind.

''Claudie, you've just met Matthew Ross, my cousin. Matt, Claudie,'' Bo said. He didn't give them time to shake hands. ''Help me with these bags, Cuz. I need food. Claudie refused to stop for dinner. She said we'd wasted too much time at the bridges.'' He opened the rear passenger door and withdrew a large white box, which he handed to Claudie.

Matt followed him to the rear of the wagon. ''What bridges?''

''Don't ask,'' Bo and Claudie replied simultaneously.

Naturally, Matt couldn't wait to pry the story out of Bo.

Bo passed Matt the smaller of the suitcases and a small, lumpy backpack. ''The place looks great. You did good, Cuz,'' Bo said, clapping a hand to his shoulder.

''The only other choice was a motel by the highway. This looked more like what you wanted,'' Matt said, trying to watch Claudie without appearing to. She stopped at the foot of the steps to take a deep breath. The wraparound porch was outfitted with a big swing and half a dozen wicker chairs. Light from the divided windows spilled out in a warm, inviting way.

When he noticed her shiver, he said, ''We better get you inside to warm up. I picked up some take-out chicken in Topeka, so you won't have to go out again.''

"Awesome," Bo said, following a few steps behind.

Matt slipped the strap of the backpack over his left shoulder to free up his right hand for the banister. The small weakness embarrassed him so he covered it by telling Claudie, "I'll show you to your room."

From the step ahead, she looked back, her expression droll. "It's up, right? I should be able to find it."

Matt blushed.

"Let him do it, Claudie," Bo scolded playfully. "His mother was a stickler for manners. Mine wasn't that picky."

She shrugged, her shoulder barely moving the bulky sweater that looked more college student than reformed hooker. By concentrating on his knee, Matt cleared the four steps successfully.

Once inside, there were more introductions when Mr. and Mrs. Green joined them. Mrs. Green offered them the use of the kitchen and went ahead to set things out.

Since there was no elevator, they were obliged to trudge up the wide, carpeted stairs. Each step was a potential pratfall for Matt. He tried to cover his discomfort by giving Bo a spiel about the town.

"Otter Creek was settled in 1886. There are conflicting stories about how it got its name, but legend has it there once were otters in the nearby waterway, which, by the way, is not named Otter Creek. Did we bet on that?" he asked, pausing to look at his cousin.

"Put it on my bill."

"Zach told me he saw an otter in the creek behind our house one day," Claudie said. "Yancy insisted it was a dog. They got in a big fight over it and my fa—

Garret made them hoe the entire garden as punishment.''

Matt pictured the wealth of information he'd accumulated about the man whose name she could barely bring herself to speak. Sympathy for what she was facing made him say, ''Bo told me you met with your brothers and sister. Weren't they interested in coming back with you?''

She flashed him a sharp look. ''I started this. It's my problem, not theirs.''

He stopped before a door painted a deep burgundy and adorned with a pumpkin-size stenciled apple framing the word, Winesap.

''My room. Bo, yours is over there.'' A similar door in a different shade of red bore the name Jonathan.

''Cool,'' Bo said, using his key to open it. He lugged his suitcase inside and dumped it on the bed then poked his head out. ''I'm going to freshen up a bit. I'll meet you in the kitchen in ten, okay?'' he asked Claudie.

She nodded.

Matt led the way to the small flight of stairs at the end of the hall. Since he still held the key, he went first, trying not to wince.

He opened the pretty yellow door at the top of the stairs and walked inside. He placed the suitcase on a rack beneath the window and set the backpack on the bed. Facing Claudie, he said, ''Mrs. Green says there are extra blankets—'' He was stopped by the look on her face. ''Is something wrong?''

Clutching her odd box as if it were a shield, she said, ''I'm not the right person for your cousin, but he won't listen to me. He thinks he's in—'' She swallowed without finishing the sentence. "If you care about him as much as he cares about you, you'll make him see that."

Matt's stunned response was an ambiguous nod. It was the best he could do because—for the first time—he understood what his cousin saw in this woman. Honesty. Integrity. And something he couldn't quite define.

CHAPTER EIGHT

CLAUDIE WEDGED the phone under her ear and used the hem of her T-shirt to wipe a tear from her eye. *You're being stupid, girl,* she silently scolded herself. A part of her was thrilled that One Wish House could go on without her, but another was hurt that the residents showed so little concern at her extended absence.

"Take as much time as you need, Claudie," Maya said, her voice a hollow echo from using the speakerphone in Claudie's office.

"Yeah, we'll be just fine. Don't you worry about us," Sally Rae seconded. "Not one of us has missed a single meeting since you left."

Claudie had spoken with Sara a few minutes earlier and been told everybody missed her, but obviously her friend had neglected to add the women of One Wish House were blossoming without her.

"It would be nice if you could make it back in time for the fund-raiser, but, don't worry, we can handle things if you don't," Maya said—although Claudie thought she detected a hint of trepidation. "You're going to be so proud of all the money we make."

"If I don't kill Babe Bishop first, you mean," a voice growled.

"Is that you, Rochell?" Claudie asked. "Is Babe

giving you trouble? Do you want me to call her? I could—''

Maya interrupted about the same time a loud ''Oof'' sound came over the line. ''Babe's been great, Claudie. What a trooper! She's really gotten behind the dim sum dinner. In fact, it was her idea to hold an auction, too. She and Rochell have their moments, but that's because they're so much alike.''

Claudie choked on a laugh. She pictured Ren's mother's reaction to being compared to a six-foot ex-hooker.

''Claudie,'' a Hispanic accent cried. ''How is your little sister? Did Meester Bo find you?''

He found me and he's treating me like a child, Claudie told herself. *Or a princess.* ''Bo's here, along with his cousin from New York. I haven't seen my sister yet—her class was on a field trip to Washington, DC. They were supposed to get home last night. Guess what? Bo got his hands on her school yearbook and Sherry's class president.''

Her friends' cheers felt good for some odd reason, even if they were for Sherry—a beautiful, smiling stranger in a one-inch-square photograph. ''So when do you think you'll be coming home?'' Sally Rae asked casually.

Maybe a bit too casually? Claudie thought with a spurt of hope. ''Bo says he thinks we can make contact this afternoon, if I'm ready.'' *Am I?* She knew she couldn't put it off any longer. Her life was waiting for her back in California.

''Is Bo going with you?'' Davina asked.

Claudie smiled. She and Bo had fought long and hard over this issue. In the end Bo had won—or she let him, Claudie wasn't sure which. All she knew for sure was she couldn't face Garret alone. Last night's nightmares proved that.

"Matt and Bo are setting it up so we meet in a public place where they can monitor things," she told them.

The chatting continued a few minutes—each woman doing her best to reassure Claudie that everything was perfectly fine without her. She hung up feeling torn—glad they were showing the independence and backbone to take on new tasks but a little sad, too. One Wish House was her baby. She wasn't ready for it to stand alone.

The sound of crunching gravel drew her to the window. The rental car pulled in behind her station wagon. Bo burst from behind the driver's seat with his usual exuberance; Matt slowly extricated himself from the passenger side.

Matt had intimidated Claudie the first night they met. So tall and stern—a cop in casual clothing. She could sense his disapproval. She didn't blame him and had hoped to enlist his help in deflecting Bo's misguided love. Strangely, Matt had loosened up in the two days they'd been in Otter Creek and even seemed to like her. She didn't get a sense he was making any headway with his cousin, either.

Matt looked up. He started to wave but grabbed the door when his knee buckled. Claudie saw what Bo chose to deny. Bo, who loved his cousin like a brother, seemed blind to Matt's pain, his bad knee, the back twinges that came after sitting in one position too long and his deep sadness.

Her gaze went to Bo. He also looked up, his smile

bright as the autumn sunshine. Putting both hands over his heart he mimed a swoon then blew her a kiss. The playful gesture made her stagger backward, her heart fluttering. Damn, that man could be infuriating, she thought. She didn't know how to make it any clearer that she wasn't interested in a long-term relationship with him. Even though he'd promised to back off until she had this ordeal behind her, he still showered her with attention.

Even Mrs. Green commented on his obvious devotion. "That boyfriend of yours sure does love you," the woman had told Claudie last night when she delivered clean towels. "Reminds me of the way Mr. Green used to be, back before his affliction."

A knock on the door shook her out of her reverie. "Come in, Bo, it's open."

"It's not Bo. He stopped to take a leak," Matt said, entering the room. He left the door open. Claudie didn't know if that was gentlemanly protocol or he was protecting his reputation. "Did you get hold of Sara Bishop?"

That had been her excuse for not accompanying the two sleuths on their reconnaissance mission. "Yes. I even talked to Brady. He loved the shirts I sent…and the dinosaur. He calls it a 'T-weck.'" She couldn't help smiling.

"Bo talks about him a lot. I think he'd like a couple of kids himself."

Claudie's stomach turned over. "Then he'd better find himself a nice woman and get married." She pulled together as much bluster as she could muster. "That's how it's done in the Midwest. You meet a woman—someone *appropriate*. You date, then you marry and have kids.''

His lips thinned. ''Then she meets someone better and you start over from scratch.''

His bitterness was unmistakable. She sighed. ''I don't think either one of us should apply for jobs at Hallmark,'' she said dryly.

He looked at her and smiled. ''I hate to tell you this, Claudie, but I think it's too late.''

The camaraderie in his friendly smile threw her. ''Too late for what?''

''Too late to *save* Bo.'' He said the word with wry inference. ''He's a goner. Head over heels in love with you.''

''Goddamn it,'' Bo said, stomping into the room. ''I told you not to tell her that. She has enough on her mind without worrying about my feelings. We've already had this conversation, haven't we, Claudie?''

The first time they had this conversation she'd been tempted to bolt. This time she laughed. ''Yes, but you're incorrigible. I should have known you'd blab to the whole world.''

Smiling, he strolled toward her. ''Not the whole world. Just Matt. And Sara and Ren.''

She jumped back before he could touch her. ''You told Sara and Ren?'' *That would explain Sara's overly cheerful attitude on the phone.*

He grimaced. ''Yes. But they already knew.''

She noticed Matt was stifling a grin. ''How'd they know?''

Bo shrugged. ''I'm transparent?''

She barked out a laugh. ''You always told me you

were invisible. It's not the same.'' She looked to Matt for confirmation. ''Is it?''

Matt chuckled. ''In Bo's case it might be.'' He walked to the chair by the desk and sat down, then said soberly, ''If you two could drop the debate for a few minutes, I think we need to discuss this afternoon's strategy.''

Claudie looked at Bo, and it took every ounce of willpower she possessed not to run to his arms and disappear.

''DO YOU THINK she'll be okay?'' Bo asked his cousin while they waited for Claudie to join them in the parlor.

''She'll be fine. She's strong, Bo. God, when I think of all she's been through…'' He shook his head. ''She's doing fantastic.''

Matt's approval meant a lot to Bo and his endorsement of Claudie was gratifying, even if it surprised Bo a little. ''You sure turned around fast,'' he observed.

Matt looked down to check his watch. Bo thought he detected a blush—something you didn't see too often on Matt. ''Yeah, well, maybe my experiences with Sonya left me prejudiced against women. Claudie's a decent person. And you have to respect her motives for coming back here. I give her credit for that—even if I'm not sure it's the right thing.''

Bo frowned. ''I don't think she appreciated that bit about 'letting nature take its course.''' Word on the street had it that Garret Anders was dying of prostate cancer. Claudie wasn't moved. ''Good,'' she'd said when informed of the rumor. "I hope that means he has erectile dysfunction, too."

Matt shrugged. "It was her call. I only wanted to give her an out if she was having second thoughts. You know what it's like once you open a can of worms." Matt started toward the kitchen where Mrs. Green kept a pot of coffee going at all times. "I'll be back in a minute."

Once he was gone, Bo walked to the window. Pulling aside the lace curtain, he stared unseeing at the yard and the empty street. He wasn't going to argue with Claudie about meeting Anders, but he wondered if he'd done the right thing by not giving her all the details he and Matt had learned about the man. According to the Topeka radio station that sponsored Anders's weekly "Man in God" radio program, Anders was one of their most popular evangelists. "He's a saint, but human," the programming coordinator had told Bo.

When Bo had tried summarizing the results of their investigation last night, Claudie had railed at him. "That's total bullshit, Bo. I knew him for seventeen years and he was a jerk. A pissant, little jerk. He kept my mother barefoot and pregnant. He was a rotten father—cruel and mean and so *un*-Christian it's pathetic."

They'd gone for a walk after dinner because she'd told him she was having a hard time sleeping and he thought the fresh air would be good for her. The air was a little chillier than he'd counted on. "I'm not saying he was a good father," he'd countered, feeling guilty about not divulging the extent of the man's philanthropy. "Zach said the same thing, but—"

"Did Zach tell you about the time Garret hit him with a shovel?" she'd asked her voice as bitter as the breeze.

"No."

Her small laugh sent a shiver up his spine. "One day—we were living in Illinois, I think—we had a snowstorm. It was Zach's job to shovel the sidewalk before school, but we overslept and would have missed the bus if he'd taken time to do it, so Mom said he could do it after school."

Bo had used the slight tremor in her voice as an excuse to hold her hand. Her fingers were like icicles.

"When we got home, Garret was already there. I told Zach I'd help him shovel it real fast. Garret waited until the school bus was out of sight then he came outside and started yelling."

Bo had felt a tremor pass through her body. Since they'd almost reached the inn, he pulled her up the steps and led her to the porch swing where he could wrap an arm around her shoulders. To his surprise, she'd cuddled against him for one brief minute then stiffened, putting an inch between them before going on with her story.

"I was closest to the door when he came outside, but for once he wasn't interested in me. He grabbed the shovel out of my hand as he walked by and marched to where Zach was shoveling. Zach didn't hear him coming. Garret hit him squarely between the shoulder blades with the flat part of the shovel." She clapped one hand to the other in a crack that echoed in the stillness.

"Didn't your mother try to stop him?" Bo had asked, his stomach twisting at the image.

"No. But I did."

Her words chilled him to the bone. "What happened?"

"He pushed me down and held my face in the snow. I couldn't breathe. I thought I was going to die, but Mom saw what was happening and came outside. He let me go the minute she said his name—it was like throwing a switch. Jekyll and Hyde."

Bo had pulled her close and gave the swing a push. The gentle rocking motion seemed to help her relax. "That's why I'm going to be with you tomorrow," he'd told her. "Your mother isn't here to flip switches."

He'd waited for her to argue, but she didn't. Instead, she snuggled a fraction closer and pointed to the night sky.

"Do you see those stars?" she'd asked. "The three in a row?"

He'd had to lean down to see past the roof. The proximity brought him her scent—lemon shampoo and baby powder. "Do you mean Orion's belt?"

"Mom called them the Three Sisters. She said whenever she looked at them she thought of her three girls—Valery, Sherry and me."

"Which one is you?" he asked, brushing his lips over her silky hair.

"The big one, of course," she'd answered with a giggle. "Big and bossy."

He hadn't been able to stop himself from leaning down and kissing her. Her lips were cold but not unwelcoming.

To draw her closer, he'd slipped his hand inside her open jacket and splayed his fingers against her spine.

She'd stiffened momentarily then sighed against his lips, a deep throaty hum that made him a little crazy.

He'd trailed kisses along her jaw to her neck, thrilling when she tilted her head back to give him access to the pulse point throbbing at the neckline of her sweater. A kiss, a nibble, a car rumbling down the street.

Claudie had bolted like a shoplifter caught in the act, not stopping until she reached the porch railing. Her angry scowl looked accusatory.

"Claudie," he'd said as equitably as possible, "it was only a kiss."

Stubbornly, she'd shaken her head—the angry, suspicious woman he'd first met ten months ago in Sacramento. "I told you this wouldn't work. Sex ruins things."

Bo's heart had crimped from the pain he heard in her voice. He'd have given anything to take her upstairs and prove her wrong, but he knew she needed time to learn to trust—not only him, but also her feelings.

She'd braced her shoulders for an argument, but he rose and walked to her before she could speak again. After delivering a quick, friendly peck on the lips, he'd told her, "I love Claudie. And if you need time to learn to love her, too, then I'll wait."

As he opened the door of the inn, he'd heard her mutter something about "hell freezing over." Grinning, he'd called over his shoulder, "Lucky me. I packed my ice skates."

"Here she comes," Matt said, bringing Bo back to the present. He hadn't even heard his cousin return. *I must be in love. I'm totally out of it.*

Bo turned and looked toward the open staircase. She'd dressed with care—navy woolen slacks and a burgundy sweater set. Her short blond locks were feathered off her face courtesy of a blow dryer. Her only jewelry was the gold locket.

"You look perfect," Matt said, beating Bo to the punch.

Bo gave him a dirty look and grabbed her jacket from the hall tree. "You'll dazzle him. Are you feeling dazzling?"

She gave him a plucky smile. "Yeah—like a forty-watt bulb."

He held her coat for her and added a quick hug before she could escape. "Don't worry," he whispered. "I won't let him hurt you again."

CLAUDIE REPEATED Bo's promise like a prayer the whole way to Harrah's, the nearby Potowatami casino where Matt had set up the meeting, without telling Garret the true agenda. He'd used the ploy that he was a freelance writer working on a piece about God and gambling.

Claudie had balked at the idea of meeting in such a busy locale, but Bo had convinced her the location worked to her benefit. "Midweek. Midafternoon. It won't be that busy. Besides, we want people around. He's got a reputation to protect. He can't afford to lose his temper in such a public place."

She'd been tempted to argue that the more people present meant more witnesses if she went bonkers and wound up killing her stepfather with her bare hands, but she knew Bo would protect her from her own demons as well as Garret's.

Matt drove. Claudie chose to sit in the back seat. She tried to focus on the rolling landscape, picturing it in spring—her mother's favorite season. The trees would have made lush green ribbons that followed the contours of the creeks and hollows. Farmers would have turned the rich black earth and started planting corn or soybeans.

"Are you doing okay?" Bo asked solicitously. He'd been so kind, so patient. She'd never known a man like him before.

"I'm fine."

He cleared his throat and looked at Matt. "You know, Claudie, Matt has a lot more information about Anders than what we told you. It was my call. Your issues haven't changed even if Anders has. But I could brief you more thoroughly if you'd rather know."

What could Bo tell her? That Garret was a different person than he was ten years ago? So was she, but that didn't alter what he'd done to her.

"No thanks. This is about the past, not the present."

Matt turned toward a large, brightly hued building that hadn't been there when Claudie lived in the area. He pulled under the massive porte cochere so she and Bo could get out. He would park and join them once Garret arrived. A blue-uniformed giant with a broad smile opened the door for her. Bo's hand at the small of her back kept Claudie from barreling in the other direction.

Noise and bright lights bombarded her overly acute senses; the acrid smell of cigarette smoke provoked a wave of nausea. "I need to use the rest room."

As if anticipating her panic, Bo led her to the appropriate door. "I'll wait right here."

Knowing Bo was waiting helped calm her nerves. She washed her hands and dried them, then touched up her lipstick. She looked in the mirror and wondered what Garret would see when he looked at her.

The plan was for Matt to meet Garret at the door and lead him to an alcove where hopefully only one or two gamblers would be. I can do this, she told herself and walked out to join Bo.

"He's here. Matt just gave me the sign. Do you want Matt to bring him over to you or would you prefer to join him and Matt in a few minutes?"

"Let Matt bring him."

Her heart was pounding so loud she barely heard the chatter of gamblers, the whir and spin of machines, the music piped over a loudspeaker.

"We're in luck. Nobody's close by. Matt and I will make sure the place stays that way," he said, his tone forbidding.

She squeezed his hand and smiled at him. "Thanks. I don't think I could have gone through with this without you."

His smile made a funny knot form in her throat. He leaned close enough to whisper. "I know. It's because you love me, but don't tell anybody. It's a secret."

His impish grin made tears prick behind her eyes. She pushed him away. "Such ego," she tried to mutter, but even to her ears it came out like a caress.

His smile widened, but only for a second, then his game face fell into place. "Show time," he said under his breath.

Claudie spotted Matt, but she didn't recognize the

man at his side. Her first thought was disappointment—Garret had sent someone else in his place, and there was a woman with him, too. Claudie glanced at Matt and saw him make a gesture with his hands that seemed to say, "Your call."

Claudie started to turn away when a voice from her past said, "Claudine?"

She spun around, bracing for an attack. Garret. Her arch nemesis. The man opposite her looked old. Gaunt and gray, his legs seemed to give out. He might have crumpled to the ground if not for the support of his companion. "What's this?" the woman asked, helping Garret to a nearby stool. "Is it who I think it is? Can it be Claudie? Praise the Lord, it is."

Her odd way of answering her own questions made Claudie forget this wasn't the way she'd planned the scene.

The woman bussed the man's almost bald pate and exclaimed, "Garret, honey, our prayers have been answered."

Claudie looked at Bo, and they both said, "Prayers?"

"Yes," Garret said his voice sounding stronger than his body suggested. "As Dottie knows, ever since I was diagnosed with cancer five years ago, I've prayed every day that I would have a chance to see you once more before I die."

An unexpected jolt from his simple, matter-of-fact statement made Claudie step backward. "Don't worry, sweetie," the woman said, reaching out imploringly. "He's not contagious. Started in the prostate but by the time they found it, it'd spread to the bone. Ain't no stoppin' it now."

"Who are you?" Claudie asked, unable to help herself.

"His wife," she said, with a beatific smile. "My name's Dottie. We've been together nine years."

A year after I left. A year after he ruined my life.
"Did you know you married a rapist?" Claudie asked, the spite in her tone nearly choking her.

"It's the first thing he told me," Dottie said. Her large gray eyes seemed full of sympathy. "You poor girl. I used to work in a hospital and I saw rape victims come in all the time. My heart would just break in two."

"Then how could you bring yourself to marry somebody like him?" She pointed to where Garret sat—his skeletal frame outlined by the neon aura of a nickel slot machine.

"I forgave him," Dottie said simply. "That's what you do when someone makes a mistake—even the most awful mistake in the world. If that person truly regrets it and he gives his life to God, what else can you do?"

Claudie could think of a dozen things—all hideous and painful. "Well, that's easy for you to say. You weren't the one raped."

"No. Not by Garret. But my first husband raped me—right before he took a gun and killed our three-year-old baby girl then turned it on himself. He told me that was my punishment for not being a better wife."

Dottie dropped her chin; tears fell on the carpet like fat raindrops. Garret reached out and took her hand in a gesture of comfort. He slowly rose and advanced two steps closer to Claudie. She felt Bo edge beside her. "Claudie, girl, I accept your hate. I deserve it and I'm not looking for your forgiveness—not for myself, anyway. The Lord knows what I did and why. My anger at losing the woman I loved more than life and knowing I was to blame for her death consumed me like a fire. Even before your mother died, I was a poor excuse for a father, but from the day of Peggy's funeral, I went crazy and drank myself stupid. Instead of easing my pain, it stoked it until I wanted to hurt somebody else as much as I hurt."

Claudie backed up, trying to block the memories that stalked her like a panther on the prowl. "I was in the kitchen putting away some food the neighbors had brought. More charity." Her voice sounded miles away.

"Yep. Everybody in town knew I'd lost my job and the bank was getting ready to foreclose. I was mad about that, too. Poor pitiful me. Alone with five kids to raise." He paused, shaking his head slowly from side to side. "I came home that night and there you were. Mad as a hornet about missing some dance."

He ran a hand over his face, as if washing away a film. "That's when I did the most despicable thing anyone can do to another human being short of murder. And in truth, I killed something inside you that night. I saw the light go out in your eyes before you ran away to your teacher's house. I wasn't just a rapist, Claudie, I was a murderer. First your mom, then the part of her that was in you—the sweet, loving part."

He broke down, weeping like a child. Dottie comforted him and helped him back to the stool. For a reason that made no sense to her, Claudie almost wished she could tell him it was okay. But it wasn't okay. He'd ruined her life, and he deserved the hell, the cancer and pain he had to endure. She only wished it would last longer.

"I didn't come to hear your apologies or excuses or whatever this is. Nothing you say can make up for what you did and what I became because of you. I'm here because I want to make sure you don't ruin another girl's life the way you did mine."

Garret looked at Dottie. Their mutual confusion angered her. "Sherry," she hissed. "My sister is almost seventeen. That's how old I was when you—"

Dottie gasped as if she'd heard pure blasphemy. "You can't possibly think Garret would hurt Sherry. Oh, goodness, child, no. You're so wrong. No."

Claudie scowled at her. "Why should I believe you? He—"

Garret seemed to rally strength from some deep source. He stepped forward, more the man she remembered and feared. "What I did to you was the last scene in a black chapter of my life, Claudie. At first, I tried to pretend to myself it never happened, but God doesn't work that way. When you told that teacher about what I did, and all hell broke loose, I lied and said you made it up. I was prepared to fight it in court. I cleaned up my act and put on a nice show for the judge.

"But when you disappeared, the truth of what I had done came back to haunt me. Less than a month after you left I ran straight into a brick wall. Literally."

Claudie was struck mute by the honesty she heard in his voice, and something else she couldn't define. Remorse? Salvation?

"I crashed the car, and to be honest I don't know if it was on purpose or an accident. Paramedics had to use the Jaws of Life to get me out, but I was awake long enough to tell them not to bother. I didn't want to go on living. And I died on the way to the hospital."

Claudie looked at Bo, who nodded. He knew about this.

Dottie took over the narrative. "I was on duty when they brought him in. That's how we met." She lowered her chin and said, seriously, "Now, I'm going to tell you something you probably won't believe, but it's God's honest truth. I saw an angel come to Garret and breathe him back to life."

"Breathe him...?" Claudie repeated.

"A white figure—it was glowing and kinda fuzzylike so I knew it wasn't another nurse. It leaned down and put its face close to Garret's and the next second he was breathing. I swear on all that's holy."

Garret nodded his confirmation. "I was dead, then I was alive. All I know for sure is that when I was dead I saw my life for what it was—a barren desert of my own making. My soul was black and shriveled like a dead bug. I'd wasted my chance at love. My greed killed my darling Peggy. It killed the child in you. And it killed me."

"You look fairly alive to me," Claudie said, trying her best to stay unmoved by his confession.

"God gave me a second chance. A chance to change. And I did."

Dottie took a step closer and clasped Claudie's hand with an exuberant cry that made Claudie shrink back. "It's true, Claudie. I witnessed it with my own eyes.

He was hurt real bad, and the doctors said he'd never walk, but he did. The lawyers told him not to bother fighting for custody of his kids, but he did and he got Sherry. Valery didn't want anything to do with him, so he let her go to the family she wanted. The boys could have come home but chose to go out in the world instead. You were the only one we never could find.''

Claudie yanked her hand free. ''Well, I'm here now, but I don't know how much of this I believe. And even if it's true, I don't really care that you're reformed and holy and all that crap. I still wasted ten years of my life selling my body for nickels and dimes because you made me believe that's all I was worth.''

Garret swayed. Bo rushed forward. ''Do you need a drink of water?'' he asked.

Garret nodded. Bo motioned to Matt who slipped away into the casino. Hunched like a wizened gnome, Garret said, ''I feared that might happen, Claudie. I saw a therapist regularly for two years. He helped me come to grips with my anger—a product, we learned, of my foster father's somewhat psychopathic benevolence.'' His rueful chuckle sent a chill down her spine. ''My therapist told me that prostitution was one trap you might fall into given the abuse—verbal, emotional and physical—I'd inflicted on you over the years.''

His frank assessment of his behavior seemed too staged to be true. Until she looked into his eyes. The man behind those eyes was in pain. Not the physical pain of cancer but emotional pain caused by guilt and regret.

''He told me rape is an act of violence. I took my

self-loathing out on you, Claudine—the child I'd envied for sixteen years.''

"Envied?''

"Dear girl, you alone had the one thing I desired more than anything—my sweet Peggy's love. Oh, I know she cared for me, and she proved it by giving me six wonderful children. But I wanted her *love*. The love she felt for the boy who was your father. Unfortunately, it took her death—and mine—to understand she'd loved me the best she could.''

Claudie's breath caught in her throat; an ache started behind her eyes.

"I'd sell my soul to take it back—to change what happened, Claudie, but that's not the way God works,'' he said, his sad eyes boring into her. "I was given a second chance, and I used it to be a good father to Sherry. And I think I can honestly say I accomplished that.''

Dottie nodded with verve. "That he did. You can ask her yourself if you don't believe us.''

Claudie's mouth was too dry to speak. Fortunately, Matt arrived with a tray of glasses. She guzzled one. Garret took two small sips and handed it back. "Thank you, Matthew,'' he said politely.

Then he looked at Bo and said, "We haven't been introduced. You know who I am, but I don't know you.''

Bo put out his hand. "Bo Lester.''

Claudie looked at Garret and his wife. "Bo and Matt are friends. They're also private investigators. I ran across your Web page on the Internet, and they helped me—'' The smile the couple exchanged made her ask, "What?''

Dottie answered. "The Web page was my idea. I told Garret you might get curious some day and come looking. I promised him I'd keep the page up and running even after he's gone." Her bottom lip trembled and Garret squeezed her hand. "We like to think his message is important to other lost souls, but we were really looking for you."

Claudie didn't like the way that made her feel. She resisted the softening she felt toward these people. "If I'd have wanted to find you sooner, I would have come looking."

Dottie blinked in surprise. "But we only moved back here last year. Before that we took our ministry on the road."

"How did Sherry go to school?" Bo asked, taking the words right out of Claudie's mouth.

"Home schooling," Garret said. "Dottie's a wonderful teacher. Sherry is at the top of her class. She's class president, you know," he said with a father's pride.

Suddenly Claudie was at a loss for words. She didn't know where to go with her anger, her pain. She couldn't use it to protect a girl who didn't need protecting.

Bo interceded. "I'm sure Claudie would like to talk to her sister at some point, but right now I think we should go."

Claudie didn't resist when he took her elbow.

"Wait," Garret said. "Just one more thing. Claudie, child, I was the worst father imaginable, and I don't expect you to forgive me for what I did to you. But I pray—like I've prayed every day—you'll find a way to forgive yourself."

"For what?" she cried.

"For being human. For loving me as a child loves a father. For whatever it is that you think you're to blame for. Let it go, dear girl. It wasn't you. It was never you. You were the most wonderful daughter a man could ever hope for. You helped your mother without complaining. You took all the guff I had to give with spunk. You protected your brothers and practically raised Sherry those early years. None of what happened was your fault."

Claudie would have sagged if not for Bo's support. She fought the tears that blinded her. In her mind she could see that night. Her sadness, yet there was anger, too. She was tired of being his substitute wife. She wanted to go to the prom and he'd told her they couldn't afford a dress, yet somehow there was money for booze. "If only I'd kept my mouth shut," she said, not realizing the words were spoken aloud until Garret answered.

"If not that night, then some other. My rage was so great, it was just a matter of time."

"But you called me a slut because I wanted to go to the prom with Darren. You said you knew we'd made love and I was a whore and you—"

He shook his head. "I don't remember what I said, but I'm sure it was bad because I had to make you look bad so I could justify what I was doing to you. You were never that kind of girl, Claudie, and I knew it. If you and Darren experimented sexually, it was because you were looking for someone to love you. I'm just sorry you chose someone weak like Darren. He told the police about leaving you alone in Oklahoma."

Dottie nodded sagely. "He's been divorced twice and can't keep a job. He's a mama's boy—always has been. You were his chance to escape but he didn't have the gumption to go through with it."

"You talked to Darren?" she asked.

Garret nodded. "So did the police. They put out a missing persons report and put up your picture all over the western states. We really wanted to find you." Claudie looked at Bo. Was this the part he didn't tell her about? Would it have made a difference if she'd known?

Garret went on. "Like I said, at first I denied what I did, but after my accident I called the police and told them the truth. A judge gave me probation and ordered counseling as part of my sentence. Dottie was the one who took care of Sherry until I regained custody." He looked at his wife.

Short and round, dressed in her good, Sunday dress and sensible heels. Her scrubbed cheeks were ruddy in color, her cap of permed curls threaded with silver. "My second husband, Bill, passed away shortly after Sherry came to us," she said. "A heart attack. He and I had been foster parents for ten years on account of I couldn't have children. The authorities wanted to move her to another home, but I told them she was the angel sent to keep me from despair. And that she was."

She looked at Claudie. "You did a fine job raising that little girl."

Claudie blinked fiercely, the pain behind her eyes unbearable. Her throat ached with unshed tears. Bo pulled her to his chest and comforted her until the dry silent sobs passed.

"I'd like to see her before I go," Claudie said, her voice low and husky.

"How 'bout you all come for supper tonight?" Dottie suggested.

Claudie shook her head. "No. We're leaving tonight."

Garret spoke. "Sherry gets out of class at three-fifteen. I'll call the school and give them a message to tell her you'll be waiting by the track. Would that be better?"

Claudie nodded. She faced the man who had been her father. There was more to say, but she didn't have the words. "Goodbye."

He put out his hand but stopped short of touching her. "Thank you for coming, Claudie. Now I can meet my maker in peace."

Claudie turned away. Bo's hand never left her back; he paused when she did. She looked over her shoulder. "I can give you Zach's and Yancy's addresses if you want them. I guess you know where Val lives."

Garret gave his wife a look that seemed so full of joy it made Claudie flinch.

Sniffling, Dottie answered. "We'd like that very much. You can give them to Sherry when you see her."

Claudie started to leave, but Dottie gave a small cry and—almost as if she couldn't stop herself—barreled across the short distance to envelop Claudie in a hug. Repelled, yet somehow also comforted by the motherly gesture, Claudie gave Bo a helpless look. He put a hand on Dottie's shoulder and she backed away apologetically. "I'm sorry. I just couldn't contain myself. You truly are the answer to our prayers and you're so much more wonderful than I ever dreamed. I see your mother's spirit in you. From what Garret's told me, Peggy was a beautiful woman who loved too dearly."

Claudie looked from Dottie to Garret. "I have to go," she said flatly. Her anger was gone, but so was her focus. Without her hatred what did she have? A wasted life. An empty shell.

Bo took her hand and led her through the busy casino. Pausing to let a man in a wheelchair pass, Claudie's gaze was drawn to a brilliant Jackpot sign. A revolving board promised her a chance to be a Big Winner.

"A *winner*," she said, bitterness dripping like acid from her tongue. "What a joke! It turns out I raced halfway across the country to save poor little Sherry from squat. I make Don Quixote look sane." Her attempted laugh caught in her chest, doubling her over.

Bo pulled her to him, stifling her sobs. "You're the bravest person I've ever met, Claudine St. James," he whispered fiercely. "If that doesn't make you a winner, I don't know what does."

She swallowed her anguish and pulled back, wiping her cheeks with the shirttail he offered. Beneath the soft plaid shirt she glimpsed a hideous green-and-brown camouflage T-shirt. *Oh, Bo, you are so...*

The understanding look he gave her made her breath catch. He touched her eyebrow and smiled supportively. "Come on, sweetness, it ain't over, yet. Let's get your game face back on—we have one more stop to make."

CHAPTER NINE

CLAUDIE RECOGNIZED her sister the instant the girl stepped through the door of the school. Tall, blond, her carriage proud and graceful, she looked like a young Grace Kelly. Her outfit looked like something a businesswoman would wear—a sober black wool skirt and white turtleneck sweater with knee-high boots. Her calf-length coat of deep teal was topped with a hand-knit scarf of scarlet and gold. She carried a black leather backpack.

She never hesitated on her walk across the paved trail—a path Claudie remembered as mud and gravel. While she'd only attended this school for a year and a half—and had failed to graduate with her class, Claudie still thought of it as her alma mater.

Sherry didn't hail her or display any outward excitement. Her smile seemed curious, but not apprehensive. Claudie surmised Garret had informed Sherry of her sister's arrival.

Claudie rose from the metal bleachers and stepped down to greet her sister face-to-face. "Hi," she said, grimacing when her voice came out garbled. "Do you know who I am?"

Sherry's blue eyes seemed to sparkle with some underlying emotion that Claudie couldn't read. "You're Claudine. My sister."

"Half sister," Claudie corrected. "We had the same mother, different fathers."

Sherry's smile took Claudie's breath away. It was their mother's smile. "You're younger than I pictured. They said you left home when you were my age, and I guess I thought you'd be older by now." She ducked her chin slightly. "You're prettier, too."

Claudie's heart skipped a beat. "Well, that makes us even. You're older than I pictured. My last memory of you was wiping your runny nose. You always had a cold."

Laughing, Sherry exaggerated a sniff. "Allergies. Mom took me to a dozen doctors before they finally pinpointed the problem. Problems. Wheat, pollen, cat dander—you name it. I've outgrown some, but I still sneeze like crazy when the lilacs are blooming."

"Almond trees do me in," Claudie confessed. She took a breath and pointed to the bleachers. "Could we sit and talk a few minutes?"

Sherry frowned. "Daddy said you weren't staying. I don't think it's fair that you just got here and have to leave right away."

For the first time, she sounded her age. "I have to get home to my job." She went on before Sherry could ask her what she did. "Do you have plans for after graduation?"

She took a seat on the cold metal bench—thankful for Bo's jacket and the too big gloves he'd ordered her to wear. Sherry sat down folding her woolen coat around her in a ladylike manner that Claudie found endearing. "I've applied to three schools—two Christian colleges and Kansas State. Partly, it will depend on Daddy's health. I hate to be too far away in case he gets worse. But he's adamant that I go off and live my life, not hang around watching him die.''

Her matter-of-fact statement of Garret's mortality struck Claudie as almost too healthy to be real. "Do his doctors give him long?" she asked.

Sherry rolled her eyes. "They told him he'd be dead two years ago. He says the Lord doesn't necessarily consult with doctors when He makes His plans.''

Claudie was curious how much her sister knew of her reasons for running away. Oddly, she didn't want to damage Sherry's feelings for her father, so she asked, "Do you know why I left home?"

Sherry looked down. "Yes. It's hard to have too much privacy when you're living in a travel trailer.''

This was Claudie's cue to unload her anger and bitterness, but for some reason she asked, instead, "Where have you traveled?"

"Just about everywhere." Sherry made an encompassing motion with her hands. She had the poise and delivery of a professional speaker. *Did she get that from Garret?* "We started in northern Maine and worked our way down the eastern seaboard then across the south and Texas. We spent a year working with the Navajo—that was amazing—then we drove from the bottom of California to the top. It took us six months.''

"Did you go through Sacramento?" Claudie asked.

Sherry nodded with enthusiasm. "For sure. I homeschooled, and Mom was a stickler for geography and history, so we'd always spend two or three days in every state's capital city.''

Was it possible they were in Sac when I was work-

ing the streets? Pushing the disturbing thought aside, she said, "I notice you call Dottie, Mom. I'm not surprised since she's the only mother you've ever known, but I wonder if you'd like to know anything about your real mother."

Sherry tilted her head thoughtfully. Her shoulder-length blond hair curled gracefully against her coat. "I'll probably think of a dozen things once you leave, but...not really. I mean, Daddy's told me a lot about her. How they met, how he talked her into marrying him." Her smile seemed soft and romantic. "Daddy said he took her a different kind of flower every time he passed through her town until he hit on the right one—a yellow rose."

Claudie couldn't remember ever seeing yellow roses in any of their homes.

"We have a big map on the wall at home showing all the places we traveled. The towns where you and the other kids lived when you were growing up are marked in red," Sherry said. Her soft chuckle was full of fondness. "Daddy had the wanderlust even then, didn't he? Only then he was selling appliances and baby furniture and pharmaceuticals. Now, he's selling God." She made it sound like a noble thing.

Claudie didn't want to talk about Garret. She was still having a hard time understanding what happened in that casino. *Who* was she suppose to forgive? *Why?*

As if reading her thoughts, Sherry said, "Daddy told me on the phone the only reason you came back was to find me." Her blue eyes filled with tears. "Claudie, I think that is the sweetest, most wonderful thing I've ever heard. My heart nearly broke in two when he told me."

The thing to do was hug, but Claudie held back for some reason. "I wanted to make sure you were okay. I didn't want you to have to go through any of what I've done. You deserved a chance at a normal life and…"

Wiping her tears with the tips of her gloves, Sherry sniffed and said, smiling, "That's so brave. I'm so glad you're my sister."

Claudie closed her eyes against tears of her own. *Oh, hell.* She looped one arm across the young girl's shoulders. With a small cry, Sherry turned and embraced Claudie with both arms, squeezing ingenuously. "Thank you for coming back, Claudie. You don't know how much it means to me…and my dad."

Claudie stiffened. She couldn't help herself.

Sherry pulled back. She gave Claudie a look too empathic for her age. "I'm sure it's hard not to hate him after what he did."

How does someone so young see so much? Her silent question must have shown because Sherry said, "I'm a peer counselor in school, and we had a girl who was date raped by a college boy. It was awful. She had all kinds of problems afterward dealing with her self-worth."

She smiled. "But now she's got a new boyfriend— he's a junior—a really sweet guy, and she seems happy."

Claudie didn't know what to say. *I've got a boyfriend. I'm happy…some of the time.*

"Dad told me two men were with you today. Is one of them your boyfriend?" Sherry asked.

Claudie swallowed. "He thinks he is." Her answer came out sharper than she'd intended.

Sherry giggled. "Don't they all? I'm going with a guy who thinks he's God's gift to women."

"Have you been together long?"

She shrugged. "Two months. We're at that stage where he wants sex but hasn't come right out and asked."

"What will you tell him when he asks?" Claudie asked, knowing it was none of her business.

Sherry smiled serenely. "Same thing I've told all the boys who want me to do things I'm not ready for—God will tell me *when*—and I'll know it's right because of the ring on my finger."

Claudie shook her head, mystified. "Wow. I wish I'd have had half your poise when I was your age."

Sherry's smile faded. "God gives us our path, Claudie. Yours was much harder than mine has been, but it was the one you needed to travel. Part of who I am is because you loved me and cared for me when I was a baby. I went from you to my mom. You made that possible even though you didn't know it at the time." Claudie blinked against the cold breeze that was making her eyes tear up.

"My mom—Dottie—is a wonderful lady, Claudie. She's an angel, really. You'd like her if you stayed around and got to know her."

Claudie swallowed. "I have to go. My job, my friends…" All true, but she suddenly realized leaving this beautiful young woman wasn't going to be any easier this time than it had been when she was six. "My friends are waiting," Claudie said, rising.

Sherry stood up. Although a good five inches taller, she suddenly seemed small and sad.

"You can e-mail me," Claudie said.

"Really?" Sherry brightened. "Cool. I'm online a lot with my Christian chat groups, and I'm taking an advanced humanities class from K.S.U. in Lawrence."

They talked about her plans for college as they crossed the now abandoned parking lot. Sherry pulled out a pen and paper from her pack and wrote down Yancy's address and Claudie's e-mail. In the far distance, Claudie saw a late model sedan with the engine running. Dottie, no doubt. When they stopped beside the station wagon, Claudie spotted her little camera on the dash. "Can I take your picture?"

"Sure," Sherry said, smiling. "Daddy says I'm half ham."

After snapping three shots, Claudie glanced once more at the waiting car then said, "I'm sorry your father's ill. Tell him…not all my memories are bad."

Sherry's eyes filled with tears and she hugged Claudie fiercely. "You are so wonderful. That will mean so much to him. Thank you. I love you."

"I love you, too, Sherry," Claudie said, stumbling on words she hadn't used for what seemed like a hundred years. "Take care. Keep up those grades, and tell any boy who gives you a problem your big sister will come back and make him very, very sorry he was born male."

Sherry laughed and waved goodbye before dashing across the parking lot. Claudie watched her go. This wasn't the way she'd seen any of this little drama unfolding, but she wasn't sorry her trip had been in vain. Sherry was a beautiful gift, and Claudie felt a tiny bit of pride that she'd helped raise her.

Smiling, she hopped in the car and turned on the heater full blast.

"I'd forgotten how much I hate winter," she said, shivering. "I wanna go home."

STRETCHED OUT on his bed, Bo glanced at the alarm clock. Four-thirty. His bags were packed. The bill paid. Matt was on the phone in his room, trying to arrange a flight to New York. If he couldn't get a plane until morning, he might opt for another night at the inn, but regardless, Bo and Claudie were headed west. And, frankly, Bo couldn't wait.

He didn't know what to expect from Claudie when she returned from meeting her sister. He figured it could go either way. She'd either be a basket case who needed him to comfort her or a clam—her nefarious alter ego.

A swift knock preceded Claudie, who rushed in and slammed the door behind her. She shed her coat and gloves before turning around to lock the door.

Bo sat up, reclining on his elbows. "Are you okay?"

She kicked off her shoes. "I'm fine," she said, strolling forward. "I'm better than fine, actually."

Bo swallowed. "Good," he said, his voice cracking. He cleared his throat and sat up straighter. "Are you packed? We should probably hit the road."

"Not just yet," she said, kneeling at the foot of the bed. She slipped off the dark-plum cardigan leaving the short-sleeved sweater top behind. For Claudie, this practically constituted a negligee.

"What are you doing?" Bo asked, scooting back until his shoulders encountered the old-fashioned beaded headboard.

"Healing. I think."

If she'd have left it at "healing" he might have been able to buy it, but that little quaver in her voice that accompanied the "I think" told him she wasn't ready for this.

"I don't think this is a good idea," he said, even though his body thought otherwise.

She stretched out her hand, lightly brushing the front of his canvas trousers. "A part of you disagrees."

He snorted, crossing his left leg over his right the best he could. "Well, sure, but if I listened to that part of me there's no telling what kind of trouble I'd be in."

"Trouble can be fun, if it's handled right," she said, not so subtly stressing the double entendre.

He shifted positions. "Really, Claudie, after the hell you've been through toda—" He choked on his words when she shifted to all fours, a graceful feline, stalking her prey. The scooped neck of her sweater afforded a great view of ivory lace and peachy skin. The golden locket swung like a pendulum between her breasts.

"Claudie…"

She ran the tip of her tongue across her upper lip.

His damn knees parted without so much as an "Open, sesame," and she moved forward, straddling him.

Bo groaned. "Sweetheart. Please. Don't do this."

She nuzzled the side of his face, her hair tickling his nose. "Why? Isn't it what you want?"

"Yes. Of course. But you need time to get some perspective on what happened."

She sat back, her weight resting in the most perfectly designed position imaginable. Bo felt his control slipping. His mind started charting the fastest way to remove her slacks—until he looked in her eyes and saw the shattering pain and doubt he'd always known haunted her.

"Oh, honey," he whispered, sitting forward to wrap his arms around her. He rolled them to the side so they were facing each other. Without her resting quite so provocatively against his groin he could actually think. "You just got back from hell, baby. It's natural to want to prove to yourself you're still alive, but maybe we should wait until—"

She exploded out of his arms, scrabbling back to the far corner of the king-size bed. "Goddamn it, Lester. Make up your mind. When I don't want you, you want me. When I throw myself at you, you play hard to get." Her chest was heaving and he could see she was close to tears. "What are you?" she growled. "A woman?"

Bo would have laughed but he was afraid she might find his gun and use it on him. He bent his elbow and rested his head on his palm. "I'm a coward."

That shut her up. For a minute. "No, you're not."

He nodded. "Yes, I am. Where you're concerned. I'm so afraid I might screw up I don't know what to do."

Her frown looked doubtful, so he sat up, kneeling across from her. "Sweetheart, there's nothing in the world I'd like more than to make love with you, but a quickie before we hit the road isn't quite what I had in mind."

Her eyes narrowed. "Men are supposed to want it any time, any place."

"I don't just want your body, Claudie. I want you."

She looked down. "I thought this would prove—" She gulped. "I don't know what I thought it would prove."

Bo reached out and pulled her to him. She laid her head on his shoulder and put her arms around him. Nuzzling her neck, inhaling the fresh outdoor smell in her hair, he whispered, "Can you tell me what happened?"

When she nodded, he moved them backward to the plump eyelet lace pillows. She snuggled into the space beside him, her head still on his shoulder. Bo closed his eyes and listened to her relate the news of her sister. His heart swelled with her joy, twisted with her pain. He tried to keep from thinking too far ahead— the long drive home where they'd spend three nights on the road. Time he planned to use to convince her to marry him.

"Will you marry me?"

Claudie leapt to her feet as if a bomb had gone off beside her. The mattress jiggled as she danced from foot to foot. "What? What did you say?"

Bo felt a rush of heat to his face. "Oops," he muttered. "Did I say that aloud?"

"You didn't mean to say it?" She stopped dancing and gave him a suspicious glare.

"Well, yeah, but not right this minute. Damn." He put his hand to his head.

Her giggle caught him totally off-guard. When she bent over laughing, he didn't know whether to be hurt or laugh, too.

She collapsed to her knees, tears in her eyes. "That is too funny," she sputtered. "An accidental proposal." Wiping her cheeks with her hands, she looked at him and asked, "What would you have done if I'd said yes?"

He sat up, facing her. "I'd have considered myself the luckiest man in the world." Her smile faded. He touched her damp cheek. "I wasn't kidding, Claudie. I want to marry you and start a family. I want to help you open a second and third halfway house. I want to be at your side when the governor awards you a plaque for your contribution to society."

Her eyes spoke the words he knew she couldn't say to him. Not yet, anyway.

He leaned forward and kissed her. "They call those dreams, Claudie girl. Now that you've kicked the bogeyman out of your nightmares, you can dream, too."

She tilted her face to kiss him. Her tears added a salty flavor to her taste. When her hands moved to his shoulders, he hauled her to him, his pulse racing with hope, love.

The knock on the door shattered the moment. She pulled back guiltily.

Bo silently cursed his cousin, the only person it could be. "What?" he barked.

"Let me in. I just got a call from my mother. It's about your dad, Bo. He's in the hospital."

CLAUDIE'S OPINION of Matt skyrocketed as she watched him handle Bo with a stalwart calm she couldn't begin to match. Not that Bo flew off the handle, but Claudie could tell he was upset and not thinking as clearly as usual. For one thing, he was under the mistaken impression she would let him fly off to New York without her.

"It makes perfect sense," he told her for the third

time. "I'll switch Matt's ticket to my name and he can drive you home."

She rolled her eyes. "No way am I spending three days on the road with Matt, even if he is your cousin. No offense," she said, looking at Matt who seemed equally serious.

"None taken." He looked at Bo. "She's right. That wouldn't work. I can't just jump into your life, Bo. This is my weekend to have Ashley."

"What's three lousy days, you jerk?" Bo growled. "I'd do it for you."

Matt's complexion darkened a degree. "I'm not saying I won't help out. I just think we should think things through. You haven't even talked to your mother yet. You know my mother—she's an alarmist."

Bo's mouth fell open.

Matt ducked his head, sheepishly. "Well, maybe not, but it still might not be that bad."

The sound of a phone made them jump. Bo clutched his chest pocket, where he'd put his cell phone after retrieving it from his briefcase. "Hello," he cried. "Mom. How is he? Aunt Irene called a few minutes ago."

Claudie watched his face, her nerves skittering along the top of her skin. She couldn't believe anyone could go through so much emotional turmoil in one day and survive. She'd already decided if this was a false alarm, she'd ask for her room back so she could go to bed. California could wait.

Bo walked to the small desk on the other side of the room and scribbled something on the rose-embossed note pad. "I got it. I'll be there as soon as

possible. How are you doing?'' He paused to listen.
''Well, don't let yourself get too run-down. Listen to
Irene, she's a nurse.'' He nodded, already on the move
with that purposeful, focused style of his.

A chameleon, he called himself, able to blend into
a crowd. Also, as forceful and dynamic as Ren or Matt
when he chose to be. ''I'll call you when I get in,
Mom. Take care. I love you.''

He pressed a button and pocketed the phone. ''He's
in intensive care. Pretty much touch-and-go for the
next twelve hours. I gotta go. Will you two stop fighting me on this so I can get out of here?''

Matt rose. ''My flight's the only one out and it
leaves at nine-forty-five. That's four hours from now.
The airport's an hour away, so we might as well take
it down a notch. There's nothing you can do at the
moment.''

Bo's upper lip curled. ''There should be.''

Claudie started to the door. ''I'll get packed. Matt,
would you see if there are two more seats on that
plane?''

Bo swore.

When the phone rang, Claudie spun on her heel and
picked up the receiver by the bed. The voice on the
other end wasn't one she was expecting.

''Hello, Claudie? It's Garret.''

She sat down abruptly. ''Yes,'' she said, mouthing
the word *Garret* to Bo. ''What do you want? We're
in a bit of a hurry here….''

''I know. You're anxious to leave for home, but
there's something I forgot to tell you this afternoon.
I'm so glad I caught you.''

She didn't like the softer feelings his raspy voice

provoked. She couldn't seem to draw up the image of him she'd held for ten years—drunk, slobbering, stinking of sweat and booze. Over the years, she'd added features of other men, other cruelties and coarseness until he was a demon too hideous to conjure in the daylight hours. Now he was none of those things. Somehow he'd become nothing more than a pathetic shell of a man waiting for death.

"We're leaving soon."

"Well, I won't keep you. I just wanted you to know about the insurance money. I thought it might make a difference to you, if you broke down and needed it for anything." His odd hesitation made her look at Bo, who'd walked to her side.

"What insurance money?"

Garret cleared his throat. "Your mom's folks bought her a paid-up insurance policy when she was a girl. After you were born she made you the beneficiary. She never changed that, so when she died, you inherited it."

"How much?"

"It was for $2500. Of course, it's worth quite a bit more now."

Claudie frowned. Bo's inquiring look made her reach out and touch his arm. Matt appeared with a piece of paper and a pen upon which she scribbled a dollar sign.

"I don't get it. Why is it worth more now?"

Garret coughed again. "Well…Peggy never told me about it. After she passed away, I found it in with some papers." He paused. "I was really upset and hurt that she— There were a lot of times we could have used the money if we'd have cashed it in, but she never mentioned it." He paused as if to catch his breath. "It's possible she just forgot about it, but at the time I was consumed by rage."

Claudie closed her eyes. She understood that kind of anger.

"Anyway, after you left home I cashed it in. Since I was your legal guardian, nobody questioned it. I'd planned to spend it, but then I had my wreck. By the time I got out of the hospital, I knew I couldn't live with myself if I touched a dime of it, so I gave it to a friend who was an investment banker."

This pause was different. Expectant. She gave Bo a tentative smile. "Did he run off to Brazil?" she asked.

Garret's laugh ended in a painful-sounding cough. When he had his voice back, he said, "No. Glen's as honest as the day is long. He did pretty well for you, Claudie. I just got off the phone with him. It's a nice tidy sum. Enough to put down on a house if you and Bo were to get married."

"Married?" she choked out, unable to contain herself.

Bo looked up, a quizzical expression on his face.

Garret stuttered. "Umm…er…I'm sorry to have presumed. Maybe you could use it to buy a new car. Dottie said yours was—"

"Car," Claudie cried, vaulting to her feet. "My car. What am I going to do with my car if I go to New York?"

She looked at Matt, who shrugged. Bo gave them both an "I-told-you" look.

"What do you mean?" Garret asked.

She recounted Bo's news.

"Just leave your car right there," Garret said. "Give the keys to Mrs. Green. Dottie and I will come get it first thing in the morning and keep it here for you until you can come back for it."

"That's very nice of you to offer, but—"

Bo groaned.

"No, buts, Claudine," he said severely. "I've waited a decade to be able to help you in any way I could. I don't think I've got another decade left in me, so you'd better let me do this."

Claudie took a breath. "All right. Tell Sherry she can drive it. A girl needs her own wheels from time to time."

When Garret answered, his voice sounded thick with emotion. "That's very good of you, Claudie. She will be thrilled to pieces." Claudie hated to admit how nice his praise sounded to her ears. "Now, about the money. Do you need any to help you get to New York? I'm sure Glen could advance you some—"

She smiled. "No. Bo can buy my ticket and I'll pay him back later." *Some way or another.*

She told her stepfather goodbye and hung up the phone. To Bo she said, "The car is taken care of, and I'm independently wealthy." To Matt, she said, "Go make another reservation. I'm going to New York."

MATT TUCKED his carry-on bag beneath his knees, glad to find three seats together in the small waiting room. Claudie took the spot beside him. Bo, still restless as an edgy lion, turned on his heel. "I'm going to the john."

Claudie put her bulky leather purse on the empty seat to save it.

They sat in silence surrounded by the low hum of other passengers and an occasional flight announcement. Compared to JFK this airport was low-key, but Claudie peered around like a kid in a museum.

"Is this your first time?" he asked.

She gave him a droll look that made him blush. "On an airplane," he qualified.

"Isn't there a law against doing it on an airplane?" she asked impishly.

"Claudie," he snapped. He wasn't in the mood for teasing. He was rarely in the mood for teasing these days. Although Matt had enjoyed the stimulation of working in the field, he still felt unsettled and useless. He couldn't even deliver the one thing his cousin asked for—an extra few days to drive Claudie home. He'd been so damn relieved when she insisted on going to New York that he'd almost kissed her.

She lightly brushed her hand against his sleeve. "Sorry," she said. "I get a little goofy when I'm nervous. And, yes, this is my first plane ride."

The way she said it made him smile.

"You should smile more often, Matt," she told him. "It's a lot less scary than your big, bad cop frown."

He gave her his toughest squint. She shrank back in her seat. "Sorry," she peeped.

He shook his head, and heaving a sigh, slumped down in his chair. He closed his eyes. "You're a good person, Claudie. I'm glad you're here. Bo's gonna need you."

"Tell him that. I think he's really pissed," she said.

Matt turned his chin to look at her. He wasn't easily impressed, but the way she handled the confrontation with her stepfather had been something. Now, jumping in blindly to help Bo took guts—especially considering the way Bo was acting. "You gotta understand. Things between Bo and his dad were never good. Robert B. is a cold man. He used to scare the hell out of me."

She looked doubtful.

"Scout's honor. One time in college, I bumped into him at some family function and asked him about an investment opportunity some friends of mine were all hot about." He grimaced. "The man had me backed up against the wall before Aunt Ruth rescued me."

"What'd he say?"

"Basically, he told me to keep my money in my pants because I was too damn dumb to invest it in anything more complicated than beer."

"What'd you do?"

"I bought ten thousand shares of my friend's stock. Which, basically amounted to pissing it away, because the market crashed and the company folded. Uncle Robert was right. I'd have been better off with the beer."

She smiled uneasily. "He sounds complicated. How'd he wind up with a son like Bo, someone so…real."

Matt looked toward the main corridor, which was visible through Plexiglas partitions. It took him a minute to find Bo, who moved in and out of the crowd like a wraith—unnoticed, Matt guessed, by the majority of the people he passed. For as long as Matt had known him, Bo had gone out of his way to blend in—understandable, Matt thought, given Bo's larger-than-life father. But Bo was far from ordinary.

"This is probably a dumb thing I'm doing," Claudie said, slumping down lower than Matt.

Matt shifted enough to face her. "Cool it. Here comes, Bo. And he's going to need you in New York. I guarantee it."

She looked to the scanning machine where Bo was waiting for a lady and her dog to pass through. "But he doesn't want me here," she said.

"Right. Just like you didn't want him to find you. But he did, and you're glad, right?"

She smiled. He closed his eyes. He didn't begrudge Bo and Claudie any happiness they could find, but as far he was concerned, love was for fools.

BO PULLED OUT the in-flight magazine from the seat in front of him and tried to focus on the pictures— words were beyond him. His mind bounced from one topic to another like a golf ball on pavement. One second he was thinking about his father, the next Claudie's stepfather and her sudden windfall.

Craning his neck, he looked around to see if he could find her. Since they'd booked so late, none of their seats were together. A full house, but no sign of Claudie.

Shaking out his hands, he depressed the button to recline his seat and loosened his seat belt. No way around it, this was going to be a long flight.

To his left, in seats A and B, was a young couple nestled against the window like baby lemurs. Behind him, the drink cart began its tortuous rumble up the aisle.

With a sigh, he closed his eyes. His mind jumped to Claudie—its favorite topic. He couldn't believe she'd insisted on accompanying him to New York. That Matt had refused to back him up still irked a little, but he understood why Matt wasn't anxious to drive to California. And, secretly, the idea of his handsome cousin spending three or four days with the woman he loved didn't exactly thrill Bo, either.

Chagrined by his unwarranted jealousy, he looked down. To his amazement, a hand slipped between his seat and half-empty seat B. Curious, he leaned into the aisle to look behind his seat.

"Claudie?"

Grinning, she jerked her hand back. "I was going to pinch you."

Her mischievous smile took his breath away. "Why?" he whispered.

"To get your attention."

He motioned her closer. "I thought you didn't like my attention."

"That was before."

"Before what?"

"Before I was rich."

Her little-girl tone unloosened something painful inside him. "Honey, I hate to tell you this, but forty grand isn't all that rich."

She rolled her eyes. "Maybe not by Ren Bishop's standards, but it is by mine. It's enough to make me an entirely different person."

His happy mood slipped away. "I like the person you are."

She scooted closer. "Do you?" she softly asked.

He nodded. She was almost close enough to kiss, but of course he couldn't. Not in public.

"Then maybe I won't change," she said, her gaze pinned to his.

Bo's heart thudded in his chest. He swallowed and glanced over her shoulder where a nine-year-old boy watched them intently. He cleared his throat. "How'd you manage to switch seats?" he asked.

Her pout was followed by a pensive look. "I saw the man in this seat go to the rest room, so I followed and asked if I could sit here."

"And he agreed?"

She nodded.

Bo didn't buy it. "Why?"

Her gaze slipped from his. "I told him we were eloping."

The lie took Bo's breath away. It took him a minute to put together a comeback. "Claudie, nobody elopes to New York City."

She made a face—so Bradylike he almost laughed. "We're only flying to New York. From there we're taking the train to Niagara Falls. A *sleeper,* remember?" she teased.

Bo had to duck back into his seat to avoid being mowed down by the drink cart. *Niagara Falls? Where did that come from?* He would have loved to ask her, but for the moment all he could do was stew.

When the flight attendant asked him for his order, it was on the tip of his tongue to ask for scotch—until a slim hand materialized between the seats and pinched the fleshy part of his arm. Snickering, he said, "Orange juice, please."

CHAPTER TEN

CLAUDIE PEERED through the hospital's glass doors to the street beyond. The steady drizzle that had accompanied her and Bo on the taxi ride earlier that morning was beginning to turn solid. The weather forecaster on the television in the waiting room predicted a severe winter storm. If she wasn't feeling quite so tense, Claudie might have enjoyed the snow. But she couldn't relax—not when Bo was acting so funny.

She sighed and squinted, trying to make him out. He'd escorted his mother downstairs from the eleventh floor where his father remained in intensive care. Although Ruth had protested that she was perfectly capable of obtaining a taxi without his help, Bo had insisted. Claudie had tagged along without being asked.

Talk about a fifth wheel. She rubbed a spot on her forehead trying to alleviate the ache. Hanging around a hospital would have been difficult enough even if Bo was acting normal, but Claudie barely recognized the man she'd joked with on the airplane just days earlier. Ever since he'd learned that his father's medical emergency wasn't a heart attack at all but a concussion from a fall he'd taken while in-line skating, Bo had turned inward—as rigid and unapproachable as the urban towers that surrounded her.

Claudie opened her purse and took out a bottle of water. She wanted to help, but Bo wouldn't let her in. *If he'd just talk to me—tell me what he's feeling...* she thought, jumping aside as two men in blue jumpsuits hurried past. She took a gulp of water and replaced the bottle in her bag.

A moment later, Bo appeared—his shaggy, uncombed mop wet with snowflakes. His haggard appearance made her ache to comfort him, but his somber demeanor didn't invite closeness.

Claudie scooted sideways. The bleak but determined look in his eyes made her uneasy.

"I need a magazine before we head upstairs." She pivoted and walked to the gift shop counter.

Bo followed. He stood close enough for her pick up his scent—coffee, a hint of fresh air and that familiar, comforting essence that was pure Bo. "Claudie, we need to talk," he said, his tone serious.

She blindly grabbed a *People* magazine and dug in her purse for money. Bo slapped down a five-dollar bill and took her elbow. "Now."

If anyone else had acted that bossy she'd have leveled the guy, but Claudie sensed the depths of Bo's frustration. She shoved the magazine in her purse. "Do you want to sit in the lobby or go outside?"

"Not down here. It's a madhouse," he said, his tone flat. His fingers tensed on her elbow. The contact felt good even though she wasn't certain what he wanted from her.

"Upstairs, then," she suggested. This giant city within a city fascinated her as much as it repelled her. Certain gross smells could ambush without warning.

Loud noises were prone to explode in any direction. Pathos seemed to outweigh hope.

Bo ushered her toward the bank of elevators. Moments later they stepped into the medicinal-smelling chrome box. Side by side they squeezed into the closest corner. Bo pushed the appropriate button.

The elevator shimmied and Bo's shoulder brushed hers. Claudie tensed.

"Most muggers stay out on the street," he said—a faint touch of the old Bo in his voice.

Confused, Claudie glanced at him. His eyebrows wiggled and he nodded toward her hands. White knuckles gripped her pocketbook. She loosened her grip but kept her chin down to keep Bo from seeing her embarrassment. Never had she felt more like a hick from Kansas.

"This can't be much fun for you," Bo said. His voice was low to avoid being overheard by the other occupants.

"I didn't come here for fun."

"Why did you come, Claudie?"

Claudie's distress level rose. She wasn't sure she could answer that in the time it took to ascend eleven floors. "Payback," she mumbled, refusing to meet his gaze.

"I beg your pardon?"

She inched closer to the wall, taking care not to bump the bandaged foot of the man in the wheelchair behind her. Bo moved, too. His arm brushed against hers, and Claudie had to fight not to react. She no longer loathed touching—especially Bo's touch—but she didn't trust herself not to wrap her arms around him and try to pretend this medicinal-smelling world didn't exist.

"You were there for me in Kansas. This is my chance to pay you back," she said softly.

His harsh curse was uttered under his breath. "You don't owe me anything, Claudie."

She closed her eyes and sighed. She had too much to say—and too little—to get into it here. She changed the subject. "Matt told me Ashley's overbite is going to cost three thousand dollars. Apparently, that's cheap. His ex-wife's husband's cousin is an orthodontist, so they get a family discount."

Bo stuffed his hands in the pockets of his wrinkled Dockers and eyed her as if she'd just changed colors. Her cheeks warmed under his scrutiny, but she continued, "And he's spoken to Mrs. Kriegen several times. You'll be glad to know she's decided he's not the anti-Christ out to usurp your business."

A flicker of emotion touched his lips. Encouraged, Claudie said, "It sounds like the business is running pretty smoothly without you, but Matt said things could get hairy if you don't get back to work soon."

Bo shrugged with a carelessness she knew he didn't feel.

Claudie also knew she was to blame for Bo losing a week away from his business. "It's my fault, Bo. That time you spent chasing after me—"

He didn't let her finish. "Don't." His voice was unusually stiff and stern. Businesslike. "Matt just got a call from an old friend in the D.A.'s office. They're throwing some work our way. A couple of the cases include some decent rewards. I'll send a couple of my guys out here after the first of the year to work with Matt. That should keep us solvent.''

The acrid twist he put on the last word made her flinch. ''Bo, what's going on?''

He glanced at the display panel—two more floors. When the doors opened, Claudie started toward the waiting room, but Bo took her elbow and led her to one of the long narrow windows away from the nurses' station.

Feeling overcome with dread, Claudie pressed her forehead against the cool glass. Below her a panorama of white sparkled as fresh and pristine as a child's snow globe. ''Wow, that's kinda pretty.''

Behind her, she heard Bo's droll, ''Tourist.''

It was the first glimpse in days of the Bo she knew—and possibly loved. She didn't peek for fear he'd be gone—his bleak alter ego returned—so she stared outside. *I wonder if it's snowing in Niagara Falls?*

BO WATCHED the wind drive waves of fat white flakes against the window beyond Claudie. Gusts curled upward shaping a miniature drift along the building's ledge. If he focused on the weather, he could almost block out the image of his father lying helpless and diminished in the room down the hall. Almost.

''Has there been any change?'' Claudie asked, not turning around.

Her breath steamed up the window like a ghost track. Bo felt surrounded by ghosts. The only way to keep them at bay was to stoke the fire of his anger.

''Nope. Whacking your head on a curb will do it every time. I know. Tangled with a few curbs myself.

Although that was from drinking. Even *I* wasn't dumb enough to go in-line skating without a helmet.'' He snorted. ''Wait. I forgot. This was a *heart attack.*''

Bo flinched inwardly at his snide tone but found himself powerless to summon one iota of the compassion he'd initially felt when learning of his father's hospitalization. He'd completely lost it when he arrived at the hospital and Trisha—his father's girlfriend—told him the truth. Bogus headlines were one thing, lying to your son was another.

''Trisha told me she lied to the media to protect your father's image,'' Claudie said softly.

Bo pictured the five-eleven, model-thin blonde. At least she was thirty, not nineteen as he'd first pictured, and she worked for a public relations firm, but that did little to ease Bo's prejudice. Tricia was the first lover his father had publicly acknowledged by moving into her condo. Did she mean more to him than the others before her? Bo didn't want to know. He didn't care.

''What kind of woman takes a sixty-eight-year-old man in-line skating?'' he muttered. ''I can't believe I fell for it. I should have known better—after all, you need a *heart* to have a heart attack.''

Claudie turned sharply. Her brow was wrinkled with concern. ''I don't think he did it on purpose, Bo.''

Her mild censure annoyed him. She was supposed to be on *his* side. ''Yes, he did. He waited until I fell in love to take up in-line skating and screw up—''

She interrupted. ''What do you mean? What's screwed up? Isn't that why you followed me to Kansas? Isn't that why I'm here? Because we—we're there for each other.''

Her reluctance to name her feelings infuriated him. Bo knew he was being childish and irrational, but he couldn't help it. And anger helped justify his decision. ''Speaking of being here...I think you should go home. The doctors won't say when—or if—Dad will come out of this coma. *I* can't leave Mom to deal with this alone, but it's ridiculous for you to hang around.''

Her sweet lips pursed in a frown. ''I don't mind, Bo. I mean, it would be a little easier if I had a feeling you wanted me here, but—''

''That's just it, Claudie. I don't want you here. I have too much on my mind to deal with your needs, too.''

Her eyes grew wide—a flash of hurt evident before she righted her shoulders regally. ''I'll get my things and leave. My coat's in the waiting room.'' She turned away before Bo could move.

He closed his eyes and leaned into the window. The glass sent a shiver through his body as if part of his soul had been ripped away. His stomach clenched at the shot of acid that hit full force. Frustration, anger and fear duked it out as he followed her down the hall.

''I'll take a taxi to your mother's then call the airport to see about a flight,'' Claudie said, not looking at him. She was seated, gathering her *stuff*—a paper cup, a crossword puzzle book, playing cards and several candy bar wrappers. ''I hope this storm doesn't get worse. They had to close the airport last week, remember?''

Was that only a week ago? Bo thought, sinking into

the chair beside her. How could he possibly have gone
from the person tracking down the woman he loved
to this empty, disconnected shell in so short a time?

She reached for her parka—the one his mother had
lent her to replace Claudie's woefully inadequate West
Coast jacket.

"Wait."

Her hand hovered—trembling—above the jacket.

Bo closed his eyes, suddenly drained. How had his
life gotten so screwed up? "I'm sorry, Claudie. I
know I've been a jerk."

He felt her hand on his forearm. His skin was
clammy with sweat. Despite the chilly weather outside, the hospital kept the rooms just above boiling.
"Don't beat yourself up about it," she said. "I know
how to roll with the punches. I thought I could help,
but it's obvious I'm just in the way. No biggie."

He recognized that voice. It belonged to the woman
he'd met six months ago—cool, contained, streetwise
and world-weary, not the woman who had joked with
him about going to Niagara Falls. He opened his eyes
and looked at her. "Claudie, I don't want you to
leave." The instant spark of hope in her eyes made
his stomach turn over. "But it's crazy for you to
stay."

She shrank back as if struck.

Turning in the chair to face her, he said, "I should
never have let you come. This place is like the twilight
zone of my life. I walk into my father's room and
leave *me* behind—the Sacramento me, the person I am
when I'm with you. Gone. History."

Her obvious concern twisted his gut in a knot.

What's wrong with me? Why can't I take what she's offering?

She put her palm to his cheek. Her scent brought comfort at a primal level, but his brain rejected the succor. "Tell me what to do, Bo. Go or stay. It's up to you."

A disturbance in the hall made him look away. Matt leaned in the doorway and motioned him to come. Bo shot to his feet. "Go." Her shattered look made him hesitate. "No, stay." As he hurried to the door, he called over his shoulder. "I don't know. We'll talk about it tonight."

SEVERAL HOURS LATER, Claudie stomped her boots on the inch-thick mat inside the door then unlaced them and set them to one side to dry. Her stockings were soaked from the ankle-deep slush she'd encountered on her walk from the subway. Dashing on damp tiptoes she sprinted across the glossy marble floor of the apartment's foyer to the carpeted hallway then hurried to the guest bedroom where she'd spent two sleepless nights. Maybe a bath and a glass of wine would help, she thought. With any luck, she might even sleep.

She grabbed her sweatpants and flannel nightshirt from her suitcase and walked to the bathroom across the hall from her room. A palace of topaz-veined marble—its pristine beauty was softened by two dozen wax pillars in various shades of lavender—all with blackened wicks. That lived-in look took the edge off the distress she'd felt when she saw for the first time the great disparity between her childhood and Bo's.

She turned the two golden handles of the jetted tub and went in search of a glass of wine. Two open reds waited at the discreet bar just inside the book-cluttered living room. Bo's mother obviously indulged in her literary passion. Claudie checked the label on each bottle, selecting the one that looked the cheapest.

Carrying her glass in one hand and a book on painted-lady architecture in the other, she returned to the bath. As she stripped, she studied the instrument panel on the side of the tub.

With a sigh, she added a measure of luxuriant lavender-scented bath crystals to the water. After lighting six candles, she turned off the overhead light and slipped into the fragrant water. She took a sip of wine—rich and smooth—and closed her eyes. Slowly, the tension that had been building all day melted away.

Fortunately, Bo's father had pulled through his most recent medical crisis. Mr. Lester's heart had stopped for several minutes before a team of doctors and nurses was able to revive him.

Her confrontation with Bo that afternoon lingered. Suddenly Claudie knew what she was going to do. If the weather cooperated, she'd grab the first plane for home in the morning.

Home. "Where is home?" Claudie muttered, polishing off her wine. Not Kansas—even though both Sherry and Garret made it clear she was always welcome there. Not Minnesota or Wyoming.

She sighed, her breath sending a ripple across the water. Even though she'd reconnected the pieces of her past, Claudie felt more alone than ever. Home was with Bo, but he didn't want her.

BO FOLLOWED his nose. He wasn't surprised to find Claudie in the kitchen—his mother had ordered him to go home and "have a nice bite to eat with Claudie," but he hadn't expected her to look quite so domestic.

"Hi, there," he said softly. She wheeled about, nearly spilling her wine. "Whatever you're cooking smells good. Did you make enough for two?"

She nodded, her eyes big. He didn't blame her for being cautious after the way he treated her that afternoon.

"Is your dad better?" Claudie asked, her tone somber.

"Stable, but Irene said this afternoon's crisis might be a precursor to other little episodes before his body eventually shuts down."

Her face showed profound sadness, and he knew it wasn't for a man she'd never met. She's here for me, Bo thought, and all I do is push her away. Am I as stupid and callous as my father? Am I?

He opened the refrigerator and grabbed a can of soda. He'd face those questions when he got back to Sac—*one identity crisis at a time.*

"What's cookin'?"

Stirring the pot on the gas range with the intensity of a witch from *MacBeth*, Claudie said, "Clam chowder. From a can, but I doctored it up."

Bo walked to the counter and pulled out a stool.

Claudie filled a bowl at the stove and carried it to him. Her bottom lip was caught between her teeth in concentration. The childlike mannerism hit him below the belt. Why was he acting like such an idiot? This was Claudie—the woman he loved.

Once the bowl was safely in place, she looked at

him and smiled. "Matt told me Thanksgiving is the busiest air travel holiday of all, so I'm thinking of leaving tomorrow if possible."

"When's Thanksgiving?"

"Thursday."

"No way."

She nodded toward the calendar.

He ran a hand through his hair; it felt dry and coarse like a clown's wig. The soup smelled inviting, but his mouth tasted as though he'd been on a three-day binge. He wanted a drink.

Claudie filled her bowl and joined him at the counter. "Sara wants me there for Thanksgiving and we've got the dim sum fund-raiser the following week," she said, taking the stool next to him.

Sacramento seemed a million miles away. Another dimension.

"What exactly is dim sum?" Bo asked, idly stirring his soup.

Claudie made a face. "I'm not sure. Maya said the name means 'little treasures.' I guess it's like won tons and egg rolls but more involved."

He swallowed a spoonful of soup. The heat loosened the knot in his chest. "Sounds like a lot of work."

"It's keeping them out of trouble. And Babe's *soliciting*—Rochell's term—things for a charity auction. The girls got a big hoot out of that."

They ate in silence until Claudie asked, "Are you going back to the hospital tonight?"

Bo shook his head. "Nope. Trisha's going to be there."

He didn't want to think about the woman or her

place in his father's life. Bo didn't understand how his mother could tolerate the woman's presence. Bo sure as hell couldn't swallow it.

He looked at Claudie. "How come your hair's wet?"

"I soaked in the tub." She closed her eyes and sighed. "A luxury I won't have once I get home."

She whispered the word. *Love and home—stumbling stones in the road of life,* he thought sourly.

"This tastes great," he said striving for sincerity.

Her weak smile seemed as disingenuous as he felt.

He pushed back his stool and stood up. "I think I'll take a shower and go to bed," he told her. "The storm's getting worse, but Mom said she'd call if anything changes."

Claudie rose and began to gather up their dishes. Bo's gut churned. "Matt told me he talked to Ren today," Bo said, not able to keep from following her with his gaze. "Sara wants Matt to go to Atlanta."

"Why?"

"They still haven't heard from Eve." Bo shrugged. He hadn't been listening too closely to what Matt told him. "Sara's convinced the South is a black hole. Life goes in but never comes out."

She looked over her shoulder and smiled. "I know. I think it has something to do with her time in the military, but Keneesha lives in Georgia and she's doing great. You'd think Sara could show a little forgiveness."

Forgiveness. That was the main tenet of what his mother was preaching tonight before he left. *If I can forgive him, son, I would think you could show a little compassion.* But Bo didn't forgive his father. Not for cheating on his mother. Not for valuing work over family. Not for being a pathetic excuse for a father.

Bo spun on one heel and stalked out of the room. He marched through the living room to the corner bar that he knew would be stocked with every kind of booze available—a good New York bar. He filled the ice bucket from a tray in the mini refrigerator, then dropped two cubes in a crystal highball glass. As he surveyed the gold mine of choices before him, he caught a glimpse of Claudie in the doorway.

"What are you doing?"

"It's been a lousy day and I feel like a drink." He grabbed a red-label scotch.

"Life sucks, right?" She stopped a few steps away. "You hate your father, and he might die before you can tell him off. Is that it?"

"Close enough," he snarled, wrenching the cap off the bottle. "But let's not forget that the bastard's soon-to-be ex-wife is solicitously wailing by his bedside along with his current girlfriend who just happens to be ten years *my* junior." He dumped amber liquid into the glass.

He picked up the glass and drew it to his lips. The smell almost choked him, and he had to pull back to catch his breath. A sudden movement made him look toward the couch. Claudie's sweatpants flew through the air to land on the floor beside him.

He turned his head sharply. Her oversize plaid flannel shirt stopped at midthigh, only bare leg continued. Her toes curled in the plush carpet. She started unbuttoning her shirt.

"What the hell do you think you're doing?"

She shrugged. The shirt gaped, displaying the tops of her breasts. "This is what we do, right?"

Confused, furious, he watched another button succumb to her nimble fingers. "What are you talking about?"

"Vices," she said—her voice flat. "Yours is booze. Mine is sex. When things get tough, we fall back into the old patterns." Bo cringed at the resignation in her tone. "I'd kinda figured that might happen, which is why I didn't think you should get involved with someone like me."

"Claudie, this has nothing to do—"

She didn't let him finish. "Bo, think about it. If this is enough to push you over the edge—after twenty years of sobriety, how long will I last?" Her mocking laugh hit him like a punch in the gut.

She freed the final button.

Bo swore. The glass slipped from his fingers, landing haphazardly in the sink. Whiskey splashed everywhere—the smell a toxic flashback to the floor of a college bar where he once spent the night facedown in his own vomit. Wiping his hand on his pants he started toward her just as she shrugged out of the chamois-soft shirt. It pooled at her feet.

"Oh, God, Claudie," Bo whispered, taking in her naked form. Beautiful. Breathtaking. And Bo couldn't have been more furious. "Put that back on."

"No."

He reached for the shirt, but she jumped back and sent it flying off the tip of her toe. "Don't worry," she said flippantly, hands on her hips. "I won't charge you."

Bo's stomach heaved. "Claudie, stop it. You're scaring me. You're not a prostitute anymore."

She turned to face him. Her hands dropped to her sides. "And you're not a drunk."

Bo closed his eyes against the tears that hit him.

"I'm not the same girl who was raped by my stepfather—a man who could never love me no matter how much I wanted him to. And you're not the same boy whose father failed you in ways you can't even talk about. We're not those people any more, Bo. Are we?"

"No love, we're not." He put out his arms. She flew to him, wrapping her arms around his neck, kissing his wet cheeks.

"Then who are we, Bo? Do you know?"

Kissing her eyes, her nose, her lips with feverish need, he whispered, "We're two people who love each other."

Her sigh was the only answer he needed. Bending down, he scooped her into his arms and started toward his room. Right or wrong, there was no turning back this time.

CHAPTER ELEVEN

WHEN HE PICKED HER UP, Claudie's heart almost jumped out of her chest. The gesture was so romantic—such a long-held image of the romantic hero—tears sprang to her eyes.

As if sensing her sudden disquiet, Bo nuzzled his lips against her hair and whispered, "I need you, Claudie. More than I've ever needed anybody, but we won't take this any further if it doesn't feel right to you."

His hands, so big and hot against her skin felt connected—not invasive strangers taking, but old friends, giving.

She dropped her head back to look at him. "I'm fine, Bo. Really."

She framed his face with her hands and kissed him with the same fire she sensed burning inside him. "My place or yours?" she asked, trying to sound sexy.

To her surprise, his step faltered. "Where do you prefer?"

She threw back her head and laughed. "It's not the where that matters—it's the who. I'm with you. That's what counts."

His smile had a Harrison Ford quality, as if he couldn't quite believe his good fortune. "My room, then. I packed a few—you know—just in case."

That he couldn't say the word made her smile inside, but she nodded seriously. "Good. Playing it safe is what kept me healthy."

He flinched, and Claudie realized there were still things that needed to be said. When they reached the bedroom, she closed her eyes as he carried her across the threshold, imagining herself a new bride. In a way, she was. Their first night together would be her first time since leaving her old life behind. Her excitement was tempered by a voice that asked, *What if this is no different? What if I can't feel anything?*

When he set her down on the bed, Claudie kept her arms around his neck reluctant to let go.

"They're in my bag," he said, his eyes questioning.

She pushed away her fear and released him. Bo walked to the closet where his bags were sitting, still half-packed. He unzipped his leather shaving kit and pulled out a strip of three foil-wrapped disks.

When he turned around, he was frowning. "Claudie, maybe this isn't—"

A sudden shiver made her look down at her naked body. Even her mother's locket was missing—safely stored in her travel bag while she'd soaked in the tub. Spotting a cashmere throw at the foot of the bed, she grabbed it and looped it across her shoulders. The fluid material provided instant modesty, but oddly she felt herself blushing, as if her true feelings were even more visible.

She patted a spot beside her on the bed. "You're right. We should talk first."

His wiry brows collided above his nose. "Talk about what?"

She took a deep breath. "Like how many men was

I with? Were they any good? Did they all have dicks the size of a horse and is it true size doesn't matter? How long could they last? Did I ever come? Am I going to see their faces when I'm with you?''

Bo's stricken look made her yank the silken cloak over her head and pull her knees to her chest.

''Claudie,'' Bo whispered. She sensed him dropping to his knees in front of her. ''Look at me.''

She shook her head. How could she ever have thought this would work? They might be adults and her hooking life was history, but he was still a man and men were weird about things like virginity and virility.

He looped his arms around her back and cuddled her as a father might a small child. His warm breath penetrated the fibers of the material near her ear. ''We can do that if you want,'' he said softly. ''I'll even go first. I'll tell you everything I've ever done with other women—the ones I can remember, at least. The size of their breasts. The way they moaned or screamed or barked.''

She drew her chin up sharply. The blanket slipped to her shoulders.

One corner of his mouth twitched.

''Oh, you—'' If her arms had been free, she would have slugged him.

''The point is,'' he said, laying his cheek against hers, ''we can do all that crap if it will make you feel better, or we can leave it behind us and see what happens.''

He pulled back to look into her eyes. ''I don't have any answers, love. To tell you the truth, I'm scared spitless, but that has nothing to do with other men. I only care about you. What if I hurt you? What if this is the right thing, but the wrong time?''

His empathy loosened her inhibitions. She worked one arm free and touched his face, running her index finger over his lips—manly lips, a little skinnier on top, but well-shaped and usually full of humor.

''Oh, Bo, I've missed your smile.'' Closing her eyes against a rush of sudden, unexpected tears, she threw her arms around his neck and leaned into him. Her knees parted and she locked her ankles across the tops of his buttocks.

The blanket disappeared, no longer needed once Bo's hands replaced it. He laid his head against her chest and pulled her to him. His long sigh connected with something deep inside her.

Lowering his chin, he nuzzled the tops of her breasts, first one then the other. ''You are incredibly beautiful,'' he whispered.

She arched her back as his mouth closed around one nipple. When he suckled, shock waves vibrated through her center core. A soft moan slipped from her lips. Silence had always been her credo—never give anything away—even pain, but with Bo she couldn't keep still.

He cupped the other breast and gently kneaded it, working loose emotions she'd never allowed into her world. ''Oh...'' she shyly volunteered, ''that feels...nice.''

His low chuckle caught her off guard. Were lovers supposed to laugh? Did she already do something wrong? ''Just 'nice?''' he asked. ''I was hoping for something like *wonderful, fabulous*. You're tough.''

His playful tone further unlocked the rigid control

she'd always kept in place. She pushed him away and scrambled back, moving to all fours. "And here I always thought I was easy," she teased.

Momentarily stunned, his gulp of laughter was followed by a frontal assault like something she once saw when she'd worked as an usher at a professional wrestling show. Before she could so much as scream in mock outrage, she was flat on her back with Bo stretched out on top of her.

"How come I'm naked and you're still dressed?" she asked, her nose touching his.

His rumbling chuckle jiggled his belly against hers in a most provocative way. She felt a buzzing sensation that triggered a warm moist response. Her wiggle was automatic, unplanned, but it provoked a kiss that took her breath away. A lover's kiss. Possessive, demanding.

Comforted by his weight, yet reassured by the fabric separating them from actual consummation, she reveled in the sensation of his kiss, the taste and texture. She freely explored his mouth before giving him access to hers.

As the pressure of his erection intensified against her pelvis, she lifted her hips, grinding them upward. His low groan sent a shot of adrenaline through her veins. She played her hands down his back, pulling the tails of his shirt free so she could touch his skin—moist with sweat, yet smooth and taut. His muscles worked at her touch, reminding her of his strength.

Lifting up on his elbows, Bo lowered his head and looked into her eyes. "You're torturing me and you love it, don't you?"

The humor in his gaze was tempered by the fire she

felt ripple through him. She contracted her abdominal muscles to lift her pelvis higher. "You're on top," she said, watching him grit his teeth for control. "What does that say about you?" She ran the tip of her tongue over her top lip. "You like a little pain with your pleasure?"

His hoot made her heart soar. He wrapped his arms under her back and rolled them both to one side. "I love you, Claudie St. James. You are incredible."

She started to say something about it being too early to tell, but the words died on her lips when Bo ran his tongue from her clavicle to her bellybutton. He pressed his face against her belly.

Claudie worked her fingers through his hair, content to have him holding her—not sure she was ready for him to go any lower. As if hearing her silent debate, Bo pulled back. His understanding smile took away her tension. She suddenly knew she could trust him to hear her, to know her.

"I don't expect my mother back any time soon, but just in case..." he said, slipping off the bed. He crossed the room and locked the door. On his way back, he stripped off his shirt and belt then sat down on a cane-back chair opposite the bedside table to re-move his shoes and socks. Before standing, he leaned over and unplugged the phone.

Claudie levered to one elbow. "Is that a good idea? What if something happens?"

Bo happened to be looking down, carefully guiding his zipper past the bulge in his pants. When he looked up, he grinned. The pants fell to the floor. "Didn't you hear? There's a blizzard out there. Even the phones are down, and the battery on my cell phone needs recharging.'' The impish glimmer in his eyes made her smile back.

He stripped off his Jockey shorts and walked toward her. ''Besides, Dad's got two worshipful women at his bedside. Don't you think I'm entitled to one?''

''Did we say anything about worshipful?'' she teased.

He gave her a hurt look then shrugged. ''I'd settle for tolerant and forgiving of my middle-aged love handles.''

She looked at his fit, trim midsection and couldn't help from noticing his very erect penis. ''I don't see anything worth complaining about,'' she said. ''In fact, on a scale of one to ten, I'd say you're a twenty.''

His soft chuckle brought a grin to her lips. He stopped to pick up the foil-wrapped condoms that had fallen to the floor. When he looked up, their eyes met. ''You're too kind, but I appreciate that in a woman. Especially when she's the woman I love.''

His words hit her deep. He'd said the words before, but for some reason, it never truly registered at a gut level. This time she felt it—in her gut and below. ''I love you, too, Bo,'' she said, her voice hushed with the power of her emotions. Fear, loss, hope and joy warred within her breast. Her heart beat so fiercely she had to turn on her side and cross her arms to keep the pain from consuming her.

Bo was there in a flash, molding his body into the curved C she formed. His breath against her neck and shoulder was warm and soothing, his body a shield from external forces. But who would protect her from the demons within? Too many memories, so much pain.

"I never wanted to love anyone, Bo," she choked. "Love sucks. It killed my mother. She loved my father and never got over him. It ruined her life. What if—"

His strong arms tightened around her. "I won't let that happen. We'll figure out a way to get past all this bullshit. I know I've been a jerk since we got here, but that's all about me and my old man. Not you, Claudie." He kissed her ear. "You are my one reality."

She believed him, and she trusted him, but could she trust love? She rolled over to face him. "Could we say we're just a little in love?" she asked, trying to make sense of her fear. "For now at least. We could do this—make love, and it won't be like any of the others because we care about each other, right? But the idea of being totally, forever in love, scares me."

He pulled back enough to look into her eyes. He didn't answer right away. Claudie held her breath, wondering if she'd blown it.

"You just love me a little bit?" he asked.

His tone told her how much she'd hurt him. He sounded like Brady. "No," she said, hugging him fiercely. "I love you more than I dare. I love you so much it terrifies me because I have no control over it and I don't want to wind up like my mother."

She felt him relax. He stroked her back in a way that almost made her purr. "You're afraid to love because you think it's what killed your mother." He made her look at him. "Claudie, negative emotions kill people, not positive. Love is what gave her you. How could that be bad?"

Her sudden tears seemed as inappropriate as her

earlier laughter, but Bo held her and kissed her and when the moment passed she found she was still naked and in the arms of the man who loved her and obviously wanted to make love with her. And to her amazement, for the first time in her life she felt ready. Truly ready to make love, too.

IN THE IMMEDIATE aftermath of their lovemaking, Bo felt a high unlike anything he'd ever known. His heart seemed to swell to the size of his chest cavity and that was good. Very good. Claudie's head on his chest, her breath floating across his chest hair felt very right.

But out of nowhere came a voice, a harsh hurtful voice that said he probably totally screwed up not only Claudie's life but also his own. He knew it wasn't true. Anything as wonderful as making love with the woman he'd spent his whole life looking for couldn't be bad, but the old voices knew just where to dig.

What happens if Dad dies? What if he lives? Either way Mom's going to need me. For how long is anybody's guess. But Claudie's life is back in Sacramento. People are depending on her. She needs the validation the halfway house gives her. She deserves to revel in its successes.

"Bo?" her sleepy voice asked, interrupting the chaos in his head. "Is that you in the picture on the mantel? The little boy in a cadet's uniform?"

Bo pushed aside his dark thoughts to bring the photo in question to mind. He smiled ruefully. Grindham Academy. Elite, pretentious, expensive and bleak in every sense of the word except structurally. "You mean the fat kid in the neo-Nazi drum major suit? No. That wasn't me. That was my twin brother Mike. We sold him to the gypsies when he was eleven because he wouldn't even try to learn to play rugby like the other rich kids." He snorted. "I mean, come on, what the hell good was he?"

She was silent a long time and Bo wondered if she'd fallen asleep when she suddenly asked, "Do you ever hear from him?"

"Who?"

"Mike." The way she said the name made him realize she was holding back tears. He didn't want his past to intrude on what they'd just shared so he tried to keep it light.

"Sure. All the time. He's a big used-car dealer down in the Keys. Smuggles a few cigars on the side. Never been married but he's got three kids."

"Do you ever wish you'd been the one they sold?"

Bo closed his eyes against a sudden shaft of pain. It took him a minute to regain the use of his vocal cords. "Why would I? I had it good—three squares, finest education money could buy, enough pocket money to score booze off the doorman. I couldn't complain," he finally said. But in truth, he'd dreamed of running away so often, in a way, a part of him was that imaginary brother living on some balmy Caribbean beach.

She sighed, her breath whispering across his chest. "Maybe we could go visit him someday."

He kissed the top of her head. "Before or after Niagara Falls?"

She lifted her head. "It's your call. He's your brother."

Bo tried to smile but his mouth wouldn't work right. She moved to take his face in her hands, and she told him, "You just gave me something I didn't think I'd ever find—my heart. Maybe someday you'll let me return the favor."

He squeezed his eyes tight and nodded, not trusting himself to speak. With a light sigh, she kissed his lips then sank back down. Bo held his breath, afraid any movement might create a ripple in the calmness. His heart was fine, thank you. As was his libido. His conscience was another matter, but he was just too damn tired to get into that.

Pulling her closer, like a shield, Bo gave in to sleep.

MATT RUBBED the sleep from his eyes and stumbled out of the elevator. It wasn't that late—probably about ten, but he'd fallen asleep watching some lame sitcom and might still have been curled up in his recliner if not for the phone call that jolted him awake.

His mother had been short and to the point. "Robert's being taken into surgery. They need to relieve the pressure in his brain. It's highly risky and we can't reach Bo."

He hadn't bothered arguing with her that if Bo didn't answer the phone it was probably because he was dead to the world and needed his sleep. More than likely the phone lines were down in that part of Manhattan and the cell phone's battery was low. Whatever, Matt knew his duty. As his Jeep negotiated the slippery streets and slush-covered potholes, Matt realized the storm had blown itself out. Stars were visible as moonlit clouds scattered before an icy wind.

Stalled cars, idiot drivers and a couple of impassable streets combined to slow him down. When he reached his aunt's apartment building, he had to use his badge to secure the okay from the building's door-man to leave his car in the loading zone. Stomping snow from his feet, he pushed the doorbell and waited.

When no one answered, he used his fist. "Bo, open up. It's me, Matt."

Concern was starting to build when he finally heard a noise on the other side of the door. "Matt?"

"Claudie. Open up. The phones are down and I need to talk to Bo."

Two locks clicked and he hurried in. To his utter shock, Claudie was standing to one side, wrapped in a blanket—with quite obviously nothing under it. Her hair was tousled, and she had that just-loved look about her.

He felt his cheeks grow hot and he looked down the hall toward Bo's room. "Is he here?" *Well, duh?*

She nodded. "He's asleep. I'll get him."

Matt had to force himself to stare at his boots to keep his eyes off the fetching figure she made tiptoe-ing down the hall. *Angelic* was the word that came to mind.

Bo joined him moments later, zipping his pants as he walked toward the foyer. "What's going on?"

Matt gauged the changes he saw in his cousin's demeanor. More the old Bo than the bitter man of late. Maybe she was an angel, he thought.

"Your dad's having some kind of crisis. Mom didn't go into the details on the phone, but the bottom line is they're taking him into surgery. Sounds touch-and-go. Your phone's out, so they sent me."

Bo swore. He ran a hand through his hair impa-tiently. When he looked at Matt, he said, "I'll be right back."

The bedroom door slammed behind him and Matt walked into the living room. A trail of clothes littered the carpet, but before he could analyze it too deeply Bo returned. "There's no need for both of us to go. I can call a cab."

Matt handed him the keys. "It's stopped snowing but the roads are a mess. There aren't many cabs running. I'll just crash here."

"Okay." Bo took his jacket from the coat closet and felt around in his outer pocket. "Damn," he said, producing his cellular phone. "I meant to plug this in the minute I got home."

He tossed it to Matt. "Take care of it, will you?"

Matt nodded, but Bo had already turned away. "I'd better tell Claudie goodbye. This will probably be an all-nighter. No telling—"

Before he could finish the words, she appeared, wrapped in a too big robe, obviously borrowed from Bo's closet. Barefoot, she dashed to him and threw her arms around him. "Are you sure you don't want me to come with you?"

Bo shook his head.

"Call if you need me, okay?" She kissed him.

Matt looked away. The tender scene hurt. He loved his cousin and was glad he'd found someone to help him through this turbulent time, but a part of him was bitterly jealous.

"Go back to sleep," Bo whispered, kissing her. "I won't call, unless—"

"Call," she ordered sternly. "I won't be able to sleep until I hear."

Bo nodded then took a deep breath and left.

Matt and Claudie stood in silence a moment. He

sighed. ''Well, hell, I'm awake now. Want some ice cream? Aunt Ruth always keeps ice cream in the house.''

CLAUDIE HEARD Matt's question, but it didn't register. She stared at the door, kicking herself for not insisting on going along. Did his refusal to include her signal a reversion to the stranger she'd been seeing for the past two days instead of the tender, caring lover she'd been with an hour earlier?

''Umm, here,'' Matt said, tossing something to her. Claudie reacted instinctively, catching the soft bundle to her chest. Looking down, she saw her sweatpants and flannel shirt. Heat instantly consumed her cheeks.

''You might need these,'' he said. ''The snow stopped, but now it's colder than hell.''

''I suppose it's pretty obvious that we—''

Matt cut her off. ''Bo and I have an agreement. I don't make up stories about my nonexistent sex life and he doesn't tell me about his. If something happened between you two, I'd say it was about time, but I'd really prefer not to talk about it. Envy isn't a pretty emotion.''

She couldn't help but smile. He returned it with a wink then headed for the kitchen. ''I'm a top-notch sundae maker. Wanna risk it?''

Claudie took a deep breath and let it out. ''Okay. I doubt if I can sleep. I'll be right back.''

''Take your time. A perfect sundae is a work of art. It can't be rushed.''

Hugging her bundle of clothes, Claudie returned to Bo's room. The sight of the bed—a jumble of blankets and pillows—made her sigh. She sat down on the side

Bo had occupied and reached beneath the sheets searching for any residual heat. His smell—soap, body talc and something intangible that seemed to define him in her mind—made her flatten her body against the covers.

"You are a treasure chest of wonders," he'd told her. "Glittering gold baubles, sparkling jewels. I feel like the richest man on earth when I'm in your arms."

She'd believed him. How could she not when he took her over the brink of the most glorious feeling her body had ever known? Their connection was too special, too perfect to be anything but love. For the first time in her life, she understood what her mother had felt for her father.

Propelled by an impetus she couldn't name, Claudie pulled on her warm clothes and dashed across the hall to the bathroom where her toiletry bag sat on the marble counter. She fished inside—impatient to find the one tangible link she had with her mother.

"Ah," she sighed, pulling the golden chain from the bag. Claudie faced herself in the mirror as she placed the necklace over her head. "I'm sorry it didn't work out better for you, Mom. I truly am," she whispered.

With that concession came a sense of pity for her stepfather. "Poor Garret," she said, drawing the locket to her cheek. "I'd be bitter, too, if I couldn't—"

Superstitiously, she bit her tongue. Things were too unsettled to predict what would happen between her and Bo. What if his father doesn't make it? she wondered. What if Bo never gets the chance to tell him how he feels?

She couldn't predict what might happen because, despite what they'd shared and how much she loved him, she didn't know him well enough.

With a sigh, she turned off the light and went to find the one person who did know Bo—maybe even better than Bo knew himself.

"How's the art project coming?" she asked, poking her head inside the doorway of the kitchen.

"The bowls are on the coffee table," Matt called back. He was standing in front of the microwave, his back to her. "I decided to make some tea, too. Do you like sugar in yours?"

"No, that's Bo's cup of tea."

Matt snickered, glancing over his shoulder. "I forgot napkins, grab a couple, will you? They're in the buffet by the liquor cabinet."

She took two from the top drawer of a built-in buffet. She wondered if Matt had noticed the mess. She tucked the napkins in the waistband of her sweatpants and hastily cleaned up the spilled whiskey. The smell almost sent her racing for the bathroom.

"Close call?" Matt asked, walking past her with two steaming mugs.

Frowning, she rinsed the rag. "You could say that."

"I've been worried about him the past few days, but I honestly didn't expect him to turn to booze," Matt said conversationally. "Once Bo makes up his mind about something, that's it. I haven't seen him take a drink in ten years."

Claudie joined him at the cozy grouping of overstuffed furniture. Two damask upholstered sofas faced each other while a pair of pale-yellow leather recliners sat side by side facing the fireplace. She took the chair at right angle to Matt.

Claudie laid a napkin beside one giant bowl of ice cream then reached for the bowl Matt had scooted toward her. Art was an understatement. Wavy lines of chocolate syrup drew to mind a child's painting, but strategically placed cherries gave it more a Picasso look. "This is gorgeous."

"Thanks."

She swallowed a bite of ice cream and sighed with pleasure.

Matt cleared his throat then said, "You know, Claudie, Bo's a great guy and I love him like a brother, but he *is* a guy."

"No argument there," she said, unable to keep from grinning.

Matt's swarthy complexion darkened. "What I mean is that's why Bo's been such a jerk lately. He's tweaked about his dad, but he can't talk about it. Guys don't talk about their feelings."

He sounded so sincere Claudie asked, "To each other or to anyone?"

"Pretty much anyone. Used to drive my ex-wife crazy. She was sure I was holding out on her—you know, keeping my inner thoughts private. Truth is, men don't have inner thoughts."

Claudie burst out laughing. "That's not true."

"It is. They might exist, but we're genetically programmed not to hear them."

She almost choked on a cherry. "Baloney. We sell a ton of books at the bookstore about men getting in touch with their feelings. Just because you're a little deaf to those kinds of emotions doesn't mean you can't learn to hear.''

He gave her a horrified look that made her sit back laughing—until the little twinkle in his eye let her know he was putting her on. ''You're just as bad as your cousin,'' she said, taking a sip of tea.

He scraped the last bit of ice cream from his bowl. ''I know. But it's nice to see you smile. It's been awhile.'' He set the bowl down and leaned back. ''This has been a pretty crazy week, huh? First, your family, then Bo's. I guess you could call this trial by fire.''

''I guess.'' Claudie fingered her locket, trying to picture the image of her father. She wondered what her life would have been like if he'd been strong enough to disobey his father and marry her mother.

Suddenly, something Sherry said came back to her. This was her path. If the misery of the past hadn't happened as it did, she wouldn't have known Bo.

Sighing, she looked at the cluster of photos on the mantel. ''Matt, do you know who Mike is?''

''Mike?'' He frowned as if racking his memory banks. ''What's his last name?''

Claudie shook her head and rose. ''Never mind. It's not important. I'm going to try to sleep. Are you staying?''

He nodded. ''Yeah. I'll hang out in case Bo calls.''

Claudie smiled, but deep inside she knew he wouldn't call. He'd shared his love with her but not his demons. And what that meant for their future was anybody's guess.

CHAPTER TWELVE

THE MUTED HUM of a vacuum cleaner shook Claudie out of her dead-to-the-world sleep. She leapt from her bed, confused and a little dazed. The unfamiliar surroundings momentarily brought a burst of panic—*some guy's hotel room,* but the sight of Bo's suitcase with his shaving kit spilled open gave instant relief.

"Whoa," she murmured—the adrenaline in her system slowly dissipating. "I actually slept."

She grabbed the robe she'd used the night before and left the room. Somehow, the normalcy of a vacuum seemed out of place given all that had happened. She and Bo had made love. And it was good. Very good. Claudie couldn't repress the grin that spontaneously blossomed.

Her smile faded when she saw Matt and Ruth standing at the living room window against a backdrop of blue sky. Brilliant sunlight poured across their shoulders. They were speaking in low tones, their body language tense. The vacuum switched off and Ruth turned to say something to the maid. She spotted Claudie.

"Claudie, you're awake. I'm sorry if the vacuum—"

Claudie shook her head, walking forward to join them. "No, that's all right. I didn't mean to sleep so long, but I had a hard time falling asleep last night. Did Bo call?'' she asked Matt.

Matt glanced at Ruth before answering. ''Yes. I told him you were asleep, and he ordered me not to wake you.''

''How's Mr. Lester?''

Ruth reached out to pat Claudie's arm as if she were the one whose husband was in critical condition. ''He came through the surgery fine, but they've got him heavily sedated—a sort of precautionary coma this time. Irene said the doctors are optimistic.''

Claudie's initial relief was tempered by a sense of underlying tension. ''Is Bo at the hospital? I'll grab a shower quick then...''

She started to leave, but Matt's look stopped her. ''What?''

Matt started to speak but Ruth cut him off by reaching out and taking Claudie's arm. ''Would you care for a cup of coffee? There's pastry and fruit in the dining room. Let's go sit down.'' Ruth's smile was so like her son's, Claudie almost hugged her.

''I have some calls to make. I'll join you in a few minutes,'' Matt said, excusing himself.

Claudie watched him walk away. *Something's wrong.*

When they were seated, Ruth handed Claudie a cup filled with dark, fragrant coffee. Claudie sipped the bitter brew then set down the cup and pushed back the wide sleeves of the robe. ''Okay,'' she said, ''tell me what's going on?''

Ruth closed her eyes a moment and sighed. She'd aged since Claudie met her last summer. ''I hate nosy people, Claudie. I've always made every effort not to intrude in other people's lives, particularly my son's. But I don't feel as though I have a choice in this case.''

She drew in a breath, then said, ''Claudie, Bo loves you. And I'm guessing that you love him, too.''

Claudie looked down. Her feelings were too new to share in public. Especially like this.

''I'll take that as a yes,'' Ruth said, her tone gentle. ''And, Claudie, I'm very glad because you've done something no other woman ever has. You've gotten under Bo's skin—touched his vulnerable underbelly.''

''Is that bad?'' she asked, glancing up.

Ruth shook her head. ''No. It's wonderful. You've exposed the Bo that exists beneath all those silly disguises he's so fond of. Have you ever asked yourself why Bo chose to become a policeman and then a private investigator?''

Claudie shook her head.

Ruth made an encompassing motion. ''As you can see, he didn't want for much growing up. He led a very entitled life—the kind of upbringing that usually spawns lawyers and doctors and investment bankers, not private investigators.''

Claudie didn't bother looking—the *old-wealth* opulence had been the first thing to hit her when she'd walked in the door.

Ruth smiled. ''I'm sure you've wondered about that, too. Well, I believe Bo purposely chose a career he thought his father would detest.''

''There's nothing wrong with being in law enforcement,'' Claudie said, although Ruth was right. The thought had crossed her mind.

''Of course not, but Robert B. Lester, God love

him, is a very pretentious person. He was raised that way and truly can't help himself. If it weren't for his amazing intellect and an almost childlike need to be loved, I never would have looked twice at him.''

Claudie didn't want to be rude, but she couldn't help wondering what this had to do with her.

As if reading her thoughts, Ruth said, ''Claudie, dear, the point I'm trying to make is that my son is a smart man, but he's never looked very deeply into what drives him. Bo has a number of issues to deal with where his father is concerned, and I'm afraid he won't do that if you're here.''

Claudie sat back. *She wants me to leave.* ''Have you talked to Bo about this?''

It was Ruth's turn to look away. ''I wanted to speak with you first. If you're determined to stay, I won't stand in your way. As I said…'' She reached out and touched Claudie's hand. ''I want what's best for my son, and I honestly believe you're that person—just not at this moment.''

Is she right? Is my being here keeping Bo from dealing with his problems? Maybe that's what Bo meant when he asked me to leave.

Claudie looked at Ruth's hand still resting on her own. Deep down she knew Bo's mother was right. Hard as it would be, Claudie had to let Bo deal with his own problems first.

She rose. ''I'll call the airport about a ticket. But,'' she looked sadly at Ruth, ''I can't just leave without talking to Bo.''

Ruth nodded in agreement. ''Of course not. Matt's going to the hospital, so he can take you there as soon as you're ready.''

Claudie rose. "I should get organized." She started to step away, but paused and impulsively asked, "Ruth, could I borrow that photograph of Mike, uh, I mean, Bo? The one on the mantel? I'll make a copy and send it back."

Ruth cocked her head, curious no doubt about Claudie's gaff. "Of course, dear. Keep it. I've been trying to give all my photos to Bo for years, but he wouldn't take them."

Claudie started to leave but stopped at the doorway. "I really hope Mr. Lester gets well soon."

"Me, too, dear," Ruth said, softly. "For all our sakes."

Bo LIKED his father's new room. Without the wall of high-tech equipment behind the bed, Bo felt reassured his father's health was improving.

Not that you can tell by looking at him, Bo thought.

Robert was still unconscious. A new bandage had replaced the old. Bigger, but more evenly conformed. His face looked bruised, with dark smudges beneath each eye. His long narrow cheeks were sunken, but the breathing apparatus was gone, as were the many tubes.

The doctors predicted a full recovery—although none would speculate how long that might take. What that meant for him and Claudie—whose lives were in California, Bo didn't have a clue.

Claudie. An image of her, naked in his arms, her breath coming in short, sweet bursts as she climaxed, caught him in the solar plexus.

He'd just talked to his mother and she said Claudie was on her way to the hospital. With any luck they could grab a few private moments in the coffee shop or the chapel. Maybe they could...

The sound of the door opening interrupted his wayward thoughts. And the focus of those thoughts walked in.

"Hi, there, sleepyhead," he said walking to her. Her hair was messy from the breeze and her cheeks still held a kiss of winter. "How are you?"

He started to put his arms around her, but she sidled to the left. She crossed to the window and stood with her back to him. She kept her jacket on, he noticed, despite the locker room heat.

"What's wrong?" he asked, starting toward her.

"Matt's driving me to the airport, Bo. My plane leaves in two hours."

Baffled, Bo shook his head. "What are you talking about?"

She took a deep breath; her hands fluttered nervously. "I called the airport and apparently the Thanksgiving rush has started, plus the storm last night compounded things. The only seat available before Friday leaves in two hours. I...took it."

A panicky sensation made his underarms tingle. "Why?"

Her shoulders lifted and fell.

Bo cleared the distance between them. He put out his hand but didn't touch her. "Claudie, is this because I left so abruptly last night?"

Her eyes flashed in anger. "Of course not. I know what an emergency is. You were...you are needed here. And I have to get back to work. To One Wish House."

Bo threw his hands out. "Now? You're leaving now? Didn't last night change anything?"

She flinched. "For me, it did," she said softly. "I'm not sure what it meant to you."

He blew out a sigh of relief. Jitters he could understand. They'd missed that whole waking up in each other's arms thing. He took her by the shoulders. "If we could find a quiet corner, I'd show you what it meant to me," he said playfully.

She jerked free of his touch. "Bo," she said, sharply. "This is a hospital. That's your father."

"Yeah, I know. Don't remind me. They're starting to decrease his medications. He'll be back on his feet in no time—although it may be a while before he goes skating again."

Bo was watching Claudie's face; he swore he saw a flicker of sadness or regret that reminded him of their time in Kansas. "Claudie, what's this about? Really?"

"I talked to your mother this morning. She's worried about you—your feelings toward your father."

Bo shrugged. "I'm here, aren't I?"

"Yes. And we both know you'll stay as long as your mother needs you, but she thinks having me here will be a distraction."

Bo snickered and pulled her close. "She's right. A beautiful one."

Her sigh warmed his chest, but a shiver passed through his body. Instead of melting against him, she held herself back.

"That's what I was afraid of." She touched his cheek. "Bo, last night was the most wonderful experience of my life. But every moment we're together is one less chance you have to fix this thing between you and your dad.'' She took a breath. "You can't keep putting this off, Bo. I know what I'm talking about."

Bo pulled back. A heavy weight pressed on his chest. He spun on his heel and strode to the window. "This isn't the same as with you and Garret." He gestured toward the figure on the bed. "That man was a lousy father and a pathetic excuse for a husband but he never smacked me around or anything. Hell, half the time he acted as if I didn't exist. Besides, what does that have to do with us? It's ancient history."

"Is it, Bo?" she asked. "I don't think so."

Before he could go to her and take her in his arms, the door opened. Matt popped his head in and looked around. "Claudie, if you want to make that plane, we have to go. Traffic'll be a bear."

She nodded and started to leave, but Bo intercepted her. "Wait. You can't go. Not after last night."

She kept her chin down. "I have to."

The scent of her cologne filled his nostrils, bringing with it a memory of her uninhibited response to his lovemaking. "You can't just leave me, Claudie. Good Lord, woman, I tracked you all over hell to be by your side when you needed me. Now you want to take off like a scared rabbit the minute things get too intense."

"That's not why I'm leaving, and you know it."

He ignored the pain he heard in her plea. "No, I don't. Last night was real, Claudie. Maybe too real for you."

He thought for a moment she might change her mind, but instead she reached up and removed her locket. She held it out to him.

Bo kept his fists tightly clenched at his sides, but she reached down and took his hand in hers. "Open," she ordered.

When his fingers unfurled, the gold chain spilled into his palm. The locket felt warm and heavy. His heart lifted and fell. His sinuses prickled from the emotion churning within.

"I'm trusting you with my heart," she said, rising up on her toes to press a quick kiss to his numb lips. Then she left.

Blinking at tears that refused to go away, he closed his fist around the talisman. He clasped it to his chest, as a racking pain drew out a long groan.

A noise made him look up. His father's eyes were open and he seemed to be staring at Bo.

Bitterness rose up like bile and Bo growled, "Are you satisfied now? You weren't content to ruin the first forty years of my life, you had to screw this up, too."

Bo WAS SITTING AT THE FOOT of the bed dully threading Claudie's necklace between his fingers when his mother walked into the room.

"She's gone," he said flatly.

Ruth took off her coat, laying it neatly over the back of a chair. "Yes, I know. Matt took her to the airport. Both Matt and Claudie care a great deal about your welfare. You know that, don't you?"

He shrugged, not really listening.

"Robert B. Lester, Junior," his mother said sharply. Bo so rarely heard that tone of voice he almost jumped to attention. "I'd appreciate it if you'd listen when I'm talking to you."

Bo called that her librarian's voice. "I'm sorry," he apologized. "What did you say?"

She pulled up a chair beside the bed and sat down. "Do you remember when your Grandmother Lester passed away?"

Bo shook his head. "No, I can't say as I do."

"Pity. It might have helped you deal with this."

Puzzled, Bo looked at her. "Why?"

"Your father acted the same way you're acting right now. He pushed me away when I tried to help him. It wasn't six months later that he had his first affair."

Bo gaped. "You knew about it?"

She gave him a droll look. "Just in case you're ever tempted to cheat on Claudie, let me tell you—the wife is *not* the last to know. Not if she's paying attention."

Bo couldn't have been more stunned if his father suddenly jumped up and started dancing a jig. "I don't get it. Why'd you stay with him all these years?"

Ruth sighed and looked at the man in question. "I loved him, son. I still do. The heart doesn't always listen to what the head says."

Bo knew that for a fact. His head had been telling him for years that he hated his old man, but here he was—waiting, hoping, caring. He couldn't say for sure what he expected once his dad opened his eyes— they'd been strangers to each other for years.

"Who's Mike?" his mother asked.

Bo's nerves scattered like quail. "What?"

"You heard me. Claudie asked if she could take Mike's picture with her when she left. It was a slip, but it made me wonder."

Bo smiled. "It's nothing. We were joking around."

He could tell by her look anything short of the truth wasn't going to fly. "I was kinda chubby in that picture, and she couldn't believe it was me, so I told her it was really my twin brother, Mike." Talking about Claudie and last night brought him perilously close to panic. *She's gone.*

"I always regretted that we couldn't have more children," his mother said wistfully. "I think it would have made your childhood so much easier. Growing up the way you did probably made you feel like a bug under a microscope."

He lifted one shoulder. "It wasn't so bad, Mom."

"No, but it wasn't so good in some ways. I remember the day you were born. Your father was so proud. He called a buddy of his at the Times and asked for a whole column to announce your birth."

Bo snorted skeptically.

Ruth sighed. "Bo, your father and I both made mistakes. In our marriage and with you."

"You've been a great mom."

She reached out and patted his hand while shaking her head. "I've always been more comfortable around books than people, but your father thrived on public attention. Sometimes I wonder if I acted out of pure selfishness. When he wasn't around, I was free to read, to study, to escape into my books. Perhaps, I'm the one who was unfaithful first."

Bo was stunned by her confession. "Mom, it's not the same..."

She cut him off with a sharp gesture. "Yes, it is. If you love someone, you try to meet their needs, and you hope they'll meet yours. If you don't meet them halfway, you have no right to expect them to be there when you're ready."

Her words sounded ominous, a portent of the disaster he'd created in his own love life. Claudie had tried to help him in the way she thought best, and he'd yelled at her. Accused her of being a coward.

When he started to rise, Claudie's locket slid to the stark white blanket. Claudie's mother's locket—the most precious thing she owned.

"She gave me her heart," he whispered—his voice cracking.

"So you could find your way home to her," his mother said softly.

Blinking at tears that refused to go away, he closed his fist around the talisman. He clasped it to his chest, as a racking pain drew out a long groan. His mother enveloped him in her arms. "It's okay, baby. Everything will be okay."

MIDWAY THROUGH the movie she wasn't watching, Claudie grabbed the glossy in-flight magazine from the seat pocket in front of her and flipped through it searching for a map. She used her right index finger to mark New York, then traced one of the myriad lines to San Francisco.

If this is us, we fly right over Kansas.

As discreetly as possible she opened the plastic window shade beside her. She was tucked in a corner and no one grumbled when she opened it so she guessed she was safe. Pressing her nose to the window she peered below. Nothing but a gray blur. Either they were too high or low-level clouds were blocking her view.

With a sigh, she closed the shade. She felt restless,

yet lethargic. Anxious and tense, but numb. She couldn't identify her problem. *Lonely? Lost?*

People without family or friends were lost. But she had both—somewhere a mile or so below her.

Impulsively, she reached out and took the phone attached to the seat ahead of her out of its plastic receptacle. She dug in her purse for her credit card, then followed the instructions to place a call. This would cost her a fortune, but she didn't care. She found the number she'd tucked in a secret pocket of her billfold and punched in the sequence.

The voice that came on the line was so clear Claudie almost dropped the phone. "Sherry?"

There was a pause. "Yes. Who's this?"

Claudie's mouth went dry. "It's me. Claudie."

Her sister's loud wail seemed to echo in the cabin. "Thank the Lord. He heard my prayers."

Claudie blinked in confusion. "What?"

"I was just praying you'd call. We had a really bad night last night and I'm home alone and I was feeling really blue and—"

Claudie could hear her sadness. "What happened?" *Boyfriend troubles?*

"We had to take Daddy to the hospital. He was in a lot of pain the past few days, but he wouldn't go to the doctor. Finally, it was just so bad I started crying and he gave in."

Claudie's stomach twisted. "What do the doctors say?"

Her sister's voice became soft and childlike. "They've contacted the hospice, Claudie. I just came home for his Bible. We left in such a rush last night, we forgot it."

Claudie heard her start to cry. "Oh, honey, I'm sorry. I'm probably pretty close to you right now. I'm in a plane on my way home. Do you think they'd care if I opened a door and jumped out? Maybe I'd land on your house."

Her silliness brought a giggle on the other end of the phone. "I'd catch you in my butterfly net. Daddy and I used to catch all kinds of bugs and butterflies for my entomology studies. I always caught the prettiest ones."

Claudie swallowed against the lump in her throat. "Sherry, I'm sorry Garret's taken a turn for the worse. Give him my...tell him I..." She didn't know what to say. It was too soon.

Sherry rescued her. "I'll tell him you called. It will make his day."

Claudie's eyes filled with tears. "I'll call again as soon as I'm home."

They exchanged a few more words then Claudie hung up the phone. She peeked out the window again. The man she thought she hated was dying, and she felt like crying. The man she loved was half a continent away.

Claudie glanced at the movie screen and saw the beautiful leading lady in full bridal regalia kiss her groom. If she'd had anything in her hand, she'd have thrown it. Happy endings were for movies and romance novels. Real life was a whole different story.

CHAPTER THIRTEEN

"CLAUDIE," A VOICE CALLED the instant she stepped into the terminal of the Sacramento airport.

Totally unprepared for a greeting party, it took Claudie a few seconds to pinpoint the sound. Sara and Brady rushed to meet her.

Brady barreled into Claudie, nearly knocking her over. She scooped him up.

"Oh, Brady-boy, I missed you so much," she cried, emotion choking her almost as much as Brady's arms around her neck.

A moment later, he wiggled free, and she set him down. He rattled off something too fast for her to catch then beamed at his mother expectantly.

"He wants to know if you'll read to him tonight. He missed you. We all did," Sara said, giving Claudie a warm hug.

Claudie's heart expanded but she still couldn't figure out how Sara knew to meet her plane. Had Bo called?

As if reading her mind, Sara said, "Matt called. He was worried about you. He sounds like a nice guy. Brady..." Distracted, she dashed after the little tyke. "Let's get your bags. We can talk in the car."

Brady was asleep before they hit I-5. Claudie couldn't keep from smiling at his cherubic face. She definitely wanted children. She hoped Bo felt the same way. *If he was still speaking to her that is…*

"Could I use your cell phone?" she asked, suddenly desperate to hear his voice. "I should let Bo know I got home safely."

"Sorry. It's in the diaper bag which I left at Babe's," Sara said. "Do you want to stop somewhere or can you wait until we get home?"

"Sure. No problem."

Sara gave her a sidelong look. "Well, something's wrong. Did you and Bo have a fight? Is that why he isn't with you?"

Claudie regretted not spending more time preparing an answer to that question instead of spending most of the flight second-guessing her decision to leave. "Bo's mom and I talked about it and we decided he needed to spend some time alone with his dad."

Sara made a face. "How'd Bo take that?"

A fluttery sensation akin to panic made Claudie reach for her locket—her touchstone. But it was gone. Her one tangible proof of her journey. Then she remembered something. She fished in her purse for the little disposable camera. She'd used the last shot to get a picture of Matt at the airport. "Sara, could we drop this off at the one hour photo place on the way home?"

"Sure," Sara said. "And Ren can pick them up when he gets done with class. When I told him you were coming home, he insisted on a welcome home party. A little barbecue. Then a dip in the hot tub. Okay?"

Soothing water and a glass of wine sounded tempt-

ing. So did the idea of talking to Ren. Who better than
Bo's best friend to tell her if she did the right thing?

ON THE FOLLOWING THURSDAY, as the residents of
One Wish House were preparing to join the Bishops
for Thanksgiving dinner, Claudie ducked into her office. She sat down at her desk and picked up the hand-
made Thank You card that had been waiting on her
desk when she got home Monday night. Beside it,
Claudie's photos lay scattered, including the three
shots of Sherry that made Claudie's heart soar.

"You saved her," Maya said softly, taking Claudie
by surprise. She hadn't heard her approach. "I knew
you would."

Davina and Sally Rae joined them before Claudie
could respond.

"She's so beautiful. And tall. Are you sure she's
your sister?" Davina asked.

"Did she like you?" Sally Rae asked. "I mean, you
know, did you tell her about …" Her expressive complexion turned bright red.

"What I want to know is why'd you have to give
her your car?" Rochell complained, sweeping into the
room in an impressive African caftan. "How're ya
gonna get around?"

Claudie chuckled. "I didn't actually rescue Sherry.
I told you—my stepdad's dying of cancer. They're
moving him to a hospice Saturday."

The low cheers were meant to be supportive, but
Claudie was saddened by the image of Garret that
came to mind. "The important thing is Sherry's great,
and I gave her my car because my mother left me
enough money to buy a new one. I'm going to start

looking as soon as Bo—'' she bit off the thought. ''As soon as we get past this dim sum thing.''

This, of course, set them all off on their favorite topic, but Claudie held up her hand for silence. ''Let me finish. As to whether or not Sherry really is my sister—yes. She has our mother's eyes and smile. And, Sally Rae, she's going to come visit after graduation. I can't wait to introduce her to all of you.''

Claudie had received two e-mails from Sherry— including an update on Garret's condition and had forwarded both to Val, hoping to reconnect those two. And Claudie planned to keep in touch with her brothers, too. Particularly, Zach. In fact, she hoped to talk to Ren today about Zach's postprison options.

Ren had already helped Claudie by giving her some perspective about Bo's situation. ''One thing I know,'' he'd told her that night in the hot tub ''is, no matter how much you love a person, *you* can't fix him. Ultimately, that has to come from within. Give him time, Claudie. He'll understand that you did what you thought was best for him.''

Claudie hoped so. But so far, he hadn't returned any of her calls.

Something Sally Rae was saying suddenly sank into Claudie's consciousness. ''Wait. Did you say Babe has a date?''

Sally's blush returned. ''I overheard her on the phone. She said it isn't really a date. He's an old friend, and he asked Babe to help his church serve Thanksgiving dinner to the needy, so they're only coming to Ren and Sara's for pie.''

Rochell hooted and rolled her eyes. ''I swear all this do-gooder stuff is going to come back and bite her in the butt. Rich people can't mingle with us common folk for long without something bad happening."

Claudie would have argued the point, but Sally beat her to it. "Hogwash. Money sets people apart, but a good heart can overcome that. Babe told me her father was a grape farmer, Rochell. She was the Grape Queen before she met Ren's dad. And I'll tell you a secret, but you have to promise not to tell her I blabbed."

The room fell silent.

"Babe's real name is Beulah. Beulah May Smith."

Rochell's gaze met Claudie's. "My grandma's name was Beulah."

"My father's name was Smith," Claudie said softly.

On the way to the airport Matt had handed her a computer printout with a name and a bunch of dates on it. "I know this isn't any of my business," he'd said apologetically. "But it's what I do."

Claudie smiled picturing that paper. Her father's name was John Lowell Smith. Knowing that meant more to her than she ever could have imagined. Sadly, the one person who would most appreciate the significance of it wasn't speaking to her.

A car horn sounded in the driveway. Everyone scattered to collect last minute items to take to the feast. Claudie hurried, too, but she'd have been more thankful if Bo would have called that morning.

Maybe he'll call Sara's, she thought trying to smile. Maybe.

THE SMELL OF roasted turkey warred with the antiseptic smell of the hospital room. Matt had dutifully carted three plates loaded with all the traditional Thanksgiving fixings to the hospital to share with Bo and his mother. Bo's father was on a restricted diet and showed no real interest in food. In truth, Robert showed no interest in life, and Bo found his meager supply of compassion sliding beneath an overwhelming sense of frustration.

"Your mother is the best cook in the world," Ruth told Matt, wiping the corner of her mouth with a floral napkin. "I love her yams."

Matt smiled. "That's what Ashley said when she found out she wasn't having dinner at my mom's."

Bo thought Matt looked inordinately pleased by that. "Is she at Sonya's parents' today?"

Matt shook his head. "Alan's mother's place in Connecticut. I just talked to her on the phone. She said there are a million little kids around but nobody her age, so she's bored out of her mind."

Bo eyed him thoughtfully. "Tough break. Guess she'll look forward to next year with you, right?"

Gnawing on a drumstick, Matt nodded grinning.

Bo's low chuckle was interrupted by a sharp, unintelligible outburst from his father. The first time Robert had tried to make himself understood, only meaningless sounds had burst forth—guttural and strange. Irene explained that this was common for a man whose brain had suffered such an extreme trauma, but the knowledge made it no less unnerving.

Bo rose from the corner table where they were eating and walked to the bed. "Awake? Good. I think they have pureed turkey for you today. I'll call the nurse." Bo realized his formal tone probably sounded phony, but he didn't have the first clue how to talk to this man—a stranger in his father's body.

He started to turn away, but his father suddenly grabbed Bo's hand in a grip far stronger than Bo would have imagined. "Whoa, somebody's been pressing iron when our backs were turned." He leaned toward his father. "What can I get you, Dad?"

"Scotch."

The clarity, as much as the word itself, took him aback. "Mother, did you hear that?"

Ruth and Matt joined him. Bo felt his father's grip lessen. "He answered my question. He wants a drink."

Ruth frowned. "That's not possible, dear. You're on a lot of medication."

Robert's eyes closed. His fingers went slack.

"I don't think he was serious, Mom," Bo said. "But he sure got our attention."

She pressed a kiss to her husband's slack lips then said, "I've made up my mind. Tomorrow we start looking into rehab centers."

Bo was shocked. They'd discussed the timing of this decision at great length but not in front of his father. "Matthew, you may start moving into Robert's loft tonight, if you wish."

"Are you sure Uncle Robert's going to be okay with that?" Matt asked, eyeing Bo's father nervously.

Ruth patted her husband's shoulder and smiled. "It's for the best. We're both too old for any more nonsense, and the location will be perfect for your new office."

Bo agreed wholeheartedly. "It'll be great, Matt," Bo said. The disposition of his father's apartment had been bothering him until his mother suggested renting it to Matt. There was still the matter of boxing up his father's personal items, but at least this relieved Bo of having to find a renter.

They returned to the table and sat down to finish their meal.

"I don't have to move in right away," Matt said, taking a bite of mashed potatoes. "I could wait until after the first of the year."

"The sooner the better as far as I'm concerned," Ruth said. "Once we get Robert settled, Bo will be free to return to California. And Claudie."

Bo rubbed his thumb across the bump in his pants pocket. Her locket. The one tangible reminder of their night together. The longer they were apart, the less real their time together seemed.

Matt pushed his plate away and crumpled his paper napkin on top of it. "I guess you're right. I'll go home and start packing." He rose. "If you're not too tired, Cuz, stop by and give me a hand. Or are you going out to my mom's, too?"

It had been decided that Ruth would spend the night with her sister-in-law. Bo planned to stay until his father was asleep for the night then go back to the apartment. "Mom? Is it too late to change my mind and go with you?" he teased.

Matt gave him a light poke on the shoulder. "Don't come empty-handed. Bring boxes."

Once he left, Bo and his mother ate in silence until she said, "How's Claudie?"

A bite of stuffing lodged in his windpipe. "Umm...I haven't actually talked to her."

Ruth's brow rose. "And why is that? It's been three days."

Bo let out a raspy sigh. "I...don't know what to say."

She snorted. "I doubt that very much. You're the product of two people who never shut up. Robert once said the thing that kept us married so long was our ongoing dialogue—and the fact neither of us listened to a word the other one said."

Bo chuckled, but his smile faded when she gave him a stern look. "Call her. Now. Wish her a Happy Thanksgiving and tell her you miss her." She stood up. "Enough nagging. You'll pick me up at Irene's in the morning, right? The first rehab place I want to visit is on Long Island."

Bo was dreading that almost as much as calling Claudie. What could he say? I'm sorry? For what? For having a father like his? That went without saying.

After his mother left, Bo rose and stretched, stiff from so much inactivity. He glanced at his watch and subtracted three hours. "So, whatcha doin', Claudie girl?" he said aloud, drawing her image into his mind. "Just sitting down to eat?"

A moment later a voice said gruffly, "Crazy. Talk. Self."

Bo spun to face the bed. "God!"

His father shook his head. "Dad."

Bo laughed. He couldn't help himself. The shock of hearing his father speak rivaled the realization he'd just laughed out loud at something his father said—a miracle that hadn't taken place in twenty years.

Bo stepped closer. "Must have been that turkey juice they gave you. You look better."

Robert closed his eyes and breathed in. On the exhale he said, "Still want drink."

Chuckling, Bo walked to the moveable bed stand and poured some ice water into a plastic cup. "Here you go. Whisky and water. Light on the whiskey."

Feeling awkward, he put one hand behind his father's bony neck and helped guide him to the glass. A trickle made it past Robert's flaccid lips. Excess drops fled down his cheek, getting caught in the bristly white stubble. When Robert closed his lips to indicate he was finished, Bo gently placed his father's head back on the pillow and used a towel to wipe up the spills.

"Not bad," Robert said.

Bo placed the cup on the tray and moved back, resting his hip on the bed near his father's thigh. "Mom and I are going to look at a couple of extended-care facilities tomorrow," Bo said, feeling a need to say something.

Robert's eyes flew open, a look of panic visible in his gray green irises.

"It's temporary, Dad. Just until you can walk and talk again. One of the places has a hydro pool and offers Swedish massage. I'll ask to meet the massage therapists. I know you prefer tall, buxom and blond." Bo tried to keep his tone light, but even to his ears it sounded snide.

As his father's breathing evened off, Bo picked up his coat and left. He planned to call a cab from the lobby, but once he picked up the receiver he made the impulsive decision to call Claudie. His mother was right. He was making a bad problem worse. He knew she made it home safely because she'd called his mother's and left a message on the machine. He'd played it a dozen times, alternating it with the recording he'd saved from his office.

"Twisted," Matt had said, catching him in the act. "Severely twisted. Maybe that old lady you told me about on the plane was right. Maybe you are a stalker."

"Shut up."

"You know, you deserve it if Claudie never talks to you again. Notice she called your mother, not your cell phone."

"You have my cell phone," Bo pointed out.

"She hasn't called it."

"I only have your word on that. Aren't you supposed to be picking up your daughter from her riding practice?" he'd snarled, hating the way Matt could provoke him. Matt was even more annoying than Ren.

Matt had left, but the disquiet his observations raised lingered.

Bo punched in his memorized calling card code, then Ren and Sara's number. He knew from Ren's call that Claudie and the girls from One Wish House were spending the day with the Bishops.

"Happy Thanksgiving," a deep masculine voice answered.

"Yeah, whatever," Bo returned.

"Hey, Bo, what's happening?"

"Not much. Is Claudie around?"

His attempt to sound casual came off as cool as a teen asking for his first date.

"Nope. She's not here. After we finished eating, Claudie and the others offered to take Brady to rent a movie."

"Damn."

"Can I have her call you back?"

Bo sighed. "I'm helping Matt move into my dad's loft tonight. We'll be in and out. And my mom took my cell phone in case the hospital calls."

Ren was silent a minute then said, "You know, Bo, this is none of my business, but Claudie was trying to do the right thing by giving you time alone with your dad. How's he doing, by the way?"

Bo briefed his friend on his father's progress, ending with, "He seemed more like his old self tonight." Then trying for levity, added, "I guess that personality transplant thing is still in the experimental stages."

Ren's laugh sounded good, but it made Bo homesick. He missed his friends. He missed Brady. He missed Claudie.

Bo's gut churned. "Do you know where she'll be tomorrow?"

"She and Sara are going to be at the bookstore all day because Daniel's skiing in Utah. You know how busy the day after Thanksgiving is for retailers. It's the start of the Christmas rush."

Damn! Just what I need—another lousy holiday to add to the equation.

"Just tell her I called. Monday I'm getting a second cell phone for Matt, so she can call my number if she wants to get hold of me."

Bo hung up feeling more conflicted than ever. His mother needed him, and for the first time in Bo's life his father needed him; but he needed Claudie—who was back where she belonged.

STILL A BLOCK from the video store, Claudie squeezed the little hand she held, smiling down at the curly crown of the child walking beside her. She'd missed Brady so much when she was gone, but it hardly compared to what she was feeling at this moment for Bo. His presence had been glaringly absent from the long, festive dinner table in Sara and Ren's recently remodeled dining room.

Claudie thought she was doing a good job hiding her true feelings until Sara cornered her in the kitchen. "We miss him, too, Claudie. But Ren says Bo's father's prognosis is good. Bo will be home in no time," she'd whispered. Nearby, Maya and Sally Rae were mashing potatoes—a joint effort since neither seemed too familiar with the process.

"I know," Claudie had tried assuring her. "I'm fine."

"Yeah, right. Me, too. Except I'm pregnant and you're miserable."

Claudie had patted her friend's rounded tummy. "How are my godchildren?"

"Bo's kid is great. Yours is only so-so."

Claudie knew Sara was joking, but she blanched at the thought that something was wrong with one of the twins—babies she and Bo felt they'd had a hand in conceiving. After all, Ren never would have met Sara without Bo's investigative skills, and Sara wouldn't have moved in with Ren without Claudie as a chaperon. Close to tears, Claudie had grabbed a napkin just before Sara scooted her out the patio door.

Claudie refocused on the present when Rochell ushered them into the brightly lit video store. She absently picked up a video.

"Claudie?" Brady asked, tugging on the leg of her khaki slacks to get her attention. "For me?"

She glanced at the four other women who were looking at her expectantly. Claudie looked down and saw she was holding a movie. She hadn't even realized she'd picked one out. When she read the title, she laughed. "I guess this will do. What do you think, ladies?"

She held up the box with its highly recognizable title.

Maya gave an inscrutable shrug.

Sally Rae sighed wistfully and said, "I used to watch that with my big brother. He always reminded me of the cowardly lion." She frowned. "He got hit by a car and died when I was fourteen."

"Let's get it," Davina said with enthusiasm. "I never got to watch the whole thing. Ever."

Only Rochell gave it a thumbs-down. "Those flying monkeys give me the creeps," she muttered.

While Sally Rae took Brady up to the counter to pay for *The Wizard of Oz*, Rochell hunted for a second—more *adult*—selection. As she waited, Claudie resurrected a memory of lying elbow to elbow on the floor in front of the television with her siblings while Dorothy skipped down the Yellow Brick Road toward Oz. Claudie didn't know if the image was real or imagined, but she could vividly picture Garret and her mother on the sofa, holding hands. Kissing.

"The past speaks to you," Maya said quietly.

Claudie didn't dismiss her observation. She'd sensed the older woman's concern since her return. "Not everything was bad. There were good times, too, but I guess those memories got lost in the pain."

"You wish to go back again? Be a family once more?"

I'd like to spend time with Sherry...and Zach. I'm sorry Garret's sick, but... Before Claudie could formulate an answer, Brady ran up to her and grabbed her hand.

"Home, Claudie?" he asked, his blue eyes glittering with love and affection.

Claudie blinked back her sudden tears. She picked him up and squeezed him tight. Settling him on her hip, she followed the others out the door. Maya brought up the rear. Over her shoulder, Claudie softly called, "This may not be Kansas, Maya, but it *is* home."

CHAPTER FOURTEEN

RESTLESS AND TENSE, Bo prowled the confines of his father's new room at the Pennington Institute, an extended-care facility renowned for treating all kinds of neurological-motor disabilities. His father was going through an in-processing evaluation; Matt and Ruth would be along soon with Robert's personal items and clothing.

Tricia had appeared at the hospital that morning to tearfully announce that the whole situation was "too intense" for her. For some reason, her brief, awkward goodbye had left Bo feeling more unnerved than he cared to admit.

For the first time in his life Bo understood the frustration of wanting to be in two places at the same time. He was needed here—his parents needed his help and business-wise no one else could get the ball rolling with Matt—but Bo wanted to be with Claudie.

And she would have been here if not for her misguided belief about his needing to fix things with his father. *The past is ancient history* he'd told his mother. And Bo meant it—except when he looked at his father. Then all the old hurts had a way of zapping him.

He'd tried to discuss his feelings with Claudie. Unfortunately, long distance phone calls did little to promote empathy. For one thing, it had taken half a dozen attempts to finally connect with her. His first try on the Saturday after Thanksgiving had ended in a shouting match with Rochell, whom he'd woken up at seven in the morning.

"You've been off the streets for months, Rochell. Aren't you acclimated to a new schedule, yet?"

"I'll give you acclimation, Mr. High and Mighty," she'd countered with a growl. "Aren't you the fool who raced off to find the woman he loves only to send her back with her tail between her legs like a whipped pup?"

Her graphic metaphor almost made him lose his breakfast. "You don't know anything about it, Rochell. Let me talk to Claudie."

"Not before I tell you why she oughta dump your ass." Rochell made it to number six on her list—All men suck—when she finally admitted that Claudie and Sally Rae had started a new exercise program and were out jogging.

Bo finally caught up with Claudie at the bookstore later in the afternoon, but his timing was off there, too. Sara had just left and Claudie was swamped with customers. She'd promised to return his call that night—which according to the answering machine she'd done while Bo was packing up his father's belongings at the loft.

The three-hour time difference seemed to conspire against him no matter when he called. Either she was running errands or attending a city council meeting with Babe Bishop or giving an interview to a reporter about the upcoming fund-raiser. To her credit, Claudie never failed to call back. Her voice on his mother's answering machine was like candy—sweet little morsels that whet his appetite for something more substantial.

Even getting back his cell phone hadn't helped. He was out of the loop. On those rare times he'd managed to catch Claudie, she'd sounded distracted, overwhelmed by the last-minute details involved with hosting what had become a large-scale fund-raising event.

Bo sat on the edge of the bed and pictured his conversation with Claudie the night before. Even three thousand miles apart he could hear her fatigue. "You sound wiped out."

Her sigh was very un-Claudie. "I thought it was jet lag, but Maya calls it 'life lag.' Everything is catching up with me. Plus I'm worried about Sherry and Garret. I told you he's in hospice care, didn't I?"

Bo didn't want to think about Kansas...or New York. He only wanted to hold Claudie and feel her cuddle against him in her shy, sweet way. "You have too many irons in the fire. If I were there to be a buffer, they'd have to come through me to get to you."

"Any idea when you're coming back?" she asked. Before he could answer, she'd added, "Not that I'm trying to be pushy. I know this is really, really hard for you."

He sighed. He had a few too many irons of his own. "I'm shooting for Saturday, but I can't promise anything."

"I wasn't asking for promises," she said testily. "I was just curious."

They were both silent a moment then Claudie told him. "I'm covering for Daniel on Friday and Saturday. The dim sum thing is Sunday. Then I'm off Monday through Thursday—if I survive.''

"Do you need a place to hide out?'' Bo suggested, wondering if they'd ever get back to the easy repartee they shared in Kansas. "I happen to know where you could find a quaint—some might say, charming—houseboat on the delta.''

Her long pause had been enough to make him twist the phone cord into a knot. "I promised Sara we'd go Christmas shopping in the city next week—maybe even stay over. And I have to start looking for a new car, too.''

Her excuses confirmed Bo's fears. "You're really mad at me, aren't you? For the way I acted when you left. Especially after the night we shared.''

"No. Of course not,'' she said quickly, too quickly. "I'm a big girl, Bo. I knew what I was doing and I'm not trying to hold you to anything. What happened that night was just one of those things.''

"No, it wasn't.'' He couldn't prevent the desperate edge in his tone. "Claudie, tell me you don't believe that. I love you. You know that, don't you? This stuff between me and my dad doesn't have anything to do with us.''

Bo listened to her breathing; it seemed to catch in her throat. Before he could say anything else, she said, "I'm really wiped out, Bo. Can we finish this later?''

"Sure,'' he said, grimacing at the despondency he heard in her voice. "I miss you, Claudie. I love you.''

He wasn't certain she heard since the only answer was the echo of her yawn. "Good luck tomorrow,'' she said. "Bye, Bo.''

A noise at the door made him jump to his feet. Two

orderlies pushed a wheelchair into the room. It had taken Bo a while to get used to seeing his father in a wheelchair. A strap around his chest kept Robert upright, but his head lolled weakly to one side.

Even at a distance Bo could tell Robert was exhausted. The gray shadows beneath his eyes seemed far more pronounced. Bo hurried forward to help. One attendant removed Robert's leather slippers while the other unfastened the chest strap and worked Robert's striped silk robe over his shoulders. Bo turned down the burgundy print bedspread while the men swiftly, effortlessly transferred Robert's unresponsive body to the bed.

"Thanks," Bo said, taking the robe from the taller of the two. He hung it in the closet. "We appreciate your help."

"No problem," the man said. "I'm Jake and this is Francisco. Any time your dad needs something, just give us a holler."

Francisco parked the wheelchair to the right of the bed and they left. Bo stepped to his father's side. The bed, while as functional as a standard hospital bed, was lower, more discreet. The room itself was large and light. In addition to the recliner and armoire, there was a small settee and a coffee table.

Before the movers had arrived at Robert's loft apartment, Ruth had chosen a few of his favorite things she hoped would make the place more homelike. But Bo doubted the Baccarat vase and the couple of Boucher drawings would do the trick.

He checked his watch. Matt and his mother should arrive soon. "Not stay here," Robert said, suddenly.

The lack of inflection in his father's voice still bothered Bo. All words were delivered in a robotlike cadence, emotionless—sometimes clear, sometimes garbled.

Bo noticed his father's fists clenched at his sides.

"Sorry, Dad," Bo said, trying to sound sympathetic, "but you don't have a choice. This place comes highly recommended. I'm sure you'll do fine here."

The answer must not have been what Robert wanted to hear. His eyes closed, fingers relaxed. These mercurial mood swings threw Bo for a loop, too. His father had always had only one mood—serious.

Bo studied his father's face. Daily physical therapy had helped him regain some color. Although Robert still lacked most fine motor skills, the therapists had been impressed with his recuperative powers.

Bo looked up as a nurse entered the room. She carried a small tray with three tiny plastic cups.

"Good afternoon, gentlemen. Welcome to Pennington," she said, smiling to include Bo as well. Small, dark and in her midfifties—her accent sounded Philippine. She moved with quick, economic motions. "I've got some medications for you, Mr. Lester."

Without warning, Robert's arm swung wildly and caught her just below the shoulder. The tray crashed to the floor. She would have fallen, if Bo hadn't reached out to steady her.

"Sorry," Bo said.

Her look held no malice. "It's okay. Patients are often upset and confused when they first arrive." She kneeled to pick up the pills. "I'll try this again a little later. We can always go back to an IV if he doesn't settle down."

Robert's eyes were closed giving no indication

whether or not he heard her, but once she was gone, Bo saw his father unclench his fist.

"I remember you telling me once that a bad attitude was no excuse for abusing the help," Bo said softly.

"Hangover," Robert said, taking Bo by surprise.

"I beg your pardon?"

"Bad hangover."

When it dawned on him what his father meant, Bo couldn't keep from grinning. "You're right. You did say 'hangover,' not 'attitude.' But in my case, the two were practically interchangeable."

His father let out a deep sigh. Bo knew that sound: exasperation—a signal Robert was ready to throw up his hands and stalk away from whatever argument they were in the midst of.

This time Bo did the walking. He picked up a large, lush hothouse plant—a gift from Sara and Ren that had just arrived—and carried it to the window.

"Carmen," his father barked, almost making Bo drop the plant.

Bo placed the container on the sill and walked back to the bed. Bo didn't know anyone by that name but the fact his father was calling out for someone other than his mother infuriated him.

Before he could respond, his father spoke again. "Serves right."

Serves right? "I get it," Bo exclaimed. "You mean karma, not Carmen. You think this is payback for what you've done in your life."

Robert's head nodded fractionally. When he opened his eyes, there were tears. Not the tears of frustration that Bo had seen off and on all week. Tears of anguish. And fear. The kind of fear that awaited the less-than-righteous on judgment day.

Something twisted in Bo's gut. His first impulse was to turn around and walk out, but he couldn't make himself go. Instead, he stepped closer and put his hand on his father's shoulder. "Dad, that's not how it works. I think you have to die first, then you come back as an anteater or something."

Bo regretted his flippant answer when Robert's chest heaved with silent sobs. Tears ran into his pillow. Bo's fingers squeezed. "Dad, what happened was an accident. This place is going to help you get your life back. That's a good thing, right?"

Bo sensed his father struggling to speak, but was obviously hampered not only by his physical disabilities but his emotions. "Bad...father," he finally spewed out.

A flood of emotion cascaded over Bo. He pictured Claudie facing Garret—the man who'd robbed her of her self-worth. What had Robert done so wrong by comparison? Worked too hard? Been self-absorbed and demanding? Failed to keep his loved ones close?

Bo lowered his head and looked into his father's eyes. "Yeah," he said softly. "You were a lousy father...at times. But, believe it or not, I think I always knew deep down that you loved me."

Something in his father's eyes changed. Hope tempered by caution. "Always," he whispered.

Bo's heart swelled with emotion. He blinked back tears of his own. "I remember telling Ren Bishop one time that no matter what a bastard you were, I could count on you for anything. Was I right?"

Robert nodded.

"Then prove it."

"How?"

Bo pulled up the wheelchair and sat down. He rested his elbows on the mattress and said, "Get well. Soon."

His father's left brow rose—a semblance of his old self.

Bo suppressed a grin. "I don't know if Mother mentioned it, but I've met someone. Her name is Claudie. She's not like anyone I've ever known. She's totally honest, absolutely straight with the world. I love her and I'm going to ask her to marry me."

His father's smile was a little crooked but it was definitely a smile.

"Knowing Claudie, she'll undoubtedly insist on waiting to set a date until you're well enough to attend. So, the sooner you get well, the sooner I can get married." Knowing how much his father loved a challenge, he added, "Now that I think about it, you ought to pay for my wedding."

His father's wiry gray brows shot up. "Why?"

Bo bridged his fingers trying to look stern. "Well...there's still that matter of your gambling debt."

His father's eyes went wide.

"Oh, sure, try to give me that cracked-my-head-on-the-sidewalk-and-can't-remember-anything   excuse. You know what I'm talking about. That Christmas I came home from college. Mom was helping Aunt Irene with Deborah's twins. Remember? I invited those guys from the bar to the apartment to play poker, and you joined us."

Robert scowled. "Crooks."

"I had them right where I wanted them until you bluffed me out of my straight flush. If I hadn't folded, I would have won. Instead that loser dude with the tattoo won." In truth, Bo had been drunk on his butt and probably would have lost his shirt, all the good silver and the vast majority of Christmas presents under the tree if his father hadn't come home and rescued him. "I figure I lost about six hundred bucks. Invested wisely—which you would have, no doubt—we'd be looking at something in six figures by now. So, I think it's only fair that you pay for the wedding."

Robert looked at him squarely. He didn't blink. After a moment of stiff silence, Bo saw the corner of his lips twitch. "Done," his father said.

Bo smiled. "Good. I'll keep you posted on the details. There is one small problem." *Please let it be small.*

Although obviously exhausted, his father said. "Tell me."

Bo let out a long sigh. "Claudie was here with me for a few days. We were in Kansas together when we heard about your...accident. She left so I could..." Bo made a face. "She tried to do the right thing, but I was a jerk."

"Dumb."

Bo flinched. "It gets worse. We'd actually been...uh...together the night before." He felt himself blushing under his father's unblinking scrutiny. "It was the first time, and—"

Bo couldn't quite believe he was talking about this with his father.

"Tell her."

Bo cocked his head. "Tell her what?"

His father's mouth worked at forming the words. "Only...one...love."

Even given the state of his father's memory, Bo couldn't let that kind of hypocrisy go unchallenged. "Dad," Bo said, striving to keep his long-held bitterness in check, "have you forgotten about Trisha? She wasn't exactly your first extramarital affair, you know."

Robert's eyes squeezed tight. "Bad husband." Bo didn't argue. "But. Just one. Love," he said, choking on tears.

Bo caught the slight emphasis on the word *one*. He leaned forward, his elbows on the armrests. "Mom?" he asked softly.

His father nodded.

A sound made Bo turn. His mother stood in the doorway, one hand covering her lips.

"Dad, if you love Mom so much how come you had those affairs?"

Robert's lips worked at forming a sound, but in the end no words came out—just a low, raspy moan. Tears dripped into his pillow before he turned his face away.

Bo felt his mother at his side. She leaned down and took her husband in her arms. In a soothing voice, rich with emotion, she told him, "It's okay, honey. I know you love me, and you know you're the only man I've ever loved. We need to put all that foolishness behind us. We have a tough road ahead, Robert Lester, and we aren't going to waste time worrying about things that can't be changed. Do you hear me?"

Her librarian voice. Stern and commanding.

Robert looked at her. Tears glistened in his eyes. He nodded.

Bo pushed backward with his feet; the wheelchair rolled to a stop a few feet away. He watched his parents with a sense of awe and wonder. Was it possible that thirty years of hurt could be wiped away just like that?

As quietly as possible, Bo slipped away. He started down the hall but stopped when his mother called his name. He returned to her side. For her small stature, she suddenly seemed like a miniature dynamo. Her eyes glowed with an inner fire.

"Thank you, dear heart, for giving him that," she cried, taking Bo's hand.

"What do you mean?"

"The wedding. That's just what he needed to hear. Now, he truly has something to aim for in his rehabilitation."

Bo swallowed painfully. "I...uh...I didn't necessarily think he'd take that seriously. I mean...Claudie and I...we haven't really talked about...uh...I think I hurt her."

Ruth squeezed his hand. "You'll be home tomorrow. You can make things right. Claudie's a smart girl and I know she loves you. Together, you can fix it."

Bo sighed and enveloped her in a hug. If his parents could reconcile after so much marital strife, surely there was hope for him and Claudie.

CLAUDIE ADDED a sprinkle of cinnamon to the frothy cappuccino and handed the cup to the customer on the other side of the counter. She seldom worked the coffee bar, but Sara was handling the book side of the

store while their two new employees—both young
prostitutes who were struggling to leave their pasts
behind—were on break.

"How did we ever handle this business without outside help?" Sara asked, clambering awkwardly onto
a stool.

"We had Keneesha," Claudie said.

The two exchanged a look and burst out laughing.
"Claudie, Kee's a great friend, but she thought the
espresso machine came off the starship *Enterprise*."

"I know," Claudie agreed, smiling at the memory.
"But she was terrific with Brady."

"True. And at the time we didn't have Ren to baby-
sit."

Claudie prepared a fruit smoothie in the new
blender they'd installed for the popular iced drinks.
"Here," she said, setting the old-fashioned parfait
glass on the counter in front of Sara. "Drink up. It's
peaches and cream. The babies will love it."

Sara beamed. "You take such good care of me.
Mmm," she murmured. "Yummy."

Keeping one eye on the door at the far end of the
building, Claudie said, "Sara, I'm worried about Rochell. I think she might be doing drugs. What should
I do?"

Sara took a long draw on her straw before answering. "One Wish House's policy on that subject is crystal clear. She wouldn't be the first who couldn't make
it, Claudie."

Claudie nodded. Of the twelve women Claudie had
tried to help, only six were still off the streets—the
four at One Wish House and two who'd married and

moved to other cities. Five had gone back to hooking. One died from a drug overdose.

"If you'd seen her eyes this morning..." Claudie began but couldn't finish. It killed her to give up on anyone, but she knew the futility of trying to help someone who didn't want help. "I'm sure she's using. I should have busted her this morning. I don't know why I didn't."

"I do," Sara said. "She reminds you of yourself. I thought so, too, the minute I saw her."

Claudie made a face. "Sara, Rochell's black."

"That has nothing to do with what I'm talking about. She's alone and angry and smart and touchy. Just like you were."

"Touchy?"

Sara nodded. She gingerly lowered herself off the stool and stepped away from the bar. "Come here."

Claudie groaned. "I'm busy. I still have to unpack the FedEx box."

"Come."

Claudie did as she was told.

When they were standing shoulder to shoulder, Sara said, "I remember a time when the only person who could touch you was Brady."

Claudie's laugh was supposed to sound ironic, but it came out forced and harsh. "Sara, I don't know how you and Ren do it, but, believe me, what I did for a living involved a whole lot of touching."

Sara stuck out her tongue. "I don't mean that kind of touching. I mean hugs. Like this." She wrapped her arms around Claudie and squeezed. Sara's rounded tummy kept them slightly apart, but Claudie automatically hugged her back.

Claudie laughed. "You are so nuts. What does this prove?"

Sara pulled back slightly, but didn't let go. "It means you've evolved, my friend. You're not afraid to let yourself touch or be touched…by someone who loves you."

Just then, the two new clerks walked past them toward the coffee bar. Both girls gave them a sideways glance, then looked away.

Sara dropped her arms and Claudie stepped back, embarrassed.

Claudie looked at Sara and they burst out laughing. *Wait till I tell Bo,* Claudie thought, then sobered. *When, Bo? When are you coming home?*

BO LOOKED at his watch. He'd known he was cutting it close by stopping at Pennington on his way to the airport, but he'd needed to tell his father goodbye in person.

"What time do you get to Sacramento?" Matt asked from the driver's seat.

"Ten."

"Did you let Claudie know you're coming?"

Bo nodded. "I left two messages—at the bookstore and at One Wish House. I'll try again from Denver if I have time. My car's in long-term so I don't need a ride, but I'm anxious to see her." *What an understatement that is!*

"One Wish House sounds like a pretty cool place. I'm impressed that Claudie's trying to help other women. I knew a few hookers when I worked vice. It's a tough life."

Looking out the window, Bo sighed. "It still

amazes me that she survived in that business for as long as she did without giving up.''

"Yeah, I know what you mean. Underneath that tough exterior is a very soft heart. She proved that in Kansas.'' He glanced at Bo and added, ''Did I tell you I talked to Sara this morning? Doesn't sound like Claudie's stepfather is going to be with us much longer.''

It was on the tip of Bo's tongue to say ''Good,'' but the memory of the shattered look on Claudie's face when she told her family goodbye made him swallow the thought. He'd learned a few things himself about fathers in the past week. Even the worst was forever a part of your heart.

Neither man spoke for several miles, then Matt said, ''I keep forgetting to ask—do you know some guy named Mike?''

Bo's stomach lifted and fell as though the Jeep just hit a bump. ''I know half a dozen Mikes. Why?''

Matt shrugged, turning the wheel to take the airport exit. ''Just curious. Claudie mentioned the name before she left. I thought he might be someone from her past. I could check him out if you want.''

Bo's relief was conflicted. His mother had said Claudie took *Mike's* photo with her. ''No. I'll take care of it. You're gonna be busy looking for Eve.''

Matt snorted. ''Piece of cake. She's a celebrity. They don't fall off the face of the earth without someone knowing something.''

They talked business the rest of the way to the airport where Bo had Matt drop him off without waiting. He lugged his suitcase to the ticket counter only to discover his flight had been delayed one hour.

"Mechanical difficulties, Mr. Lester," the ticket agent told him.

"Will it affect my connection in Denver?" Bo asked.

The woman entered data into the terminal then smiled. "No problem. You should make it with time to spare."

TIME TO SPARE, Bo thought ruefully, as he watched his Sacramento-bound connection taxi away from the gate. Cursing under his breath, he tracked down a ticket agent who spent twenty minutes trying every configuration known to man to get him on the next available flight.

"Six-sixteen," the woman chirped.

Bo looked at his watch. "Eleven minutes from now?"

She shook her head. "Tomorrow morning."

"No way. There's got to be something else tonight. Did you try Salt Lake? Seattle? L.A.?"

She nodded. "Everything. There have been fog problems in San Francisco impacting all West Coast flights. I'm sorry, but that's the best I can do." She gave him a sympathetic look. "I can give you a voucher for a motel room, but in all honesty, you might want to stay put. You're going to be on standby and it pays to be the first one here."

Muttering his disgust, he took his new itinerary and headed for the bank of phones in the center of the concourse. Denver's new airport was sleek, modern and efficient, but it was still an airport, and he wasn't a bit happy about spending the night there.

His mood didn't improve after four phone calls.

Neither Matt nor Ren answered, so he had to leave messages, but he couldn't tell them to call his cell phone because he'd mistakenly packed it in the suitcase he checked through. A woman named Mary answered at the bookstore, but she refused to call either Sara or Claudie to the phone, telling him they were in a very important meeting and couldn't be bothered. He tried One Wish House, planning to leave a message for Claudie but the line was busy.

Someone's online, I bet. We've got to get a second phone line in there, he thought.

Sighing, Bo found an empty chair in a nearly deserted gate and sat down. He pulled out his laptop, thinking he could at least play catch-up on business, even if his life was hanging in limbo. He released the latch and pushed the power button.

He frowned. Does it always take this long to load?

The screen saver appeared—along with a little symbol telling him he was out of power. "Damn," he swore out loud.

He snapped the lid closed in disgust and slumped down in the chair.

"Low battery?" a voice asked.

Bo glanced up. A well-dressed businessman gave him a friendly smile. "There's a place over in the main terminal that gives you a power hookup, Internet access, the whole thing. They charge by the minute, but it's pretty reasonable—compared to the price of beer, anyway."

Bo sat up. "I'm interested. Tell me more."

Eleven minutes later, Bo was breathless from his trot to the far end of the main terminal. Laptop Lane, he read, checking out the small storefront. The posted hours told him he had forty-five minutes to get his battery recharged.

''Feel free to send e-mail,'' the cheerful clerk told him, handing him the key to his private office cubicle.

E-mail, he thought. E-mail. That might be the perfect way to tell Claudie his feelings. It beat the heck out of stuttering and stammering on an answering machine, and he certainly wasn't about to trust his inner thoughts to any of the residents of One Wish House.

E-mail. Fast. Private. Personal. Perfect.

CHAPTER FIFTEEN

"TRY THIS ONE, CLAUDIE," Davina said, forcing a small, dumpling-shaped morsel into her mouth. "Spinach, shrimp and peanuts in won ton dough. It's *muy bueno*."

Chewing, Claudie nodded. "Uh-huh."

Claudie looked around at the throng of people crowded into One Wish House's backyard. A steady stream flowed in and out of the gate, some looking anxiously ahead to the striped awning where Maya and her cooks were dispensing the tasty little offerings, others triumphantly carrying their aluminum-foil-wrapped paper plates to their cars or to the tables set up along the fence.

"Can you believe we pulled this off?" Davina asked. Her tone of awe matched what Claudie was feeling.

"I wouldn't have bet on it last night." Claudie shuddered recalling the chaos in the small kitchen well past midnight. Fortunately, Maya had subcontracted a dozen of the dishes so Claudie and the girls were limited in what they'd had to prepare.

A tall man carrying a messy-faced child split away from the crowd and approached them. At his side was an older woman, petite and elegant in white woolen trousers and a colorful sweater. "If I'd have known

you were going to need the backyard I'd have hired
a grounds crew to come in," Ren Bishop said apologetically. As a landlord, he was a tenant's dream.

Claudie shrugged. "The grass would have gotten
trampled anyway. I had no idea this would go over so
big. Hello, Mrs. Bishop, how are you?"

Babe's reply was cut off by Brady's yell. "Ninjas."

Claudie grinned. Maya had arranged for a troupe of
Korean dancers and drummers to perform.

Ren let Brady down but kept his eye on the ram-
bunctious youngster. "I'd better not lose sight of him.
If his mother didn't kill me mine would." He winked
at Babe then looked at Sara who was perched on a
stool taking money from eager buyers. "I just wanted
to tell you I'm very impressed, Claudie. You've done
an amazing job and from what Sara said you're making money hand over fist."

Claudie tried to smile but only one thought came
to mind: *I wish Bo were here to see it.*

Ren patted her lightly on the shoulder. "He'll be
here soon, Claudie."

Claudie started, not even aware she'd spoken out
loud.

"Knowing Bo," Ren added with a grin, "he probably hog-tied some passenger in the bathroom to be
sure to get a seat out of Denver this morning. He'll
make it."

Ren turned suddenly and let out a low groan.
"Brady, come back here, you little imp. Bye, ladies,
see you later." He took Babe's elbow. "Mother, another dim sum goodie?"

Davina followed them with her gaze. "What a

hunk! You and Sara are both so lucky. Meester Bo's not bad, either.''

Claudie made herself smile. Everybody seemed to assume Bo would show up and they would magically be a couple. Only Claudie doubted it would be that simple.

For one thing, there was the matter of the message on the answering machine.

Claudie excused herself to go inside—ostensibly to check the indoor cooks, but she slipped past the kitchen and dashed upstairs to her office. She wanted to hear his message one more time. She hadn't noticed the little flashing light last night until almost 1:00 a.m. on her way to bed. Sara had already called to tell her Bo's flight had been delayed leaving New York and he was stranded in Denver, but Claudie hadn't heard from him directly—until she checked her machine.

"Hi," his disembodied voice said "I'll keep this short and sweet. I wanted to be there tonight but that isn't going to happen, obviously. Save me some dim sum—whatever the hell that is—and I'll see you tomorrow. By the way, have you checked your e-mail?''

Claudie hadn't had time to go online, but now seemed as good a time as any. She slipped into her padded chair and pushed the envelope icon on the keyboard. A minute later, Claudie's breath caught in her throat. "A poem.''

She scooted closer to the desk; her fingers were shaking so badly she could barely manage to move the mouse to scroll downward. She read:

Silver wings took you away, but your
golden heart remained—an amulet of love

to guide the way home. Do you wait with open
arms in the almost-memory of a honeymoon
beside the roaring waters? Or did my callow act
forge a river of sorrow too wide to span
with poetry or electronic prose?
A kiss might be a vow unspoken. But the question
has yet to be asked or answered.
Will you marry me?

"Oh, my God. It's a proposal," she said dumbfounded.

"A proposal? Of marriage? From Bo?" Sara cried
rushing to Claudie's side. "Let me see."

With a shaking hand, Claudie pointed at the screen.

"It is!" Sara squealed a moment later. "He wants
to marry you. This is so romantic."

"Romantic?" Claudie wailed. "Sara, we've barely
even spoken since New York. Now, I'm supposed to
say okay, let's live happily ever after? Just because he
sent me an e-mail?"

Sara's smiled faltered. "Y-yes?"

"I don't think so." Claudie tried to sound stern but
knew she'd failed when Sara whooped with joy. She
also knew her friend was a cockeyed optimist who
lacked the pragmatic objectivity she needed.
"Where's Ren?"

"He just took Brady home. Daniel's coming over
to stay with him while Ren handles the auction." Sara
turned back to the screen. Her long sigh made Claudie
cringe. "Ren doesn't write me poems. Oh, Claudie,
this is so beautiful. Let's print it and frame it."

Claudie pushed the exit key. "No."

"Why? Don't you want him to propose?"

Claudie rose and paced to the window. Below, a mass of cars filled the street, taking up every spare parking place for three blocks on either side of One Wish House. No primer-gray Mazda in sight.

"Sara, my mother married a man who loved her more than she loved him. I let Bo into my life back in Kansas, but when I tried to return the favor, he closed up." She sighed and closed her eyes, her heart heavy with regret. "I love Bo, but I refuse to live my life like Garret—bitter and angry because the person I love doesn't love me the same way."

BO CLIMBED OUT of his car and stood for a minute just soaking up the December sunshine. The crisp breeze made him want to sing. *Home.* I'm finally home, he silently rejoiced.

Well, not quite home, he amended, trotting to Ren Bishop's back door. He tried the knob. It opened.

"Anybody here?" he called out, walking into the kitchen. He'd planned to go right to One Wish House, but after a night on a bench in the Denver airport he needed a shower.

"Is that you, Lester?" a voice replied.

Bo opened the refrigerator and snatched a cold wiener from an open package. "You got it."

"Unca' Bo," Brady squealed, racing through the swinging door that connected with the dining room. The little boy launched himself into Bo's arms, barely giving Bo time to chomp down on the hot dog.

"Hey, superkid, I missed you," he said, chewing. He hugged the little body as tight as he dared then let him drop to his feet. Kneeling in front of him, he looked the child over. "You've grown a foot. What

are you feeding this kid?'' he asked, looking up at
Ren.

''Tofu dogs. Like the one you're eating.''

Bo's stomach lurched. He scrutinized the remaining
half-eaten object then looked at Brady. ''Not bad. I
think I like 'em.''

Rising, he shook hands with Ren. ''It's good to be
home. I thought I should clean up before I head to
Folsom. Mind if I use your shower?''

''Make yourself at home. I'm heading back over
there as soon as Daniel gets here. He's going to read
to Brady while I handle the MC duties at the auction.''

Bo shouldered his tote bag and started toward the
stairs. ''What kind of things are you auctioning off?''

''Mother strong-armed a couple of dozen busi-
nesses into donating items and services. Some art-
work, tai chi lessons, a cord of firewood, a couple of
trips…'' He snapped his fingers and abruptly veered
toward his office. ''That reminds me—I almost forgot
something.'' Glancing over his shoulder at Bo he
added, '' Make it snappy. I'm due onstage in fifteen
minutes.''

BO'S MOUTH dropped open when he saw the number
of cars on the street. One of the One Wish House
residents—Bo couldn't remember her name—moved
a barricade to let Ren park in the driveway behind his
mother's car.

''Wow! Good turnout,'' he said, getting out.

''It's been like this all morning, hasn't it, Sally?''
Ren gave the blonde a friendly smile. When Bo
looked at her, she gave him a stern frown.

Bo sighed. ''This ain't gonna be a cakewalk, is it?''

Ren cuffed him lightly. "Nothing worthwhile ever is."

They entered the side gate, which had been propped open with a garbage can, and Ren took off to find Sara. Using his skill as a sleuth, Bo melted into the crowd, on the lookout for Claudie. He felt her presence before he saw her. Her back was to him. He didn't recognize the long-sleeved wine-colored wool dress, but its simple sheath cut made her look taller. Sheer gray hose set off her shapely calves, and platform heels gave her an extra three inches of height. Instead of the spiky curls he loved, her hair had been tamed to a sophisticated cap of waves.

Bo's heart leapt in his chest but a bittersweet bite of fear made him hesitate. She was engaged in an animated conversation with Rochell. Bo saw Claudie put out her hand and squeeze the other woman's shoulder. When Rochell looked up, there were tears in her eyes.

Bo knew the moment Rochell realized he was watching. Their eyes met. Hers took on a shuttered look and she dropped her chin. Claudie glanced over her shoulder. Her spontaneous smile was replaced by a cautious nod.

Adrenaline pumped through his veins. He hurried to her side.

"Hi."

Claudie looked at him a long time, her eyes checking out his face, his clothes, his hands. Bo glanced down. "I should have brought flowers," he said stupidly.

She blushed. "No. It's okay. I...um..." She suddenly looked at the woman beside her. "Bo, you know Rochell, right?"

"Hell, yeah, he knows me. He came to the house looking for you."

Bo didn't want to talk to anyone. He wanted to pull Claudie into the most private corner around and kiss her. Instead, he put out his hand and smiled. "Nice to see you. Could we go somewhere and talk?" he asked Claudie.

Claudie frowned. "I'm in the middle of something here, Bo." She turned to Rochell. "I'm sorry for assuming the worst."

Rochell shrugged. "Don't sweat it." She turned and left.

"Claudie, I—" Bo started.

She interrupted him. "I made a mistake, Bo." His stomach flip-flopped. "I thought Rochell was using drugs. Her eyes were red—she seemed really out of it." Claudie sighed. "She's been studying for her GED—burning the midnight oil. I'm such a fool."

"No you're not. You care about these women. Isn't that what all this is about?" He made an encompassing gesture. "The women of One Wish House are making good things happen, and I like being a part of that." He nodded at a man he recognized as a prominent attorney. "So do a lot of other people, apparently."

Something in Claudie's eyes softened. "If you're serious about pitching in, they could use your help in the kitchen," she said, her tone teasing.

Bo's heart skipped a beat. "Only if it'll get me some time alone with you." He moved to close the gap between them, but bumped into someone who muttered something in Spanish, then exclaimed, "Meester Bo," Davina chirped, "you came home. I knew you would. They all say you are never coming back, but I know different."

"Why wouldn't I come back?"

"If I had a rich papa who wasn't doing too good, that's where I'd be," Davina answered, nibbling on something that looked like an egg roll.

Bo stepped back as if struck. He looked at Claudie. "Is that what you think?"

Her cheeks turned the color of her dress and she looked around self-consciously. "No. Of course not. It's just that…" She shook her head. "Let's not do this here. Ren's about to start the auction."

Her diversion worked. Davina wiggled her fingers at Bo in a cute wave. "I gotta go," she said. "I'm biddin' on the Hawaii trip. Sandy beaches and mai tais, here I come."

Claudie started to step away but Bo stopped her with a hand on her arm. "Claudie, I know I was a jerk when you left but we can talk about this, right? Did you get my e-mail?"

"Uh-huh," she said, softly, her gaze not meeting his. "It's a little hectic right now and I need to talk to Ren before he starts the auction. Will you be around later?"

All Bo could do was nod. This wasn't at all what he'd planned. He grabbed the closest folding chair and sat, his gaze following as Claudie melted into the crowd.

"Hello, Bo," a clipped voice said.

Bo looked up, his heart sinking another inch into

the soft ground. He dragged himself to his feet. "Hello, Mrs. Bishop. How are you today?"

She studied him a moment then took the chair beside his. "I wanted to tell you that I'm very impressed with the way you handled things with your father," she told him, motioning for him to sit.

Bo's shock must have been written on his face because Babe added, "Family is the most important thing there is in the world. Family...and love. Sometimes those things are the most painful, too. But you didn't let your antipathy stand in the way of doing the right thing—where your parents were concerned, anyway."

Bo swallowed. "Thank you."

She gave him an odd look. "I never would have guessed you to be a poet. Isn't it odd how we so often keep the most interesting parts of ourselves hidden from view? Even from those for whom we care the most," she said softly, then rose and walked away.

Claudie showed Babe my poem? His shock was almost as great as his humiliation.

"BO'S HERE," Claudie whispered in Sara's ear.

Sara finished making change for the last dim sum customer then whipped a fat rubber band around the cash box and stuffed it in her purse. "Tahiti or the Virgin Islands? Which one do you want? I figure there's enough cash in this box to live on for a year."

"Tahiti. And I doubt if the Virgin Islands would take me."

Sara's smile didn't quite make it to her eyes, which seemed filled with sympathy. "Have you talked to him?"

Claudie gave a noncommittal shrug.

"You're going to have to, you know."

Claudie took a deep breath, rallying her spirit. "Yeah, I know. I can run, but there's nowhere to hide. He's too good a P.I. to let me get away with that."

She turned to leave, but Sara stopped her. "Um…Babe knows about the poem. She read your e-mail. Not on purpose, but—"

An odd kind of expectation made her ask, "What'd she say?"

Sara smiled, a bit wistfully. "Something about underestimating poorly dressed men." The two friends looked at each other and grinned, but Sara quickly sobered. "What are you going to say to him?"

"I don't know, Sara. My heart almost jumped out of my chest when I saw him. I've missed him so much. But I'm afraid, too."

Sara rose and gave her a quick hug. "Sometimes, you have to gamble, Claudie. A lot of people—you included, if I remember correctly—told me Ren was only interested in me because of Brady. But, I knew deep down he was the only man in the world for me."

"Ladies and gentlemen," an amplified voice said, "If you'd be so kind as to lend me your attention—and your wallets."

Claudie watched as Ren drew in the audience with his easy banter. As everything from clock radios to fancy dinners went for top dollar, she scanned the crowd looking for—but not finding—Bo. She happened to look toward the stage when Ren paused dramatically to pull an unmarked envelope out of his pocket. She'd personally tagged all the items up for auction and couldn't recall seeing that one.

"Now, here's an interesting item," Ren said, waving it back and forth. "Personally, I love this one, but then, I'm a hopeless romantic. As some of you might know, I was married recently. My lovely wife, Sara, is right over there. Sara, take a bow."

Blushing, Sara rose and waved as the audience applauded.

The crowd laughed when Ren added, "As you can see, our honeymoon was quite successful."

Sara ducked behind Claudie, trying to hide.

"Claudie!" Ren exclaimed, as if remiss in his duties. "Ladies and gentlemen, I forgot to introduce Claudine St. James, founder and administrator of One Wish House." He walked to the edge of the small deck that was serving as a stage. "Claudie, come up here a minute."

Claudie shook her head. "No thanks, Ren. I'm fine right here."

Sara placed her hands firmly at Claudie's shoulders and pushed her toward the steps. "Go. He's not going to let you off the hook."

Letting out a sigh, she trudged up the redwood steps. She gave him her most ferocious glare, but Ren smiled smoothly and put his arm around her shoulders to lead her to center stage. Claudie used the time to try to read the writing on the envelope in his hand. It looked like Sara's writing.

After the applause died down, Ren handed her the envelope and said, "Since you're up here, why don't I put you to work? Would you like to read the next item up for bid?"

Claudie slipped her finger under the tab and looked inside. A single sheet of creamy paper. Ornate calligraphy—Sara's latest hobby—made it hard to scan, but two words jumped off the page and Claudie almost dropped the paper.

Ren smoothly took it from her, saying, "You're right. This is my job. But you hang tight so we can give this to its rightful owner, once it's purchased."

Claudie looked for Sara, who was beaming like a beacon. *Oh, my friends what have you done?* Desperately, she glanced around. *Where's Bo? What if he left?*

"Now, as I was saying. As a recent newlywed myself, I can tell you the most—and I mean most—important part of a wedding is the honeymoon." The crowd guffawed. "So, what we have here is a paid trip to the honeymoon capitol of the world—I don't know that for a fact but that's what this paper says—Niagara Falls." A loud cheer went up.

Ren rattled off all the details; a stay at a bed-and-breakfast; boat trip under the falls; sleeper accommodations by train. To start the bidding, he said, "I'd say twenty-five hundred dollars isn't too much to pay for the trip of a lifetime."

A youthful voice sang out. "Twenty-five hundred."

Claudie spotted the man. A yuppie MBA with his girlfriend at his side. *Bo, where are you when I need you?*

"Three thousand," she said without thinking.

Ren stepped back in amazement. "Excuse me?"

She glared at him. "You heard me. Three."

He looked over her shoulder at his wife. "Okay." He cleared his throat and continued, "The bid's been raised. Do I hear any others?"

The man at the edge of the crowd called out, "Four thousand."

Claudie couldn't look at the couple. It made no sense, but she knew she couldn't let someone else have her honeymoon—even if she didn't have a fiancé. "Five thousand two hundred," she said, naming the portion of her inheritance she'd planned to use as a down payment on a new car. She'd worry about that later.

Ren grimaced. "The bid is now five thousand two hundred dollars. Going once, going..."

Out of the corner of her eye, she saw the woman clobber the man with her purse. "Fifty-three hundred," he yelped.

Claudie didn't dare go any higher. She needed a car. Niagara Falls was a pipe dream. She reached deep for her best what-the-hell face, but it just wasn't there. Ren's eyes were filled with sorrow as he said, "Five thousand three hundred dollars. Going once. Going twice..."

"Six," another voice said. "Oh, what the hell, make it ten. I only plan to do this once."

Bo cleared the railing of the deck with a clean vault. He walked past Ren and stopped in front of Claudie. "Can we talk now?"

She nodded. There was no way she could speak, her heart was in a million pieces.

Bo put out his hand. She gave him hers.

"Going, going, gone," Ren said, hastily, as they left the deck and entered the house. A tumultuous cheer followed them inside.

The parlor was empty so Claudie stopped, turned

and threw herself into Bo's arms. "I thought you'd left."

He kissed her hair and hugged her tight. "Never," he whispered. "I was getting bawled out by the tall blonde for letting you leave New York without me. What's her name? Sally?"

"Sally Rae," Claudie said looking up.

Bo kissed her forehead. "Were you really going to blow a big chunk of your inheritance on a trip?"

She caught her bottom lip between her teeth. "It's a trip of a lifetime," she said.

"Only if you're with the person you love. I love you, Claudie, marry me? You know it wouldn't be a honeymoon without you." His impish smile made her burst out in tears. He gathered her close. "Oh, babe, I'm sorry. I say the stupidest things when I'm nervous."

"You're never nervous," she corrected.

"That was before I fell in love. Now, I'm nervous all the time. I'm afraid I'm gonna blow it with you. Like I did in New York."

She moved back to give herself space to breathe. His hands skittered up and down her back like nervous cats looking for a place to settle. She laid her head against his chest. The sound of his heartbeat brought back a flood of memories—tenderness, tears, breathless passion she'd never expected to feel.

"I don't know, Bo. Do you honestly think we can get beyond our pasts?"

He kissed her hard, then led her to the settee. He dropped to the cushion beside her, never letting go of her hands.

Gazing into her eyes, he said gravely, "I know we

can as long as we talk to each other. I'll even introduce you to Mike.''

Her breath stopped. ''Really?''

He nodded. ''But only if I can meet Yancy.''

This time Claudie saw through his humor to the sad inner child behind his quip. ''Can you tell me what happened in New York?''

His broad shoulders sagged. ''When there was a chance Dad was going to die, I thought I could handle my feelings, my anger. For some reason dead was doable. But when it looked as though he'd pull through, all these conflicting emotions hit. Anger. Sympathy. Bitterness. Grief. And, with you, love.''

She cupped his jaw. ''That scared you, right?''

He nodded. ''Yes, but not for the reason you think. What I felt for you was so real, so pure, I was afraid it would get sullied if Dad were in the picture. Do you see what I'm trying to say? Dad lived his life without any respect for love, and I didn't want him to make what I felt less than perfect.''

''How could he do that, Bo? You're not your father. You feel things differently.''

''Am I really that different? It's easy to tell yourself that when you're three thousand miles apart, but the more time I spent with him, the more I wondered. I'm forty years old, Claudie, and I've never been in love until I met you. My dad slept with women left and right, but I wouldn't call that love.''

''But your mother—''

''She loved him, and he put her through hell.''

Claudie understood what he didn't say. ''Bo, I'm not the type to put up with that kind of thing. You even look at another woman and I will hurt you. Believe me, it's something a hooker learns how to do early on.''

He eyed her. ''You mean that, don't you?''

She nodded. ''Bo, you're not your father. And I'm not your mother. I'm not my mother, either. I want two kids, not ten. Preferably two years apart.''

''A boy and a girl?'' Bo asked, smiling.

She shrugged. ''Sex doesn't matter.''

He lowered his chin and waggled his bushy brows. ''Oh, yes, it does, my love. I'd be happy to prove it to you, if you'd care to accompany me to my houseboat.''

She plunged into his arms. ''I'll go anywhere with you, but, first, I think we should talk about...the poem.'' His body tensed.

Babe and a distinguished-looking gentleman started into the room until they caught sight of Bo and Claudie. Mumbling their apologies, the couple backed away.

Claudie sighed. She cupped Bo's smooth, recently shaved jaw and said, ''Okay. Let's go, Cookbook Man. We can talk at home...I mean, the boat.''

Bo let out a loud whoop. ''I heard that Freudian slip. You love me, Claudie St. James, and you're going to marry me, aren't you?''

A movement in the doorway caught Claudie's eye. Four familiar faces were peeking around the jamb. Ren and Sara stood to one side. ''Maybe,'' she said, trying not to give away the flood of joy she felt inside.

''That's a yes,'' he cried, pumping his arm as if he'd just scored a touchdown. ''When? Tomorrow?''

''No! Absolutely not. Good grief! I have a life, you know,'' she said, too flustered to think. ''Garret's dying. Your father's in the hospital. I have two hundred people in my backyard.''

Bo sobered. ''Garret's worse?''

Claudie nodded, her chest suddenly tight with emotion. Bo dropped to one knee in front of her. ''Oh, baby, I'm sorry. For everything. But most of all for blowing up when all you wanted to do was help with my dad. I was a coward. I didn't want you to see the real me.''

Claudie blinked back her tears. ''I've always seen the real you, Bo. Those disguises you wear wouldn't fool Brady. You're good and strong and kind and very brave when it comes to taking care of other people, but you're too hard on yourself. And you're not very forgiving when someone you love lets you down.'' She swallowed the lump in her throat. ''That scares me, Bo. I'm afraid I won't live up to the person you think I am.''

He wrapped his arms around her and pulled her close. ''You're right. I blamed myself for not being the son my father wanted. But that's behind us now. Thanks to you…and what happened in Kansas.''

Claudie blinked, questioningly.

''Oh, sweetheart, I'd have to be pretty petty to whine about my life when you were able to get past your anger at Garret.''

He dug in his pocket and withdrew her mother's locket. As he slipped it over her head, he said, ''You gave me your heart, Claudie. But you've always had mine.''

''Oh, Bo, I love you.'' She pulled him to her. Through her tears, she saw her friends sniffling and hugging each other. Sara's face was buried against

Ren's chest. Babe, who stood a little off from the rest, remained tearless, but she smiled warmly and nodded her approval.

Claudie couldn't wait to call Sherry and Val.

It was a long and winding road—and not a single yellow brick on any part of it—but, somehow, Claudie had found her way home.

EPILOGUE

THE SUN—barely past its zenith—failed to mitigate the effect of the chill December wind that swept across the rolling hills of eastern Kansas. Blue-black spruce—hump-shouldered matrons bowed from the forces of Nature—encircled the hallowed grounds. Fifty-some mourners crowded around a vivid patch of artificial green carpet with a rectangle of hothouse flowers at its core.

Garret had passed away the night of the fund-raiser. Sherry had called the following morning to tell Claudie the funeral was set for Saturday. Claudie couldn't get over the number of people who'd packed the tiny white church then followed the hearse to Otter Creek's cemetery. Sherry had tried to prepare her the night before, but Claudie hadn't envisioned this kind of support.

"In the end, Peggy came for him," Dottie said softly as they waited for the service to begin. "I know because he smiled—that very special smile he saved for Sherry, and you."

"Me?" Claudie choked.

The older woman, her kind eyes red from crying, nodded. "You were so like Peggy, how could he not love you, too?" She took Claudie's cold, numb hands in her own and said, "Brave, generous, loving Claudie. You truly are your mother's daughter. You proved that by coming back to heal the rift between you and Garret. He died in peace, and I can never thank you enough.''

Claudie squeezed her hand and looked at the casket. Oddly, she felt no anguish, no bitterness—only regret.

"My parents wanted me to tell you that instead of flowers they're sending a check to Garret's foundation,'' Bo whispered, joining her when Dottie left to take her assigned seat.

She looked at him and her heart swelled with joy. The Bishops stood beside him.

Claudie hadn't been able to talk Sara and Ren out of joining them on this journey. And Claudie would be eternally grateful for the support. Sara's sweet smile and Ren's easy manner diverted many curious, if well-meaning, friends and associates from inquiring too deeply into Claudie's past. This freed up Claudie to concentrate on her siblings.

Yancy had driven in the night before with his wife and sons, who'd reveled in Dottie's warmhearted attention. Valery, who had balked at making the trip until Bo got on the phone and applied his sweet-talking charm, arrived in her Mercedes. Sherry—overwhelmed by both the loss of her beloved father and the convocation of so many estranged siblings—was slowly finding her footing.

"Friends and neighbors. Brothers and sisters,'' a gruff, but dignified, voice said to those gathered. "Please join us in prayer.''

Claudie gazed at the man in the ill-fitting suit, bare hands folded around a worn Bible. Around his neck was a beautiful, hand-stitched stole of Lakota design. Zach. His presence here was Ren's priceless gift.

As her brother solemnly gave their communal goodbye, Claudie stared at the simple casket. Squeezing Bo's hand, she felt the reassuring pressure of the engagement ring on the third finger of her left hand. Their wedding was set for the first weekend in June— two weeks after Sherry's high school graduation. Bo's father vowed to be well enough to dance up a storm. And Sara was happy that she'd have a full month after the birth of the twins to get in shape. Everyone in Claudie's family, even Dottie, promised to attend.

Claudie looked skyward. She wanted to think Garret and her mother were somewhere up above smiling down on them. A perfect family they weren't, but, in the end, the bonds among them were strong enough to bring them all back to Kansas.

*   *   *   *   *